Halfhyde's Island

Historical Fiction Published by McBooks Press

BY ALEXANDER KENT
  Midshipman Bolitho
  Stand Into Danger
  In Gallant Company
  Sloop of War
  To Glory We Steer
  Command a King's Ship
  Passage to Mutiny
  With All Despatch
  Form Line of Battle!
  Enemy in Sight!
  The Flag Captain
  Signal–Close Action!
  The Inshore Squadron
  A Tradition of Victory
  Success to the Brave
  Colours Aloft!
  Honour This Day
  The Only Victor
  Beyond the Reef
  The Darkening Sea
  For My Country's Freedom
  Cross of St George
  Sword of Honour
  Second to None
  Relentless Pursuit
  Man of War

BY DOUGLAS REEMAN
  Badge of Glory
  First to Land
  The Horizon
  Dust on the Sea
  Twelve Seconds to Live
  Battlecruiser
  The White Guns

BY DAVID DONACHIE
  The Devil's Own Luck
  The Dying Trade
  A Hanging Matter
  An Element of Chance
  The Scent of Betrayal
  A Game of Bones

  On a Making Tide
  Tested by Fate

BY DUDLEY POPE
  Ramage
  Ramage & The Drumbeat
  Ramage & The Freebooters
  Governor Ramage R.N.
  Ramage's Prize
  Ramage & The Guillotine
  Ramage's Diamond
  Ramage's Mutiny
  Ramage & The Rebels
  The Ramage Touch
  Ramage's Signal
  Ramage & The Renegades
  Ramage's Devil
  Ramage's Trial
  Ramage's Challenge
  Ramage at Trafalgar
  Ramage & The Saracens
  Ramage & The Dido

BY C.N. PARKINSON
  The Guernseyman
  Devil to Pay
  The Fireship
  Touch and Go
  So Near So Far
  Dead Reckoning

BY V.A. STUART
  Victors and Lords
  The Sepoy Mutiny
  Massacre at Cawnpore
  The Cannons of Lucknow
  The Heroic Garrison

  The Valiant Sailors
  The Brave Captains
  Hazard's Command
  Hazard of Huntress

BY R.F. DELDERFIELD
  Too Few for Drums
  Seven Men of Gascony

BY PHILIP MCCUTCHAN
  Halfhyde at the Bight
    of Benin
  Halfhyde's Island

BY DEWEY LAMBDIN
  The French Admiral
  Jester's Fortune

BY JAN NEEDLE
  A Fine Boy for Killing
  The Wicked Trade
  The Spithead Nymph

BY IRV C. ROGERS
  Motoo Eetee

BY NICHOLAS NICASTRO
  The Eighteenth Captain
  Between Two Fires

BY FREDERICK MARRYAT
  Frank Mildmay OR
    The Naval Officer
  The King's Own
  Mr Midshipman Easy
  Newton Forster OR
    The Merchant Service
  Snarleyyow OR
    The Dog Fiend
  The Privateersman
  The Phantom Ship

BY W. CLARK RUSSELL
  Wreck of the Grosvenor
  Yarn of Old Harbour Town

BY RAFAEL SABATINI
  Captain Blood

BY MICHAEL SCOTT
  Tom Cringle's Log

BY A.D. HOWDEN SMITH
  Porto Bello Gold

The Halfhyde Adventures, No. 2

Halfhyde's Island

Philip McCutchan

MCBOOKS PRESS, INC.

ITHACA, NEW YORK

Published by McBooks Press, Inc. 2004
Copyright © 1975 by Philip McCutchan
First published in the United Kingdom by A Barker, London

Cover illustration by Douglas Harker
Every attempt has been made to contact the copyright holder of this image.

Library of Congress Cataloging-in-Publication Data

McCutchan, Philip, 1920-
  Halfhyde's island / by Philip McCutchan.
    p. cm. — (The Halfhyde adventures ; no. 2)
  1. Halfhyde, St Vincent (Fictitious character)—Fiction. 2. Great
Britain—History, Naval—Fiction. I. Title.
  PR6063.A167H375 2004
  823'.914—dc22
                                    2003024053

Printed in the United States of America

9 8 7 6 5 4 3 2 1

Chapter 1

THE INTERVIEW had been far from satisfactory: not for the first time in his career in Her Majesty's Navy, Lieutenant St Vincent Halfhyde walked out of the Admiralty onto Horse Guards Parade in a state of high indignation at the autocratic manners of Their Lordships' highly-placed representatives. Making in a chill wind towards the Mall, and feeling more than a hint of coming snow in that wind, he lifted a white-gloved hand towards a hansom cab trotting up from the direction of Buckingham Palace. The cab altered course and came alongside under the command of an elderly man, red faced and white whiskered.

"Mornin', Captain. A cold day, sir."

Halfhyde glowered: one of his so-recent interviewers had been a Rear-Admiral, red faced, white whiskered. Getting in, he snapped, "24 Crimea Row, Camden Town."

"Yessir." The ancient cabby flicked his long whip: the thong flew over Halfhyde's head like a paying-off pennant floating over the after turrets of a man-of-war. The cab moved away, came under the Admiralty Arch into Trafalgar Square. Halfhyde looked up at Nelson: Vice-Admiral Viscount Nelson, Duke of Bronte . . . Nelson of the Nile, of Copenhagen, of Trafalgar. From inside the swaying, leather-smelling cab, Lieutenant St Vincent Halfhyde brought his right hand to the brim of his full-dress cocked hat in sardonic salute. Nelson he admired: an ancestor had sailed under the great little admiral with his black patch and his empty coat-sleeve. The salute's sardonic element was not for Nelson but for the way in which he was used by the modern Navy. Almost ninety years had passed since HMS *Victory* had with sadness hauled down the Admiral's flag, and the present rulers of the Queen's Navy had laid aside the lesson of the humility that had been part of Nelson's greatness. Then a smile twisted Halfhyde's lips, a wry smile full of self-knowledge: there were people in the Service who would have said, and indeed had said, that humility was not one of his own virtues . . .

The Rear-Admiral had come close to saying it only some fifteen minutes earlier. Rear-Admiral Sir Edward Ponsonby of the red face and cabby's whiskers, body shaped like a rum tub, had walked round and round the seated lieutenant as though he were a museum relic to be studied with interest. Halfhyde had grown hot beneath the scrutiny, had felt hot words press against his closed lips. He had kept them closed, knowing his own temper. The walking scrutiny had ended at last, and Sir Edward had uttered.

"Before the *Aurora,* two years on half-pay."

"Yes, sir."

"Result of a disagreement with your then Captain."

Halfhyde continued to keep his mouth shut. The disagreement had been none of his own making, but to say so now would not help. Sir Edward proceeded, shooting a length of starched white shirt-cuff beyond the broad gold band surmounted by a thinner one bearing the executive curl. "Your Captain in the *Aurora* gave the next report upon you, as you know. Result, another nine months on half-pay—"

"I beg your pardon, sir. I'll ask you to remember that my mission was successful."

"And caused a diplomatic storm nevertheless," the Rear-Admiral said disagreeably. "Mission in a sense successful, yes. Subordination less so, and kindly do not argue with me as I gather you argued with your Captain. You're to learn respect for your seniors, Mr Halfhyde, or you'll be given no more chances."

"Do I understand I'm being given one now, sir?" There was eagerness in Halfhyde's voice, a fresh light seemed to lift the long face and soften the wide mouth. "A sea appointment?"

A finger wagged in his face. "Don't anticipate my words." A silence followed; Sir Edward Ponsonby turned away and walked with his hands behind the back of his frock-coat towards a tall window, which stood open despite the coldness of the London morning. From the direction of Whitehall came military music and shouted commands from a Corporal of Horse as the mounted guard was changed. Halfhyde turned a little in his chair and looked past Sir Edward through the window: he saw the Royal Standard floating high above the palace. Her Majesty was not yet upon her Christmas journey to Balmoral . . . Halfhyde's thoughts moved a little way from majesty and settled upon Captain the Honourable Quentin Fitzsimmons, commanding Her Majesty's cruiser *Aurora*. Fitzsimmons was an aristocrat, and had preferred his executive officers to be of similar station; he had found no mention of Halfhyde's family in Burke's *Landed Gentry,* still less in the *Peerage.* Halfhyde came of farming stock, yeoman stock, good men of the Yorkshire Dales but not good enough for Captain Fitzsimmons, and this fact explained much that could not be pointed out to the Board of Admiralty, who stood as supporting pinnacles of power behind their sea-going captains. Halfhyde listened to Sir Edward's voice as the latter turned from the window towards a massive desk of highly-polished mahogany that reflected the pale white light of a midwinter sun: listened, but did not hear, and somewhat obviously so, for Sir Edward stopped short.

"Do me the courtesy of paying attention, Mr Halfhyde."

"I'm sorry, sir."

There was a snort. "I shall repeat myself this time, not again: you are appointed lieutenant in the *Viceroy,* at present lying at Portsmouth—"

"*Lying,* sir? Did you say lying?" Halfhyde's face flushed, and he made as if to rise from his chair. "The word I would use is rotting rather than lying!"

The Rear-Admiral gave a thin smile. "Then you shall assist in unrotting her, Mr Halfhyde. There is work for her to do, and you also. I advise you to do it well and have a care for your future. Although you have not your eight years seniority in your rank, you are in fact appointed First Lieutenant. In a ship carrying no Commander, you will therefore be the Executive Officer, Mr Halfhyde. You will be under the command of Captain Bassinghorn, of whom you may have heard. Captain Bassinghorn sets high standards, and you will observe them."

First Lieutenant of a hulk . . . it was a Pyrrhic promotion, but it was, at least, intriguing: Captain Bassinghorn and the old *Viceroy* scarcely seemed to go together. Captain Bassinghorn was a martinet with the reputation of running a taut ship and a smart one, a man who was said to have missed flag rank because he was contemptuous of the emerging ideas, scornful of the modern Navy . . . Halfhyde, sitting back in the cab as it neared Camden Town, conscious of the raucous cries of the street vendors and the sharp smell of horseflesh coming from brewers' drays and bakers' carts, reflected that there was, after all, a point of contact. Henry Bassinghorn was a sailor of the old school, sail trained and hard as nails, a man no longer young. And the *Viceroy* . . . by God, she had been built in the 1850s! A development of the armoured wooden frigates built by the French following upon the success of the heavily armoured floating batteries against the Baltic and Black Sea forts, the *Viceroy* had been almost the first iron-built, armoured warship to join the British Fleet. Today she had retreated from her former glory: she had first been relegated to the reserve and then converted to a store hulk. When last at sea, she had found her motive power partly from sails, partly from steam. The sails would fit Captain Bassinghorn, but the ship herself was an insult. Halfhyde fumed, but at the same time knew that his curiosity had been well aroused. Sir Edward Ponsonby, suddenly becoming mysterious, almost furtive, had revealed no details of his appointment. These, unusually in Halfhyde's experience, would be communicated by his new Captain . . .

The cab stopped. A sleety rain had started, and to this the whiskered face above drew Halfhyde's attention. "You'll get wet, sir."

"I shall not," Halfhyde said evenly. "Down from your perch, man, and thunder on the door of Number 24. Tell Mrs Mavitty to bring an umbrella. Quickly now! I have Her Majesty's commands to execute."

"Yessir." The cabby scrambled down and did as he had been told. To the door of Number 24 came Mrs Mavitty, landlady; vanishing again into the narrow hallway upon receiving her instructions, she re-emerged with a large black umbrella, and advanced upon the cab.

"Well I never did," she said disparagingly and with a click of her tongue. "A sea gentleman to need an umbrella!"

"Full dress is expensive, Mrs Mavitty. If you don't like the rain, you should have sent Mavitty." Halfhyde stepped down from the cab, umbrella-shielded, and shook his scabbarded sword at a crowd of grinning, barefoot urchins. Not for the first time, he was seized with extreme distaste for Camden Town: what he needed was the lift of a deck beneath his feet, and oil-skins on his body, the wind in his face, and the flung spindrift flying over the guns.

He had brought despondency to Mrs Mavitty: the good lady liked the cachet of having a naval officer, even a half-pay one, as a lodger; and she had grown fond of Halfhyde who, when his temper and his seafaring ways were allowed for, was a con-siderate gentleman and a prompt payer. Now he had come from the Admiralty to bid goodbye: that very night, he told her, he was bound into Cambridgeshire for Christmas, and in the mean-time she was to pack his trunks and uniform cases. He would pick them up on the day after Boxing Day, if the coming snow did not stop the trains into London. Then he would proceed to Portsmouth Town, and Mrs Mavitty, like a battleship at the end of its commission, would be paid off.

That early evening, by way of Liverpool Street and Cambridge, Halfhyde, now in plain clothes and accompanied by one small trunk, reached the branch line station at St Ives near the border of Cambridgeshire and Huntingdonshire. He stepped down into a pool of railway lamplight and a swirl of steam and smoke, with snow lying thick beyond the platform, glistening wet in the yellow light of the lamps. The train chugged on for Godmanchester, leaving Halfhyde to the Christmas scene: there was holly around, and distantly a carol hung in the air, and then church bells. It was cold, with a biting wind that seemed to come straight from Siberia: Halfhyde had kept himself middling warm inside with a flask of whisky, but his face felt blue. He walked into the booking hall followed by a porter with his trunk on a creaking barrow, and flung his arms about his tall body. From a bench a coachman rose, and removed his head-gear.

"You're Mr Halfhyde, I take it, sir?"

"I am. You're from Captain Bassinghorn?"

"From the rectory, sir."

Halfhyde nodded: Captain Bassinghorn, a bachelor, was spending his leave with a brother, rector of the village of Elsworth. The coachman preceded Halfhyde out to the station approach and opened the door of his conveyance. His trunk embarked, Halfhyde rolled away through the small market town, turning across the Ouse into flat country on the fringe of fenland. Dank smells smote him, smells of river and marsh: the whole countryside, as seen in the dim glow from the lamps, seemed deep in snow. The journey, one of some six miles along lonely roads, was perforce slow: the solitary horse slithered and slipped dangerously, and from the coachman the air was as blue as Halfhyde's frozen face. Along the hedges the wind had shipped the snowflakes into drifts; above the hedges the trees were outlined in silver, a scene of fairyland as the moon came out from behind cloud. Fenland was a mysterious place, and new to Halfhyde except by reputation: he shivered suddenly. In Captain Bassinghorn's young days, this would have been the sort of night to watch for highwaymen. It was a far cry from racing seas and rolling ships and the roaring drunken songs of Portsmouth Town: despite his farming background, St Vincent Halfhyde was no countryman, but, rather, a throw-back to his one seafaring ancestor, Daniel Halfhyde, Gunner's Mate in the *Temeraire* under Nelson. It was not his consuming curiosity alone that brought him a feeling of relief when the coach turned into a gravel drive and crunched to a stop beneath a storm lantern slung from the ceiling of the porch: the sooner he met Captain Bassinghorn, the sooner he would, presumably, be back in more familiar surroundings.

The coachman opened the door: Halfhyde got down. In the depths of the rectory a bell jangled like a knell as though summoning the incumbent to a funeral. A streamered housemaid opened the door and briefly curtsied: behind her loomed the dark figure of the rector. Behind again, a big man, tall as Halfhyde himself, very broad in the beam, and with a heavy grey beard jutting from a strong chin. This man came forward, brushing the rector aside, half physically, half with his very presence, an emanation of authority and vigour.

"Halfhyde? My name's Bassinghorn. Come in, come in. Rufus, your study, if you please, then you can dismiss. Halfhyde, come with me." The rector hovered uncertainly. Bassinghorn held out a hand; taking it, Halfhyde felt crushed, boneless, though his own grip was no mean one. Captain Bassinghorn leaned forward and sniffed. "Whisky. I don't mind it on a night like this, but I won't have it aboard my ship at sea."

Halfhyde raised an eyebrow. "At sea, sir?"

"D'you imagine the old *Viceroy*'s not capable?"

"A store hulk, sir—"

"Come into my brother's study," Captain Bassinghorn said abruptly. He led the way: the study was book-lined, furnished with old oak and, currently, with Christmas holly and ivy. A fire burned, spreading welcome warmth, and, surprisingly in view of the Captain's recent stricture, there was a silver tray with a crystal decanter of whisky.

Bassinghorn said, "Help yourself. It's Christmas and damned cold outside. Pour me a finger, no more."

Halfhyde poured, restricting his own, prudently, to a little under a finger. Captain Bassinghorn raised his glass. "To Her Majesty's Ship *Viceroy,* which is no longer a hulk. I've been in Portsmouth myself and I've not been idle."

Halfhyde, drinking to the toast, waited. Captain Bassinghorn, staring at him hard with piercing blue eyes, the eyes of a seaman, said, "I'll tell you something, Halfhyde: I'm an old man close to retirement and I'm not going to make flag rank. The *Viceroy*'s well past her prime, though still capable and seaworthy. And you're an embarrassment to Post Captains, inclined to rudeness and insubordination—"

"Sir, I—"

"You'll be insubordinate with me at your peril, so hold your tongue. The three things I've mentioned . . ." Bassinghorn's voice tailed away and he stared down unseeingly into the dancing flames of the fire.

Halfhyde prompted: "Sir?"

Bassinghorn gestured with a hand. "Never mind, Halfhyde, never mind. It was just a thought and perhaps one better left where it is." He turned and met Halfhyde's eye again. "All of us may have our defects, but in spite of them we're sailing to be of service to the Empire and Her Majesty."

Halfhyde, puzzled by Bassinghorn's words and manner, looked back at him. There was a curious light in the Captain's eye, a light of determination and total dedication to some duty as yet uncommunicated to Halfhyde, a duty that Bassinghorn was clearly uneasy about nevertheless . . . and a light that heralded a stormy life ahead for the ship's company of the *Viceroy* if her Commanding Officer should be seized with too firmly fixed a notion that he could turn a sow's ear of a dockyard hulk into the silk purse of a first-rater.

Chapter 2

FROM ONE lodging to another, but this time in a sailor's town, a sailor's environment: Halfhyde, having watched the muster of his gear by a porter at Portsmouth Town Station, took a cab to St Thomas's Street. His lodgings, recommended by Captain Bassinghorn as fit for a naval officer, were not far from the George Hotel in the High Street where Admiral Nelson had spent his last night ashore in England before embarking in the *Victory* for his apotheosis at Trafalgar. Having left his belongings and made his number with the good woman who would be his landlady whilst he stood by the still refitting *Viceroy*, Halfhyde, in uniform once again, lost no time in making his way to the dockyard to report formally to his Captain. He went on foot: to walk was not expected of a naval officer, but Halfhyde wished to savour Portsmouth, a town that had marked his career like so many milestones over the years. Here he had joined the cruiser *Aurora* for his eventful voyage to the Bight of Benin on the West African coast; here, his duty done, he had returned, but had at once been ordered to report at the Admiralty. He had not seen Portsmouth in the interval: as a half-pay officer, he had preferred not to hang around the skirts of employed comrades. Camden Town had spelled anonymity whilst in the wilderness of heel-kicking. But now, walking along the old High Street, reflecting upon its past associations with the British Fleet, he was a new man. He burgeoned, walked with pride and a springy step past the George Hotel and, farther on, the military barracks built in the days of the Napoleonic Wars. Moving on towards the Hard, he came below the railway bridge that carried the trains to the South Railway jetty in the dockyard. Past the Keppel's Head Hotel and onto the Hard itself, smelling of the sea, busy with sailors, libertymen from the Fleet whose salutes he returned punctiliously. Men who had come back from long commissions in China, the Mediterranean, South Africa, the West Indies, or were taking their last run ashore before sailing away to join some mighty squadron overseas. Men with the proud names of their ships in gold lettering on black cap-ribbon; men with thick beards, with gold badges on blue sleeves, or youngsters beardless and badgeless yet, boys with all before them to learn and experience: Halfhyde smiled with a touch of bitterness. They would know both the good and the bad: the pleasures of lasting friendships made, the comradeship of a world of men, the lift of a deck in fair weather with a laughing breeze from ahead and the smoke lying thick astern over a tumbling, merry wake, the thrill as the great grey guns roared across the seas and the coloured bunting, run up by nimble, barefoot signalmen from the signal bridge, flew gay and free from the halliards on their sheaves at masthead and yardarm; but the breezes could turn to gale-force winds, and then a ship became a nightmare of flung water that found its way below into mess decks and store-rooms, a nightmare of men ripped bodily from lifelines to be cast into a boiling sea with no hope of rescue. Under those conditions a ship's company lived a half-life of frozen cold and wet clothes and no hot food for days on end. And the guns did not fire only in practice runs: there could come the days when high explosive ripped through a ship's plates to burst in red-spattered torment upon crowding seamen, or a hit below the waterline would blow up the magazines and spread destruction and roaring flames until the inrush of the seas brought the main deck below the level of the waves . . .

Halfhyde made a sudden grimace at his fancies: the Navy was the Navy, and men knew what they had joined for. Once, an ancient Chief Petty Officer, many years retired and chance-met in a London public house, had despite the plain clothes recognized Halfhyde for what he was, and had risked a word. One of his remarks remained in Halfhyde's memory.

"I've not had a good laugh, sir, not once, since I last set foot aboard a man-of-war."

Laughter, and mutual trust, and a knowledge of natural forces in all their moods from storm to a peaceful dawn over a calm sea in a morning watch: these were also the British Navy. Halfhyde moved on, glancing down at unhygienic but happy urchins grubbing for thrown pennies in the low-water-freed mud below the Hard. Smiling, he stopped and felt in a pocket. He brought out a gleaming half-sovereign, something more than a day's pay. He frowned: he was that often sorry object, a naval officer without proper private means. "But confound it!" he said aloud. "I'm happy. Why shouldn't one of them be?"

He flung the coin: the gold flashed in an arc, caught by sun-light. There was a gasp from the mud: many, many hungry eyes watched. As it fell and left, momentarily, a tiny hole as marker, bodies squelched towards it, lifting small feet made giant-sized by the clinging harbour filth. There was a concerted dive: the victor emerged, black but overjoyed. In his grasp he had food for a week for a large family, plus a few luxuries.

Bright eyes shone, mud-ringed, haunting: the teeth, when the mouth opened in praise as though heaven had come down to Portsmouth Hard, gleamed pure white in contrast with the face. "You're a toff, Guv'nor! A real toff."

Halfhyde lifted a hand and moved on. Extravagance sometimes carried its own reward. He came under the dockyard gate:
the policeman on duty saluted. The law had a bulky, well-fed
body and a beery face, and the face was currently severe.

"What ship, sir?"

"*Viceroy.*"

"Fitting-out basin, sir." The policeman, hands behind his
back, rose and fell on the balls of his feet, a portly, pompous
barrel of dark blue. "Those lads, sir, the mud-larks. I see you
stop, sir."

"Yes?"

"Perishin' little nuisances to the gentlemen, sir, them urchins.
Did they bother you, sir? If so, I'll—"

"No more than they should bother you, Constable." Halfhyde
gave a cold smile and walked into the yard, disregarding a baffled "Eh?" from the policeman. The man's mind was porcine,
unthinking: Halfhyde knew nothing would penetrate, for poverty
was, simply, a crime. As he went, he sniffed: the sea smell was
strong, but overlaid by the dockyard smell, a smell of nostalgia.
Tarred rope mainly, with a hint of coal-dust. Coal-dust apart,
Nelson had smelled that smell. So had Collingwood, Benbow,
Blake. The outward appearance of the ships had changed with
the years, so had their propulsive power: but the men and the
spirit and the smell remained basically the same. Halfhyde
walked on, his pace quickening now, towards the fitting-out
basin. As he rounded some tall sheds, stowages for machinery
or fleet stores, he made out the masts and fighting-tops of
the old *Viceroy.* Coming alongside, he stared up from the side
of the basin, a stare that mirrored the many emotions in his
mind. In a sense he was staring at history: the *Viceroy* had been
a powerful ship in her day. She had come from the Blackwall
yard of the Thames Ironworks and Shipbuilding Company and

the drawing-boards of Sir Isaac Watts. Originally she had been of 9,210 tons displacement, with heavy side-armour constructed from great belts of 4.5-inch iron plates with 18 inches of teak planking to back them: in her early days she could not have been penetrated by the most powerful of the world's guns. Her 380-foot length had carried the same armament as she was to carry to sea again now: four 8-inch and twenty-eight 7-inch guns, all of them at present removed from her decks and case-mates for stripping down and overhaul in the dockyard's repair shops. History, but with a future once again . . . Halfhyde looked aloft, keenly: the *Viceroy* was busily leaving the past behind. Her masts, though still crossed with their yards, looked naked; the thin midships funnels almost sinister as they stood before the narrow navigating bridge. No sail would fill with wind to bil-low and strain from the cringles, no courses would boom her along before a roaring sea-wind: her propulsion now was to be by steam alone. There was a step on the basin wall behind Halfhyde, and he turned, and saluted as his Captain came up.

"Good morning, Mr Halfhyde."

"Good morning, sir."

"You were looking at her masts. As bare as a whore in bed! I tried, Halfhyde. I told you that."

Halfhyde met his eye: there was a moist look, and Halfhyde looked away again. Bassinghorn had already told him what the Lords of the Admiralty had said to him: that he must modern-ize himself with his new command. Captain Bassinghorn lifted a hand, shading his upward glance against the sun, his blue eyes narrowed and searching and nostalgic. Halfhyde looked at the hand: he had noticed, in the Cambridgeshire rectory a week ear-lier, how immense that hand was. The rector's whisky-tumbler had been of a generous size: Bassinghorn's hand had engulfed

it, making it disappear like a magician's trick. Square, with blunt
ends to the fingers, a seaman's hand, the hand of a man who in
seniority had not forgotten how a raw midshipman had hauled
on a rope almost forty years before. Now, standing beside his
Captain in the dockyard cold, Halfhyde recalled the conversation of a week ago.

"It's to be no cruise, Halfhyde. And we join no fleet. I shall
have the help of no one save my own ship's company. I feel a
degree of . . . dispensability."

Dispensability? An odd term; there had seemed some hidden
meaning in what Bassinghorn had said, and having said it he
was silent, beard sunk upon his massive chest, the bottom of
the tumbler shining in the lamplight beneath his great fingers.
Halfhyde did no probing in spite of his curiosity, sensing that
Bassinghorn was not the man to be hurried: in any case, few
Post Captains of the Royal Navy appreciated those who spoke
without invitation. Bassinghorn had taken a turn or two up and
down the parson's study as though walking his quarterdeck, and
had then swung round almost fiercely upon the waiting
Lieutenant.

"We've been at peace now for—what?—more than thirty
years. The Fleet is unused to action, yet action is what it is
there for."

"Yes, sir. And us, sir?"

"Action is always a possibility. In the meantime there is much
to be re-learned, Halfhyde. We must be vigilant, you and I, in
ensuring that the need to re-learn the lessons of war is instilled."

Halfhyde could find nothing to say beyond, "Yes, sir." Then,
chancing his arm, added, "May I know the orders, sir?"

"You may—that's what you've come for. Sit down." Halfhyde
took an old leather chair on one side of the fire, Bassinghorn

took another on the opposite side: he thrust his hands out, warming them at the fire, then started talking. It was a simple operation on the surface, though the reasons for it involved a scientific phenomenon that Halfhyde found baffling. The Captain spoke of volcanoes, of their geographic distribution around the world. By far the greater number, he said, stood in close proximity to the sea areas, a fact that was probably accounted for by the old-age determination of the coastlines by earth folds. He spoke of the Pacific, encircled by a ring of volcanoes. Kamchatka, the Kuriles, Japan, the Liu-kiu Islands, the Philippines, Java, Sumatra, New Zealand, and Mounts Erebus and Terror in Antarctica. Volcanoes, Bassinghorn asserted, did strange things.

"They build islands, Mr Halfhyde."

"So I've heard, sir."

"A gradual process, of course—or mainly so. That is, if they are to remain rather than sink back into the sea. They start their lives as submarine volcanoes, and are gradually built up until they break surface." Suddenly Bassinghorn smiled. "A report has reached the Admiralty that nature has obliged the world with an island, Mr Halfhyde!"

"Whereabouts, sir?"

"In the Pacific, in longitude 135° 43′ east, latitude 18° 57′ north. That is, some 1,500 miles east of Hong Kong, not far to the south of Parece Vela Island, which belongs to Japan."

"And—"

"And that is where we are bound after we've refitted. The geologists and the seismologists have given the island a clean bill of health."

"It's been visited already, sir?"

"No. At this moment—and despite what I have just said—it

is not considered safe to be approached. Natural forces are still at work. The experts base their expectations upon their instruments, their past experience, and their knowledge of the area. The island, they say, will remain and is almost certainly large. In case it is suitable for use as a naval base, we are to plant the Union Flag as soon as it is notified as being expedient to do so."

"And other Powers, sir?"

Bassinghorn had given a short laugh and expanded: diplomatic circles had indicated a possibility that the Czar of all the Russias might well be interested. He might decide, once the area was safe and once his eastern ports were free of ice and became usable, to move a force towards the island; it was considered unlikely that he would despatch ships from the Black Sea and thus arouse the curiosity of the other sea powers as they steamed through waters considered inherently the province of the British Fleet, but such a move would naturally be watched for by the Admiralty. And the word had gone out, and had reached Captain Henry Bassinghorn via Their Lordships: a Russian naval presence, a possible base for her North Pacific operations and aspirations, would not be welcomed. In the meantime, however, with the Russian fleet blocked in by ice, speed was not immediately of the essence; the *Viceroy* would be properly prepared for her mission.

Halfhyde asked, "Would it not be more practical to a detach a ship from the China Squadron at Hong Kong, sir?"

"It would not, since after her refit the *Viceroy* alone will have the increased bunkering capacity that is needed—and also we shall take equipment that is currently available only at the home ports, plus certain specialized personnel from Government departments—civilians. We are to conduct a survey, you understand."

"Yes, sir. But the initial planting of the flag—"

"You have ears, Halfhyde, ears that must have heard me speak of considerations of a safe approach. The time is not yet right, the area must be allowed to settle."

Halfhyde inclined his head. "I'm sorry, sir. But you spoke of expendability. Does this make a good bedfellow with safety?"

Bassinghorn waved a hand. "Expendability in one special sense only: our reputations. I have a wide discretion—not intimated to me in writing of course!—to use my guns if necessary." He leaned forward, eyebrows drawn down. "Do you not understand? The diplomatic niceties will be outwardly preserved come what may, for the blame for any untoward incident will be laid squarely upon our doorsteps, yours and mine, to *that* extent are we expendable." There he had paused, watching Halfhyde closely. "Should you wish to decline your appointment, I would understand. Well?"

"And return to half-pay indefinitely?" Halfhyde smiled, a touch of ice in his eyes. "Oh, no, sir! I prefer to take my chance with you. And now, sir," he went on quickly before Bassinghorn could speak embarrassed gratitude, "you talked of the Russians, and this I understand. But what about the Japanese? Are they not interested?"

"They are not. Word has been received to this effect in the Foreign Office. They've no need of a mid-Pacific base extra to their existing ones, and they're well disposed towards us, as you know."

"Yes, indeed." Halfhyde had then asked, sardonically, what seemed to him the basic question: "Do *we* stand in any need of this base, sir—this barren, unknown quantity of a base, when we already have Hong Kong and the use of the 1842 treaty ports? Is there not an element of . . . dog-in-the-manger?"

Bassinghorn had looked at him with a glint of totally under-standing humour in his eye. "Mr Halfhyde, you may quench your mutinous thoughts and insubordinate questionings with one more finger of my good brother's whisky . . . I think you already have the point of our orders!"

A party of seamen in working rig came marching along the basin wall under the orders of a bearded and gaitered Petty Officer. "Swing those arms, you lubbers! Good God Almighty, you're in the Queen's service, not the Salvation bloody Army! Eyes *right!*"

Captain Bassinghorn returned the salute gravely, looked with a lingering eye as the sailors moved past. Halfhyde felt in instinctive tune with his thoughts. Men were flesh and blood, had families to leave behind. There was a cruelty in their draft to Bassinghorn's command. Should there be action, should some intrusive Russian ship suffer damage or casualties, there would be no honour for any member of the old *Viceroy's* company. Bassinghorn, in obeying his unwritten orders, would go down to posterity as an old fool who had allowed impetuosity to govern common sense, an ageing, hidebound dugout in independent command who had stupidly risked his own men . . . and a nice indignation would froth around the British Admiralty, apologies would be humbly offered to St Petersburg. Halfhyde gave a bitter smile as the working-party marched away. Their Lordships were clever, immensely so, at keeping their own noses clean, their armour shining white!

There was an enormous amount to be done before the full ship's company joined. The days were busy ones for the *Viceroy's* First Lieutenant. Halfhyde found his principal aide in Mr Pinch, Boatswain, who had joined the ship a few days before him.

Benjamin Pinch, a Warrant Officer with a considerable paunch and a fringe of grey beard, was a Plymouth man who had sailed in the *Viceroy* in her halcyon days. He had volunteered for his present appointment, the last commission he would serve before taking his pension; and he was a happy man. January and February slipped away: by early in March the ship had come alive again, her years of hulkdom dropping away as her draft of seamen and marines and stokers filed aboard with kit-bags and hammocks to infuse her with spirit. There was still much to do. Under Ben Pinch and the Chief Boatswain's Mate the men, found from the dockyard's barrack hulks and mostly green and untried, worked with a will, transforming the old ship with paint, giving the hull and upperworks their China-side colours of light grey and buff; hoisting the freshly refitted boats back aboard—cutters, pinnaces, whalers; cleaning up her mess decks and flats, her store-rooms and working spaces, ridding the ship of the evidence of the dockyard "mateys" in whose thrall she had been since the day the orders had come for her emergence from indignity. Walking her decks, Halfhyde felt in sympathy with her: he, too, had known the wilderness. She, like him, was responding to a shift of fortune. He grudged her no effort, toiling on for many daily hours beyond the normal call of duty, making every preparation for the future, arranging for her stores, her coal, her ammunition. As the time for sea came nearer, there were other matters to be attended to: the final making-up of her complement to full seagoing strength in con-sultation with the shore manning authority, and the compiling, together with the ship's Master-at-Arms and Chief Gunner's Mate, of the Watch and Quarter Bill, the formidable document that established the station of each and every man aboard under the varying circumstances and requirements of a ship in commission, whether it be cruising watches, action, or the never-end-ing cleaning of the guns. While Halfhyde went about his particular business, the Engineer Officer supervised the final overhaul of his horizontal-trunk engines, now refurbished by the dockyard's engineering shops; he promised Captain Bass-inghorn that they should not fall far short of the original trials speed of 14.35 knots. It was the last day of March before the old ship was ready, and on that day her special equipment arrived: many crates of instruments, botanical specimens for the possible establishment of some kinds of vegetation, and a vast electricity generator. At the same time three civilians embarked: a geologist, a botanist, and a pasty, moon-faced man from the department of the Director of Dockyards—a kind of nautical builder. These gentlemen aboard, the ship was nosed out from the basin by the dockyard tugs, and, once in the stream, the engines were turned over for a full-power trial. Halfhyde, watch-ing the cufuffle below the counter as the single screw thrashed up the harbour water, was aware of the heavy figure of the Cap-tain on the bridge, face expressionless but eyes lifting constantly towards his bare masts. The engine trials finished, HMS *Viceroy*, still in the care of the tugs, was brought alongside the dockyard wall two berths up-harbour from the South Railway jetty, under orders from the Commander-in-Chief to sail for the Far East via Gibraltar and the Suez Canal in two days' time. That afternoon Captain Bassinghorn sent for his First Lieutenant and spoke to him somewhat mysteriously in the privacy of his cabin.

"Mr Halfhyde, certain stores will arrive aboard shortly. You will have them placed in Number Four store-room and bring the key to me afterwards."

"Aye, aye, sir. May I ask—"

"Yes, you may, but the information is between you and me

only. The stores are not stores, they are sails, purchased privately by an agent on my behalf from the sailyard. I would prefer that the yard authorities and the Admiralty should not know. I think you will understand, Mr Halfhyde?"

Halfhyde understood, and promised his silence. It was clear that Bassinghorn, who could ill afford the expense, had bought the sails from his own pocket; any Captain was entitled to his own stores so purchased, but Halfhyde could understand the Captain's wish for secrecy vis-à-vis the Admiralty in the circumstances. The "stores," when they came aboard, were well enough disguised and duly and anonymously loaded and stowed. On the morning of the next day, the day before departure, Halfhyde, carrying out last-minute checks with Mr Pinch and the Carpenter, saw on the jetty two small figures, uniformed naval officers with white patches on the lapels of their monkey-jackets. The patches of one of them were more grey than white, denoting, to the initiated, more seniority and sea-time than was possessed by his companion. Halfhyde walked to the upper-deck guardrail and called down in a carrying voice: "Mr Runcorn!"

"Sir?" The owner of the grey patches looked, stiffening to attention. Recognition dawned. "Good gracious, sir! It's you, sir!"

"It's me, sir! I heard only yesterday of your appointment, Mr Runcorn." Halfhyde smiled, crinkling the corners of his eyes. "I'm glad."

"Oh, thank you, sir!"

This time Halfhyde's smile was an inward one. Mr Midshipman Runcorn, grey though his patches were, had not aged since leaving the *Aurora* almost in this very spot. Halfhyde, his hands clasped behind his back, thrust his chin forward. "Waste not breath on thanks. Get yourself aboard, Mr Runcorn, there's work to be done!"

"Oh—yessir!" Rapidly, both Midshipmen sped for the gangway to the quarterdeck.

Halfhyde climbed the ladder to the bridge. Looking down, he saw the drab, poorly-dressed families gathering for a last farewell, women with pinched faces, mothers, wives, and children, sad-looking people, some with babies in their arms and with anxious, tearful expressions. Above, the sky was a chill blue, and the sea beyond Fort Blockhouse was calm, but a sailor's weather-eye told the First Lieutenant that a change was not far away. Well, it would be a good experience for a new crew who had not sailed together before: it would shake them down and settle them. When they reached the Pacific, they would need to know who could be relied upon and who could not, who could stand a degree of torment and who would crumble. The sea was an excellent sorter of men. In the port wing of the bridge stood Captain Bassinghorn with a telescope beneath his arm.

"Ah, Mr Halfhyde."

Halfhyde saluted. "The ship is ready to proceed, sir. All hands aboard, cable and side party standing by and special sea duty-men at their stations."

Bassinghorn stared icily through black smoke swirling down from the funnels. "Mr Halfhyde, the ship is not ready to proceed until my Engineer reports the state of his engines. He has not done so."

"Sir—"

"My compliments to the Engineer. He is to report immediately."

"Sir—"

"*Immediately.* And he is first to wash."

"Aye, aye, sir."

Smiling inwardly, Halfhyde despatched a seaman boy. The

Captain's order had contained an element of contradiction, but such was not unusual in Post Captains, separated only by Admirals from God. Bassinghorn the martinet, upon his bridge and about to proceed to sea, was showing his other side. Halfhyde, himself loathe to see his fresh, cleanly-scrubbed decks sullied by coal-droppings and oily feet, approved the order to wash: engineers were dirty fellows. But in a sail-less ship you couldn't move far without them.

Mr Bampton, Engineer, appeared, his face still showing traces of soap, a monkey-jacket partially obscuring his overalls, the two curlless gold rings with purple cloth between them scuffed and stained. He saluted. "Sir, the engines are ready."

"Thank you, Mr Bampton. How long have they been ready?"

"Why, sir, these last five minutes, and I—"

"Then you should have reported five minutes sooner, Mr Bampton. I think you were about to say something further. Pray, what was it?"

"Sir, I called the bridge by the speaking tube—"

"Yes, Mr Bampton, I am aware of that. Except in emergency, or when cleared away to sea, I am not to be spoken to by means of a brass tube. Let that be clear. Your readiness report is to be made in person."

"Yes, sir."

"I like to see who is responsible for my propulsion, as I used to be able to see my sails." Captain Bassinghorn turned away, walked with his gold-ringed cuffs behind his back to the starboard wing, and stood staring from under the gilded oak leaves fringing his cap-peak, down into the still water. Bampton caught Halfhyde's eye, and shrugged. Halfhyde's eye was cold: Bampton, a man with a disgruntled look, the look of the sea-lawyer, would get no support from him, no furtively exchanged glances of disdain behind the Captain's back. Halfhyde had already formed a regard for Captain Bassinghorn. The Engineer went below to his inferno, and Halfhyde, awaiting the orders for sea, stared along the Viceroy's busy decks: busy, but with a controlled activity. On the fo'c'sle the cable party and the Carpenter waited, the latter with a hand on the lever of the center-line capstan, the other hand holding an oily knotted bunch of cotton-waste. Men stood ready under their Petty Officers to bring in the berthing wires. Such of the ship's company as were not otherwise required were fallen in by divisions under the Lieutenants and Midshipmen on the fo'c'sle, in the waist, and on the quarterdeck. The guns, trained smartly to the fore-and-aft line, were shards of peace, fitted with their muzzle-blocking tampions and their painted tarpaulins against foul weather when it should come as the ship proceeded on her passage east. There was a faint engine-shudder running through the ship, and a subdued hum of dynamos, as though the Viceroy's heart beat with her eagerness to return to the seas that had been her life: there was a poignancy in the very air, and an expectancy, as every man awaited the Captain's order, which came promptly and was addressed to the Signal Midshipman, waiting, with the Chief Yeoman of Signals, to bend on any flag hoist that might be required by the Captain.

"Ask permission to proceed, Mr Runcorn."

"Aye, aye, sir." Mr Runcorn nodded at the Chief Yeoman, a nod in which assurance and extreme youth were oddly mingled, a nod that said that Mr Runcorn had been trained to expect instant obedience by having to give it himself in his turn. A colourful string of flags broke from the halliards at the foretop-mast head: hard upon its heels came the answering hoist from the signal tower in the dockyard, and Mr Runcorn, snapping his telescope shut, saluted the Captain punctiliously.

"Permission to proceed, sir."

"Thank you, Mr Runcorn." Bassinghorn turned to the Officer of the Watch. "Single-up to the backspring, Mr Campbell, if
you please." He waited while the order was passed and the various ropes and wires fell slack. "Slow astern main engine, wheel
amidships."

Still standing in the starboard wing of the bridge, Bassinghorn
looked along his decks. Slowly the *Viceroy* came off the wall
and the last line was let go, to splash into the widening gap of
dirty water and be hauled swiftly aboard and coiled down. On
the jetty, a band of the Royal Marine Artillery played *Rule,
Britannia*. There were waves from the Queen's Harbourmaster,
from a handful of dockyard mateys seizing the chance to break
off from their work. Handkerchiefs waved from the crowd of
women and children, the mothers and wives and sweethearts,
saying goodbye for an unknown period. There were more tears
as the cruel gap of water widened further and the band switched
to *Auld Lang Syne*. The ship slid outwards, belching black smoke
from her shaking funnels as the stokers, stripped to the waist
below, clanged the great spadefuls of coal into greedy furnaces,
working like sweating devils in red heat. As the ship moved into
the stream a strident bugle call rose from the after shelter deck,
blown by a resplendent boy bugler of the Royal Marine Light
Infantry; and as Bassinghorn on the bridge, obeying the Still,
saluted the St George's Cross on the Commander-in-Chief's flag
above the signal tower, all hands on the upper-deck were brought
to attention by their divisional officers. It was, Halfhyde felt, a
sombre moment and one to be savoured. It was not every day
that a Post Captain, a First Lieutenant, and one of the Queen's
ships put out to sea together in mutual salvation from the
scrapheap.

Chapter 3

THE LANDMARKS were picked up and passed, one by one, the landmarks of a naval officer's life as well as the indications of a ship's position: Ushant, Finisterre after the Bay of Biscay, Cape Roca, St Vincent, Trafalgar, and Tarifa, leading the *Viceroy* along her well-remembered path to the naval base and fortress of Gibraltar. Then through the Mediterranean, leaving Malta away to starboard, for Port Said and the slow, hot passage of the Suez Canal after replenishing the bunkers from lighters in Port Said roads. By the time the ship had come through the sand and stickiness of the Canal into the Gulf of Suez, her company were already approaching a degree of efficiency as a team. Bassinghorn had conducted one exercise after another, driving himself as well as his officers and men, remaining on the exposed bridge for hour after hour, watching, noting, criticizing. Gun drills, fire stations, collision stations, abandon ship. In the night watches the Boatswain's Mates had shrilled their calls throughout the sea-sogged mess decks as the *Viceroy* had slid her great forefoot through the Biscay swell, and weary seamen had tumbled out of their hammocks, cursing, to swarm on deck and lower the sea-boat from her davits in answer to the call, For Exercise Man Overboard. In the spray-filled darkness fists had been shaken towards the bridge, where Captain Bassinghorn stood holding a turnip-shaped silver watch in his great hand. When the sea-boat was poised at the end of her falls over the heaving water and her Coxswain ready to strike away the disengaging gear, the word would be passed for the First Lieutenant to report to the bridge.

"Too slow, Mr Halfhyde. Too damn slow!"

Water poured from Halfhyde's oilskin. "The men are tired, sir."

"They shall grow tireder, Mr. Halfhyde."

The exercises continued and the mutterings increased, but so did the speed of execution: exhausted men moved like automatons, reacting instinctively to orders. After Gibralter Bassinghorn had driven them under grey skies and through heaving seas brought up by a strong wind out of the Levant. Time and again during that long eastward thrust for Port Said, Halfhyde noted the look he had seen in the Captain's eye on their first meeting, the look of determined dedication: it had grown sharper, more fixed; and it fixed frequently upon the Engineer, Mr Bampton.

"Mr Bampton, you spoke of something over fourteen knots."

"Sir, I spoke of a figure not far short of that."

"But we have made good no more than nine knots."

"Made good, sir, yes." Bampton spoke stubbornly. "We have wind and sea against us, sir."

Bassinghorn walked up and down the bridge, bulky body inclining to the wind's weight, face rock-like beneath the streaming sou'-wester. He returned to stare down at the pale complexion of the Engineer. "After Suez we shall see, Mr Bampton. In placid water I shall expect better of your engines. You will see to it that your stokers use their muscles properly." He turned away again, staring at wind and sea, looking almost instinctively aloft: Halfhyde followed his glance. Captain Bassinghorn had no liking for being in the power of engineers. Later, in the Red Sea, his driving resulted in a half apologetic visit to the bridge by the Surgeon, Dr Carter, a diffident man of middle years who was inclined to be overly conscious of relative rank.

"Some of the stokers are taking the heat badly, sir. It's like very hell in the stokehold."

"I see." Bassinghorn looked at him gravely. "What do you advise, Doctor?"

"Well, sir, perhaps longer spells of rest for the watch on duty—"

"And a drop in steam pressure?"

The Surgeon lifted his hands. "With respect, sir, it may be necessary to accept that."

"You do not give me orders, Doctor."

"No, sir—indeed not, sir. It was a mere suggestion, nothing more."

Bassinghorn said sharply, "The eastern Russian ports will shortly be free of ice and their ships will be able to move out. Upon what errand we know not—but we must be prepared. Because of this I am now under orders to reach the Pacific with all possible despatch, so that I am on station by the time the ice melts. To do this, Doctor, I am dependent upon my steam pressure, much as I may wish it otherwise." Again he glanced aloft, this time more lingeringly. "I shall not weaken the watch in the stokehold."

"No, sir. I simply felt—"

"Doctor, you have my decision. You have done your part, and your opinion is noted. Now leave me to do *my* part."

The Surgeon said no more; he saluted and left the bridge, shaking his head a little and looking anxious. The ship's company were now in their white uniforms, the officers' caps had given place to tropical white helmets with blue puggarees, but this did little to mitigate the intense heat on deck, the rays of a high sun striking down hard from a glittering metallic sky. From below, the very sea seemed to heat the hull like a kettle upon a hob. The yellow-painted ventilators, turned forward to catch the headwind made by the ship's passage and a breeze from the south, brought but little relief below-decks. In the ward-room, the gunroom, the warrant officers' mess, off-watch bodies lay inert on the chairs and settees, drenched in sticky sweat, glad at least that they were not heading the other way, in front of the southerly breeze, so that a following wind would negate the effect of the ship's self-made headwind to leave her in still air, a cocoon of blistering heat from which there would be no escape. The three civilians from Portsmouth suffered badly, unaccustomed to sea life and the rigours of the southern half of the Red Sea towards Aden: Mr Mosscrop, the builder of dockyards, already a victim of appalling seasickness, melted like a barrel of lard. Along the mess decks seamen and marines and stokers lay on bare wooden benches, stretched out listlessly in a close, foetid atmosphere filled with body smell. In the galleys the cooks dripped their sweat into the very food they were preparing. Tempers rose with the heat. Sensing trouble, the Master-at-Arms patrolled the mess decks with his ship's police, men known to the Navy as "crushers" by virtue of the action of overlarge policemen's feet in flattening the ever-present cockroaches. But when trouble came it was of a different sort from fists and oaths, and it came in the devil's kitchen that was the stokehold. Halfhyde saw the flurry in the engine-room alleyway, and caught the arm of a running Stoker Petty Officer as he emerged from the air-lock.

"What's the rush, man?"

"It's the heat, sir. I'm going for the doctor, sir."

"Tell me first."

"The hands are collapsing, sir."

Halfhyde said, "Have them carried up and laid on deck. I'll see the doctor. Where's Mr Bampton?"

"Been sent for, sir—"

"All right, carry on." Halfhyde turned and ran for the surgery. From the surgery he made his way to the Captain's cabin in the after part of the ship. The marine sentry, shouldering arms, brought a hand across his body in salute. Halfhyde burst in unceremoniously, found Bassinghorn studying the Sailing Directions for the area around Parece Vela. The Captain looked up, eyebrows raised.

"Mr Halfhyde, I—"

"I'm sorry, sir. There are casualties from heat in the stoke-hold. I've ordered them to be taken on deck. The doctor's been informed. I think we can expect a drop in steam pressure."

Bassinghorn stared, a small muscle twitching at one side of his mouth. "The men, Halfhyde. I—"

"We embarked ice at Port Said, sir. I've left word with the doctor that he can have it brought up from the beef screen. It's all we can do."

Bassinghorn nodded. "Thank you, Mr Halfhyde. I'll be on deck directly."

Halfhyde left the cabin as Bassinghorn got to his feet and turned heavily towards the great square ports and their clear view over the sea's burning blue. Reaching the deck, he found the heat-struck stokers already being carried up by their mates, and the Surgeon in attendance. The men, naked but for white canvas trousers stained black with coal-dust, were laid flat on the open deck, and an awning was hastily rigged over them by hands detailed by Mr Pinch. Halfhyde looked down at them sombrely: the body hairs were matted, the skin drenched with sweat, the faces bloodless and still. On the orders of the doctor, seamen began fanning the bodies with their hats, and Halfhyde caught the doctor's eye.

"Bad, Doctor?"

"Very bad. I have to get their temperature down—the ice is on the way."

"They'll live?"

The doctor shrugged, his own white drill uniform sweat-darkened and rumpled. "Early days, Number One. I'll be doing all I can."

"Of course. Let me know if there's anything you want." Turning away, Halfhyde found the Captain behind him. Their eyes met: it was Bassinghorn who looked away. His eyes, Halfhyde thought, were troubled, as well they might be. Later that day, two of the stokers died. On Bassinghorn's order, a sea committal was ordered for that very evening: the Red Sea's heat permitted no delays. Once again, the Master-at-Arms and his acolytes were much in evidence, and the Captain of Marines, in command of the firing-party, had his guard nicely placed between the quarterdeck and the seamen and stokers mustered by divisions in the waist. Captain Bassinghorn's voice was strong as he read the simple words of the service, but his face was bleak. When the ceremonial, stark and sad and impressive, was over, and the weighted, canvas-shrouded bodies sinking to the depths, Bassinghorn closed his prayer-book with a snap and stalked off the deck without a word. Halfhyde forebore to ask the usual formal permission to dismiss the ship's company, but waited until the Captain had vanished to his quarters and then gave the order.

"Ship's company, turn forward . . . dismiss!"

There was a slap of bare feet as the bluejackets obeyed

and broke off; but they did not immediately leave the deck. There was a mutter in the air, a rising sound of angry voices. Halfhyde waited for a moment, standing rigidly at attention, his brows drawn down, eyes staring into what looked like a mob. Then he lifted his voice to the Captain of Marines: "Captain Humphreys, face your men about, if you please."

Humphreys opened his mouth: it stayed open for a couple of seconds, for the implications of Halfhyde's order were all too obvious. Then, with a snap, he gave the order. The ranks of armed marines turned about with a crash of rifles, and Halfhyde spoke again. "You were ordered to dismiss. Master-at-Arms?"

"Sir!"

"The rope's-ends, and don't spare them. If the decks are not cleared within one minute, I promise trouble."

"Aye, aye, sir!" The Master-at-Arms began shouting, and moved in with his ship's police. Apart from their commands there was a silence, a pause: then, slowly, reluctantly, the mass of sailors got on the move, shifting themselves forward to pour down the hatches to the mess decks. Halfhyde let out a long breath, and wiped his streaming face. Catching Humphreys' eye, he gave a brief nod, and the marines clumped away with their rifles and bayonets. Halfhyde found Midshipman Runcorn beside him, his young face full of wonder.

He put a hand on the boy's shoulder. "Well, Mr Runcorn. Have you seen a ghost, or what?"

"Oh, no, sir! Not a ghost, sir."

"I'll tell you what you've nearly seen, Mr Runcorn: you've as near as dammit seen mutiny."

"Mutiny, sir?"

"You heard what I said, Mr Runcorn. Remember, it's between you and me."

"Yes, sir."

"Off you go, then."

Halfhyde turned away in the Midshipman's wake. About to follow below, he stopped: already it was full dark, and the sky was a mass of stars, seemingly so low-slung that a man could reach out and pluck them, shining lanterns from the arch of heaven. The engines, stopped in reverence for the burial of the dead, were back once again in their thumping rhythm, and the ship was moving through the dark water, sending out her bow wave to cream down the sides and join the wake in a trail of bright green phosphorescence. The day's heat had left a closeness behind it as it emanated from woodwork and metal. Halfhyde glanced up at the White Ensign drooping like a limp dishcloth from the mizzen peak: his thoughts rioted. That ensign, worn across all the Seven Seas by Her Majesty's ships of war, floated over many things both good and bad, and the worst of all was mutiny. But second to worst, perhaps, was a stupid waste of life. Captain Henry Bassinghorn had much to answer for, and Halfhyde was much troubled, for Bassinghorn was basically a good man. From now on, watchful eyes would be required of a First Lieutenant.

Days passed into weeks, port succeeded port in a business of coaling and storing and replacing the ammunition expended in the Captain's endless practice shoots. One sea gave place to another: Halfhyde had passed through the Strait of Bab el Mandeb, known to sailors as the Gates of Hell, with his heart in his mouth for more trouble in the stokehold, but none had come, and Aden had been reached without incident. Cape Gardafui faded astern as the *Viceroy* headed into the Arabian Sea for Colombo. Bassinghorn had made no reference whatsoever to the deaths, though Halfhyde, who also refrained from comment, believed that they weighed heavily upon the Captain's mind. The seamen and stokers continued more or less sullen but there was no trouble, no refusal of orders. The Master-at-Arms reported an undercurrent of hostility towards the Captain's driving methods, and that was all. Down through the Malacca Strait, the ship steamed into Singapore over a calm sea and beneath blue skies; then on north by way of the South China Sea for the British Far East base at Hong Kong, last port before moving into the Pacific to plant the Union Flag in the name of Her Majesty Queen Victoria. Heavy cloud lay over Hong Kong as the old ship steamed slowly past Stonecutters Island and, junk-surrounded, turned off Kowloon for the man-of-war anchorage. As they approached the anchorage the berthing signal was made from the Commodore-in-Charge: the *Viceroy* was ordered to proceed alongside the wall, using a newly-constructed and specially-deepened berth in the Victoria dockyard. As they came slowly in Bassinghorn stared narrowly at the great humped cloud-bank that seemed to be increasing in size.

"I don't care for the look of that, Mr Halfhyde."

"It'll blow over, sir. It's but May and the typhoon season won't be upon us until July."

"Ah—according to the Sailing Directions, no doubt! Weather can play funny tricks, Mr Halfhyde, and confound the Sailing Directions no end—I've known typhoon conditions to come remarkably early. In any event, we may expect some heavy rain at this time of the year, typhoon or no." The Captain peered over the wing of the bridge. "Those junks. Have them cleared away before I sink them!"

"Hoses, sir?"

"Any damn thing you like, Mr Halfhyde."

Halfhyde gestured down to the fo'c'sle. "Mr Pinch, fire hoses, if you please."

"Aye, aye, sir." The Boatswain moved aft, passing the order. Within the minute, jets of water were spouting from port and starboard as the ship moved inwards. There were shrieks as the jets hit, and the Chinese crews were sent tumbling. Heads bobbed in the water: along the *Viceroy's* decks, the bluejackets, fallen in for entering harbour, grinned at the sight of discomfited heathens, potential dangers to safe ship-handling. They were looking forward to a run ashore: here in Hong Kong the British sailor was king, ricksha boys competed for the honour of carrying him to his pleasures of wine, women, and song. Hong Kong was Portsmouth, Chatham, and Devonport in a romantic setting, transported to the Orient gay.

On the bridge Mr Runcorn, Signal Midshipman, had his telescope to his eye, watching for further strings of flags or wagging semaphore arms from the Commodore: they duly came as a colourful hoist crept up to the signal yard, and Mr Runcorn consulted his Fleet Signal Book. Saluting Bassinghorn, he made his report: "From the Commodore to *Viceroy,* sir. Request the pleasure of your company for dinner at seven bells. You will also bring your First Lieutenant."

Bassinghorn stared: a "request" from a senior officer was always to be regarded as an order, yet even so the juxtaposition of "request the pleasure" and "you will also bring" struck him as peculiar: something was in the wind. Recollecting himself he nodded at Mr Midshipman Runcorn. "Reply, Commodore from *Viceroy.* With much pleasure."

He turned his attention back to his ship-handling; the *Viceroy* proceeded smoothly inwards through the anchorage beneath the peaks surrounding one of the world's most beautiful harbours; and within five minutes was sending out her lines to secure alongside and receive her bunker coal from lighters already coming from the coaling depot. Coaling ship that day would be carried out with the utmost despatch, for libertymen of the watch ashore would not be piped to clean until the vital supplies had been embarked into the specially-extended bunkers.

Chapter 4

A COLD WIND came up with the dark: Bassinghorn and Halfhyde wore boat-cloaks pulled tightly over their mess dress as they made for the quarterdeck gangway. As he went over the side Bassinghorn paused for a word with the Officer of the Watch.

"I shall return aboard at four bells in the first watch, Mr Puckridge."

"Aye, aye, sir."

"If the wind should increase, back up the wires."

"Aye, aye, sir."

Followed by Halfhyde, the Captain proceeded down the ladder, embarking in a ricksha called alongside by Lieutenant Puckridge. A big "boy," slit-eyed, yellow-skinned, was between the shafts: he began loping along, muscles rippling in arms and legs. Bassinghorn, who had been China-side many times in his career, sat wrapped in his boat-cloak with an expressionless face, staring straight ahead. Halfhyde, to whom this was a new scene, looked to right and left with interest as the ricksha was pulled through mean streets towards the Commodore's residence: the ricketty-looking buildings closed in to either side, darkly mysterious and with more than a hint of strange happenings behind the façades and the banner-like shop signs with their gaudy characters. There was an occasional glimpse beneath kerosene lamps of a venerable Chinese in a long quilted garment with a square cap topping a wrinkled face. The light streaming from the small shops was yellow, like the people's skins. The Street of the Bakers, the Street of the Opium-sellers, the Street of the Wheelwrights . . . they scarcely needed Bassinghorn's terse interpretations. Equally obvious was the Street of the Prostitutes: the number of women of all ages beckoning with talon-fingers from windows and doorways was equaled by the number of sailors from the British ships in the harbour, roistering, swaggering along, filled now with drink and seeking other pleasures. Similar desires stirred in St Vincent Halfhyde: the sea had more than its share of lonely moments for a full-blooded man. He craned from the ricksha: one or two of the women, mere girls, were attractive enough after weeks at sea, would still be so even in the woman-easy environments of London and concupiscent Portsmouth Town. Bassinghorn noticed his First Lieutenant's preoccupation.

"I see you are tempted, Mr Halfhyde. Would you wish to enter the same orifice as a common seaman, or some cook's mate?"

Halfhyde laughed. "I think not, sir. Have no fear, I can contain myself . . . with difficulty!"

"There is satisfaction in continence, Mr Halfhyde."

Halfhyde smiled in the darkness: he could find no agreement with that pontifical statement. As a Midshipman, as a Sub-Lieutenant even, he had in his youthful ignorance made the large assumption that Post Captains were above and beyond such basic stirrings, but subsequent experience had taught him different: even Admirals were not immune, and had been discovered in the most embarrassing situations in the seaports of the Empire. He wondered now how Bassinghorn subdued his urges, how he had come to remain single—for he would not have been, and still would not be, unattractive to women.

During his many talks with the Captain on passage from Portsmouth, Halfhyde had found him uncommunicative as to himself; but had formed the impression that he was far from a wealthy man. Perhaps that was the reason: married officers dependent wholly upon naval pay faced a life of near bankruptcy, showered with unpaid bills, a most unhappy lot. Halfhyde, only slimly pocket-lined himself, faced a similar situation but even so doubted if he could accept a life of celibacy. True, a naval wife was but seldom accessible and marriage was not in fact looked upon with favour in the Service; but at least a wife had not to be hunted for on return to port: Halfhyde was an impatient man, to whom the necessary formalities and preliminaries were a tiresome chore.

Emerging from the Street of the Prostitutes and its pressing, uniformed clientele, the ricksha came into more salubrious purlieus, turning eventually below an archway where it was halted by a naval picket of armed and gaitered seamen under a Petty Officer. As Bassinghorn stared from the ricksha, the guard saluted.

"Captain of the *Viceroy*," Bassinghorn said, and was waved through. They went down a broad, tree-lined drive, redolent with night-flowered smells unfamiliar to Halfhyde. They stopped beside a porch, into which light poured from a wide hall. In this light stood the Commodore's Petty Officer Steward. Disembarking from the ricksha, the newly-arrived officers were escorted to the Commodore's drawing-room. In front of a fireplace and beneath a large painting of Her Majesty before one of the tartan-curtained windows of Balmoral, stood Commodore Sir John Willard flanked by his wife and daughter. The Commodore, rock-faced and withdrawn, favoured Bassinghorn with a distant nod. Introductions were made: Lady Willard, a stoutish woman with a good-natured face, murmured rather than spoke, and kept glancing at her husband. Miss Mildred Willard had a some-what loud laugh for a young lady, and facially resembled the Commodore: as if that were not enough, there seemed a ten-dency to gush. Halfhyde summed her up as a young woman to be avoided should the path of duty lead the *Viceroy* back to Hong Kong thereafter. The Commodore lifted a hand to his Petty Officer Steward, snapping the fingers briefly. Sherry was poured.

"Your health, Bassinghorn."

"And yours, sir." Bassinghorn noticed an odd look in Willard's eye as the Commodore ran his glance over Halfhyde: more and more there was the feeling of something untoward . . . for his part Halfhyde was suffering, in addition to his curiosity, an off-putting feeling of being basically unwelcome and never mind the commanding invitation of the Commodore's signal. Halfhyde had heard of Sir John Willard by repute: Sir John was known to the Navy as an unsociable man whose single-minded purpose was his duty. The Commodore now proceeded to live up to that reputation: the sherry was despatched in very short time indeed and an impatient snapping of fingers began. Lady Willard looked desperate and the Petty Officer Steward hurried from the far end of the drawing-room, to return within the minute to announce that dinner was served. Lady Willard smiled apologetically at Captain Bassinghorn, who took her arm; with equal gallantry Halfhyde gave a slight bow in the direction of Miss Mildred and led her in with the Commodore stalking behind like a bird of prey. Dinner was a trial, Halfhyde disliked small-talk and Miss Mildred, it seemed, was incapable of anything else. Captain Bassinghorn, in female company, was tongue-tied; but was forced to do his best since the Commodore sat in a lofty silence, con-tributing nothing but watching all present with hawk's eyes.

However, little time was wasted: course followed course with the speed and precision of a fleet evolution, and when the time came for the port Lady Willard rose as though hove up on an anchor-cable by order from the bridge.

"We shall go to the drawing-room, John, if Captain Bassinghorn will excuse us."

"Of course, Lady Willard." Basinghorn and Halfhyde got to their feet, hovering with napkins in their hands and smiling deferentially. The ladies left.

"Now then," the Commodore said, pouring port.

Cigar smoke filled the dining-room, as heavy as any sea mist. Through it hung the strong chin and cadaverous face of the Commodore, who had spent a good deal of time disclaiming any responsibility for Her Majesty's Ship *Viceroy* and all who sailed in her. The ship, he said, was not joining his command. Bassinghorn was independent still. He must not think he could run for safety to the Commodore, or shift any decisions in that direction.

"I would not propose to, sir."

"Then we understand one another, Captain." Sir John paused. "Port?"

Bassinghorn waved a hand. "Thank you, no."

"You are abstemious. Halfhyde?"

Halfhyde pushed his glass forward: they were alone now, the servants, both British and Chinese, having withdrawn. The Commodore re-filled the glass, and as he did so Halfhyde noticed the disapproval in Bassinghorn's face. He didn't care; the dinner had been terrible and he wished to forget Miss Mildred's gushing talk about nothing, the gush that had been a shade dammed when he had confessed to a total lack of interest in hunting. He sipped the port slowly: it was an excellent one, making up for Miss Mildred, and putting him in a better frame of mind for what must now be coming. The Commodore continued. "I ordered you to attend upon me, Captain, for one reason only: I have been instructed by cable from the Admiralty to pass certain further information that was not available when you left Portsmouth, nor even when you cleared from Singapore. Thus I act in the capacity of an agent—nothing more. This is fully understood?"

"It is, sir."

"Equally as an agent, I shall not consider it outside my mandate to offer advice if you should ask—but it will be no more than advice and is not subsequently to be quoted in any quarter. Now, Mr Halfhyde." The Commodore topped up his own glass, filling it to the brim. "We come now to the reason I sent for you as well as your Captain. The cable from the Admiralty, Mr Halfhyde, gave me certain particulars of your past service." He lifted a hand and wagged a long, delicate finger through the swirls of cigar smoke. "I doubt if this information will be welcome to you, Mr Halfhyde, but it is possible you are about to meet an old friend—for the third time in your career."

Halfhyde felt a vague stirring in his stomach and bowels: in the circumstances of a likely Russian interest in the newly-emerged Pacific island, the Commodore's words had virtually told him who this friend, who in fact was no friend, might be. But he asked, "His name, if you please, sir?"

"Gorsinski. Admiral Prince Gorsinski, commanding a cruiser squadron of the Imperial Russian Navy, wearing his flag in the first-class protected cruiser *Ostrolenka*."

Involuntarily, Halfhyde shivered, saw Bassinghorn looking at him curiously. Halfhyde had no lack of zeal for the Service and was no coward: fear he had felt, and would feel again, like any normal man; but he never gave way to it. On the other hand, Gorsinski was a very deadly enemy, a man of immense power, allied by blood to the Czar of all the Russias, a man twice bested by Halfhyde, a man who must by now be dedicating his very life to the capture of the British Lieutenant who had made a fool of him . . .

Watching his face, the Commodore asked coldly, "You are scared, Mr Halfhyde? You find the prospect daunting?"

"I am scared, sir, but I am not daunted. I shall accept what comes."

Sir John grunted, but gave an approving nod. "An honest answer—I like that. Now, Mr Halfhyde, be good enough to tell me about Prince Gorsinski."

Gorsinski: the very name, to Halfhyde, smelled of death. The first encounter with that imperious aristocrat had come years before: Halfhyde, a Midshipman in the sloop *Cloud,* had fallen into Russian hands after an unfortunate incident in the Bosporus during which Halfhyde's semi-drunken Captain had opened fire on a Russian ship entering from the Sea of Marmara. The *Cloud* had been sunk by gunfire and Halfhyde, picked from the water, had been removed to Sevastopol. Gorsinski had been the Admiral in charge of the naval port, and Halfhyde, brought before him, had impressed the Russian with his courage in adversity; Gorsinski had subsequently rescued him from imprisonment in Siberia and had him brought back to the greater comfort of Sevastopol. After a year in Russian hands, having never given, nor been asked for, his parole, Halfhyde had contrived to escape into Turkey and thence home. Reports reaching England afterwards had indicated extreme fury on the part of his benefactor, Prince Gorsinski.

"A benefactor," Sir John interrupted when Halfhyde told his story, "is not an enemy, Mr Halfhyde."

"A benefactor to me, certainly—at that stage only! But a man of great cruelty, sir. He personally ordered the most savage treatment of other prisoners when Turkish ships were taken from time to time. There was torture, sir."

"But not of you. I understand you took the opportunity of learning the Russian tongue—and also became well acquainted with Prince Gorsinski personally?"

"Yes, sir."

"Which, no doubt, was why he took your escape as a personal insult. However, go on, Mr Halfhyde."

Halfhyde's mind moved backwards again, this time to the events of a year ago. As briefly as possible he told Sir John Willard and Bassinghorn of how his actions had led indirectly to the blowing up of Prince Gorsinski's great flagship, the *Romanov*, in the wind-swept Bight of Benin; and of how Prince Gorsinski's final indignity had come when he, Halfhyde, captured and pressed under threat into service as navigator of the Russian squadron out through the shifting sands of the bight off Fishtown, had so contrived matters that Gorsinski's two remaining cruisers had resoundingly struck each other, the proud *Grand Duke Alexis* smashing her way into the after part of the *St Petersburg* so that it had looked for all the world as though a most unnatural act were taking place . . .

The Commodore nodded. "One can understand a degree of chagrin. However, Prince Gorsinski's connections have seen to it that he was not disgraced."

"And now, sir?"

"Now, Mr Halfhyde—although I'm not aware of what his precise orders may be—he has been reported as having left his base at Okhotsk before the ice closed the port and having subsequently entered Vladivostock. Three days ago, having apparently made use of a fleet of ice-breakers to free his passage out of port before the arrival of the full thaw, he was reported to have passed Tsushima making south." The Commodore put down his glass carefully. "In the circumstances, it's very possible he has received certain reports concerning your mission, and, as a result, certain hastening orders. I think you will take the point, Captain?"

Bassinghorn pulled at his beard. "A very different complexion, sir."

"Very! An over-riding necessity now for speed. This has become a race, and you have arrived in the nick of time, gentlemen. I am able to confirm that geologically the area of the island is now settled down. Captain Bassinghorn, you will—" Sir John checked himself. *"My advice is,* that you take your ship to sea immediately—tonight."

There was a rising wind and a lash of rain with it: the ricksha boy, bidden by Bassinghorn to wait, was drenched. In spite of Bassinghorn's earlier comment on the weather, Halfhyde had not expected the weight of wind: it was as though the volcanic eruptions had left behind them some latent effect upon the elements, disturbing the normal typhoon pattern. Bassinghorn pulled out his turnip-shaped watch: he would be back aboard as promised by four bells, an estimate that he would have made good even at the risk of impoliteness to his host, for he was a man who prized punctuality. As they were pulled along, the tearing gusts of wind seemed to increase even more, battering at their bodies, sending leaves whirling and, later as they entered the narrow streets of the town, scraps of paper and oddments of unnameable filth. The streets were largely empty now, the sailors from the fleet having made their choices of women for passing the time until liberty expired. Halfhyde, thinking sombre thoughts of Admiral Prince Gorsinski, had those thoughts broken into brusquely by his Captain.

"Leave was piped until eight bells, I think Mr Halfhyde?"

"Yes, sir."

"I shall want a sober ship's company."

"As sober as possible, sir."

"Precisely. Their time must be shortened. You'll send an additional patrol ashore, if you please, Mr Halfhyde, the moment we reach the ship." Bassinghorn's words were being torn from him, cast away, so that he had to bend to Halfhyde's ear. "A Lieutenant in charge . . . the men are to be *brought* back if necessary . . ."

The ricksha boy ran on; as they came out of one of the narrow ways running down towards the dockyard, a gust of wind caught them from the waterfront and blew the ramshackle vehicle onto one wheel, lifting the shafts high and the coolie with them: with Bassinghorn on top of him, Halfhyde was ejected into the lying, rain-sogged filth of the street. Winded by the weight of Bassinghorn's heavy body, he staggered out from under and stood up, swaying against the strong wind, his mess dress filthy, his boat-cloak's gold neck chain torn away from the cloth. Bending, he hoisted the Captain to his feet. The spokes of the ricksha wheel had snapped from the hub: it was now a case of walking. Heads down, they fought against the wind's strength and the cold fingers of the rain, making as fast as possible towards the naval dockyard. Reaching it, they found an astonishing sight: with thick smoke streaming from her funnels like some nightmare bonfire, the *Viceroy* was lying across the harbour, her bows and her heavy iron ram pointed towards the dockyard wall and her stern swinging with terrifying speed to the weight of wind and turbulent water. From fore and aft her parted wires hung judas over the side, clearly visible in the light of yardarm groups hoisted to her fore- and mainmast heads.

Chapter 5

"BY GOD, HALFHYDE, either she must go to sea or she must get fresh lines away . . ." Bassinghorn's voice tailed off into silence: impotently he clenched his fists. As though in some telepathic obedience to his unheard order, a cutter was already being lowered on the falls—and, in the view of the watching officers, coming down too fast. A moment later some hitch occurred, an impediment to the free movement of the cutter's after fall. With the forward fall running free around the sheaves at the davit-head and her stern held fast, she upended in a twinkling, hanging virtually up-and-down and sending her crew hurtling into the water. Bassinghorn stared, his face working. Halfhyde seized his arm and shouted into his ear.

"A boat, sir, here by the wall. I'm going out."

Bassinghorn didn't seem to hear: Halfhyde turned away, let his boat-cloak go. It sailed off on the wings of the wind, flapping like some grotesque bird. Halfhyde ran to the edge of the wall, and jumped. He took the water with a mighty splash and went under. It was icy cold. Surfacing, spouting seawater and filth, he focused on the small boat at the jetty, secured with a single rope to a ring-bolt. He swam towards it, got an arm across the gunwhale, hung for a moment taking breath, then heaved himself aboard. The boat dipped and rolled alarmingly as he moved into the bows to cast off the securing rope: as he let it go and quickly pulled the end through the ring-bolt, he was

aware of Bassinghorn leaning over above him. The Captain was
shouting, but Halfhyde couldn't catch his drift: he pushed off
from the wall, taking up the oars from the bottom-boards and
dropping them into the crutches. Disregarding his Captain he
pulled hard towards the drifting *Viceroy,* which was now some
two cables'-lengths off. His muscles, for too long unused to hard
physical labour, quickly began to ache: he gritted his teeth and
fought on through the wind-blown water of the harbour,
drenched again by rain and spray. Smoke swept down upon
him, making him choke with its foul fumes. He heard the blast
of the steam siren, sending a warning into the night: he threw
a glance over his shoulder: he was nearing the ship, upon whose
decks there seemed to be a degree of panic now. Straining upon
the oars, Halfhyde pulled closer, making for the ship's lee side
and some protection from the tearing wind which, to him in his
tiny craft, seemed to have the proportions of a typhoon, unlikely
as this would be so early in the year. After an eternity of strug-
gle he drew in towards the still-swinging bows: and just as he
approached the stern, the port bower anchor, already free of the
cathead, was let go with a rush straight from the hawse-pipe,
the party on the fo'c'sle evidently seeing no virtue in using precious time on veering it first to the waterline. Halfhyde cursed
as a plume of sea lifted and dropped upon him, almost upset-
ting his craft. He pulled violently on his oars and drew across
to starboard into the lee of the vast iron side, towering like a
wall above him. Then, shipping his oars, he cupped his hands
and shouted up to the deck, yelling hoarsely into the comparative stillness below the deflected wind:

"Send down a heaving-line and make sure the aim is true!"

From the fo'c'sle an oilskinned arm waved in acknowledgement: Halfhyde waited, his body trembling with impatience.

Aboard the *Viceroy* they knew what he meant to do. A heaving-line was quickly made fast to the eye of a heavy manilla rope; then, in the expert hands of Mr Pinch, the thin rope with its weighted turk's-head was cast high into the air, snaking up to fall with an incredible accuracy across the plunging row-boat. Halfhyde, his arm raised ready, caught it and made the end fast to a thwart, then at once bent to the oars. With nine thousand tons of iron adrift behind him he headed back towards the wharf, pulling desperately. A quick look to his right showed him that his action was being nicely backed up: from the after part of the *Viceroy* another cutter had been launched, this time successfully, and another heaving-line was being sent across. Halfhyde redoubled his efforts, blind now to the pain in arms and legs as they strained against oars and stretcher, blind to the resumed weight of the wind as he began to re-emerge from the immediate lee of the great hull, blind to the stinging lash of the rain. Everything in him was bent to the one task, the one thought: if he and the cutter's crew could get their lines ashore so that the heavy ropes could be drawn onto the wharf and made fast around the bollards—and if the anchor could be made to hold the ship away from a sudden smash against the wall—then the situation would be under control and time would be given to back up the headrope and sternrope with the storm moorings. As he came closer to the wharf and to the Captain, who was waiting to take the lines himself, Halfhyde became aware of consternation in Bassinghorn's gesturing arms, in the urgent shouts that he could not hear. Instinct made him look over his shoulder: the *Viceroy* seemed to be gathering way, was being pushed down upon him, broadside and inexorable. By now he was within a dozen yards of the dockyard wall: there was no time left in which to make for safety away from the ship's length.

Within seconds the moving mass must crush him like a beetle against the heavy stone wharf. There was one chance, and Halfhyde, spurred by a consuming fear now, rowed for it like a maniac: the ship had been berthed against two catamarans, heavy floating fenders secured to ring-bolts in the wall to keep a vessel's plates safe from chafing and grinding with any movement of wind and water. To get between them would spell salvation. With the hull now only feet behind him, Halfhyde made a last frantic effort. He had reached the first catamaran and was rounding its corner when his boat seemed to shoot from under him. There was a heavy blow in his back, a roar of steam, and shouts; and the last he heard before he hit the wharf was a terrible crunch of wood from the farther catamaran, and the desperate cries of men.

Halfhyde came to in his cabin: his head ached abominably and his mouth was dry. Coloured lights flashed before him; he opened his eyes, closed them again quickly as nausea struck and the cabin swung around him. Something cool came down on his forehead,wiping away cold sweat.

"Feeling better, Number One?"

"No."

"Give it time, then. Nothing's broken."

It was the Surgeon's voice. Halfhyde lay still for a while, recollecting, fighting back against his nausea and the bodily stiffness that held him like a vice. There was a swaying movement of his bunk, and he heard the sound of engines. He licked his dry lips, asked, "Are we at sea?"

"Yes."

"Tell me what happened."

"The ship was re-berthed. The Captain went to sea as soon

as the libertymen were aboard." The doctor paused. "Before that, he'd gone down and got you out himself."

"Gone down?"

"Jumped down to the cat. He pulled you clear."

"I'm grateful!" Halfhyde tried to smile; the effort was painful, he felt sick again. "The others, Doctor? Any casualties?"

"I'm afraid so. The cutter was smashed. Young Runcorn was in charge—"

"Killed?"

"No, just knocked out like you. Two seamen—the bowman, the sternsheetsman—they were crushed. Three more were drowned from the upended cutter. There was nothing anyone could do, Number One." Halfhyde was aware of the Surgeon getting to his feet. "I'll leave you now. Just sleep, that's all. I'll send some medicine."

He left the cabin: Halfhyde heard the click as the door was shut. He lay thinking, and his thoughts were not pleasant ones: there had been a blunder. Lieutenant Puckridge must have been slow to send out extra ropes before the big blow had come, in spite of the Captain's last order before going ashore. There had been a terrible clumsiness in the lowering of the first cutter, dilatoriness in not dropping an anchor sooner. A mishandled business from start to finish . . . had Halfhyde been in charge in Bassinghorn's absence, he would have taken the *Viceroy* straight out to sea to ride the storm in safety, and then returned to harbour when the weather moderated. His bitter reflections were interrupted by the Captain himself.

"How are you, Halfhyde?"

Halfhyde made an effort and opened his eyes. He was dizzy still, but improving, and he said as much. He added, "I think you saved my life, sir. I—"

"And lost others."

"Not your fault, sir."

"They were my ship's company, Mr Halfhyde." Bassinghorn's tone was heavy. A seaman of the old sort, he would have the age-old seafaring belief that the ship was the captain, the captain the ship, one and indivisible, a unity and a high responsibility that was always present ashore or afloat. "As for my officers, I have already made my views known. No more will be said. I think a lesson has been truly learned, and that must be counted on the credit side. There is another credit: I congratulate you on your quick reactions, and a fine example of seamanship, Mr Halfhyde."

"Thank you, sir. What are the orders now?"

"For you, to rest and recover as fast as may be. For the ship, to reach the vicinity of Parece Vela with the utmost despatch."

"Before Prince Gorsinski?"

"Yes, Mr Halfhyde, but we shall talk about that once you are fit."

"Which shall be soon, sir."

Bassinghorn nodded, hesitated as though he had something further to say, but thought better of it and turned away. As he left, he looked back; and Halfhyde saw once again the strange look of dedication, the sudden blaze in the blue eyes. Plainly, no Russian squadron was going to stop Captain Bassinghorn; but the more he thought about their prospects, the more Halfhyde saw the impossibility of success. One ship, one old ship dug out from the grave, against a first-class Russian cruiser squadron—she was surely doomed. There was no sense in it; there must be lunatics in charge at the Admiralty! Or something more sinister, something that had not yet come to light, in their orders. Halfhyde thought about the Commodore in Hong Kong and his talk of offering advice only, of not being in any way involved himself. Sir John Willard either knew, or had guessed, that the Admiralty was failing to be honest, and he was standing well to leeward of any future trouble.

Next morning Halfhyde obtained clearance from the doctor and reported himself fit for duty to Bassinghorn in the cuddy. Bassinghorn looked up from some paperwork at his desk, and gestured Halfhyde to sit. Halfhyde looked out of the stern ports: the sea was flat, the freak wind gone, and a hot sun shone. The wake creamed into the distance astern and the Captain's quarters shuddered to the screw's tumble and thrust. Bassinghorn put down his pen with a gesture of relief. "My report upon recent events, Mr Halfhyde, with praise where it is due."

Halfhyde inclined his head but made no comment.

"I'm troubled," Bassinghorn said.

"The deaths, sir?"

"Yes. But those poor fellows cannot be brought back. To reflect upon them, other than to learn a lesson, is pointless. I am troubled by the effect upon the ship's company—do you understand?"

"Yes, I understand."

Bassinghorn picked up a heavy ebony ruler, rolled it between his massive hands and stared in silence through the stern ports where Halfhyde had looked earlier. After a while he said in a heavy tone, "The stokers in the Red Sea, now this. A voodoo ship, Halfhyde—or at all events, a voodoo Captain!"

"I think not, sir."

"Do you?" Bassinghorn gave a bitter laugh. "You have noticed nothing because you have been on your sickbed—but you'll see!"

"Can you be precise?" Halfhyde's query was casual, deliberately so.

"A sullenness, a manifest resentment."

"But they're seamen, sir, and used to—difficulties, even death."

Another hard laugh. "We've been at peace so long, they've all forgotten—all but me and Mr Pinch! No, Halfhyde, these men are used to nothing but cruising, showing the flag, fleet manoeuvres and evolutions and so forth. I'll wager none of them has met death at sea before. Now they've met it, they don't like it."

Halfhyde studied the Captain's face in silence for a while, then said quietly, "With respect, sir, I believe you may be seeing trouble where none has occurred—"

"As yet. *As yet,* Mr Halfhyde!" There was anger in Bassinghorn's voice now, hard anger, even some kind of violence held in check with difficulty. "You asked me to be precise: very well—I shall be." He got to his feet, moved over to the stern ports, gazed for a moment towards the hard line of the horizon, then swung round on his First Lieutenant. He lifted a hand, fingers extended, and began ticking off items. "One, I have detected more than a single instance of dumb insolence towards Mr Campbell, who has himself taken no disciplinary action against it. Two, the Master-at-Arms, in your absence sick, has reported direct to me that there have been gatherings of seamen and stokers that have broken up quickly on the approach of the ship's police. Three, I observed a Leading Seaman spit on the deck behind Midshipman Runcorn—who was in charge of the cutter when the ship was re-berthed. As to that, the man is currently in my report, and I shall disrate him."

"I see, sir. Then perhaps that will stop the trouble."

"I think not. I think it will not be enough, Mr Halfhyde, and I propose another measure—as a timely warning."

Halfhyde felt a prickle of apprehension: timely warnings were one thing, insensitive exacerbations were quite another; and Captain Bassinghorn's eyes revealed that he was feeling extremely exacerbatory, though, no doubt, he would himself have found another word for it. "May I ask, sir—what measure?"

"You may. Lowerdeck will be cleared, and the Articles of War shall be read, and read by you—"

"No, sir!" Halfhyde got to his feet and faced his Captain. "With respect, sir, to do that now could easily be misunderstood. The feeling you speak of will quieten—"

"I think not, Mr Halfhyde."

"But if you will allow me—"

Bassinghorn stopped him with an upraised hand. "You have a certain reputation at the Admiralty. When first we met, I told you that you would argue with me at your peril. Do you propose to argue now?"

Halfhyde controlled his face and his rising temper. "I do not, sir. I shall obey your orders—if I must!"

The Boatswain's Mates shrilled their pipes throughout the ship: "Clear lowerdeck, hands to muster in the waist!" Halfhyde contacted the Lieutenants and informed them of what was to happen. There were long faces: true, the reading of the Articles of War, the Navy's list of crimes and punishments, was carried out at statutory intervals in Her Majesty's ships at sea. But a special reading was a different kettle of fish altogether, the shore-side equivalent being the public reading of the Riot Act before rebellious citizens upon the orders of a Justice of the Peace. The import of the Captain's command would be well understood by, at any rate, the longer-serving ratings. It might work the way Bassinghorn expected, or it might not. Seamen were never like soldiers: they were unpredictable and independent-minded, which was the precise reason why the marines, who were sworn men where sailors were not, were always berthed between the officers and the men.

Halfhyde watched from the quarterdeck as all men off watch proceeded to the waist, streaming from the hatches and along the walkways for the tight-packed muster abaft the bridge and funnel-casing. Mr Pinch, moving through the press of seamen and stokers, signalmen and officers' servants and cooks, climbed the starboard ladder to the quarterdeck.

"Well, Mr Pinch?"

The Boatswain's square-shaped, sun-tanned face was troubled. "I don't like it, sir. There's a nasty mood down there." He nodded down to the waist. "They're sullen, sir. Resentful."

"Of what, Mr Pinch?" Halfhyde paused, searching the Boatswain's face. There was a clear reluctance to answer, and Halfhyde pressed. "Of the Captain?"

"Aye, I think that's so."

"I'm sorry to hear it. Captain Bassinghorn is in fact a moderate man, and never mind a certain reputation for being a hard one. But if he is driven to severe measures . . ." Halfhyde said no more: to do so would have been unnecessary, for Mr Pinch understood well enough. Halfhyde brooded as one by one the officers came up to the quarterdeck. He stood silent, hands behind his back, feet apart, bracing himself against the roll of the ship to the ocean swell. It was unbelievable that only so recently the decks had been a wind-strewn shambles of wires and ropes, that she had lost men in storm-lashed water. The China seas were as unpredictable as sailors themselves! Below in the waist the Petty Officers and ship's police were moving among the mass of men, checking, passing orders. Behind Halfhyde the Captain's Clerk, a white cloth stripe beneath the single gold one on his shoulder-straps, came up holding the volume containing the Articles of War, and blinking nervously through thick-lensed spectacles. Halfhyde glanced at him, then turned his attention forward again. The Master-at-Arms was approaching the ladder from the waist.

Saluting Halfhyde, the chief of ship's police reported, "Lower-deck cleared, sir, all hands off watch mustered in the waist."

"Thank you, Master. Stand them at ease, if you please."

"Aye, aye, sir." Another salute: the Master-at-Arms turned about and gave the order. Halfhyde walked forward a few steps and stood against the rail looking down at the silent, upturned faces, his gaze moving from one to another, trying to read the many expressions and pick out those who might prove the troublemakers. He was aware of Mr Pinch at his side, and he turned towards him. "What is it, Mr Pinch?"

"Have you ever seen mutiny, sir?"

Halfhyde smiled bitterly, his long face hard. "Not in a British ship, Mr Pinch." His memories of mutiny aboard Prince Gorsinski's flagship were terrible enough: for such to be repeated aboard a British man-of-war was utterly unthinkable, yet, as he had hinted earlier to Runcorn, possible. Halfhyde braced his shoulders. "Let's not even consider that, Mr Pinch—"

"I've no wish to, sir. None at all. To have been in a ship that's mutinied, it follows a man like a Jonah . . . even into retirement." Benjamin Pinch gave a sudden shiver. Halfhyde was about to answer him harshly, to say roundly that the old Warrant Officer was warming the bell in no mean fashion, reacting unduly before he had any reason, when the Captain's head appeared, coming up the ladder from his quarters aft. Halfhyde called the ship's company to attention, sharply.

"I have been waiting for you, Mr Halfhyde."

"Sorry, sir." Halfhyde saluted. "Lowerdeck cleared, sir—"

"So I see, Mr Halfhyde. Stand the men easy, if you please, and then read the Articles of War."

Upon Halfhyde's order, the massed sailors stood easy: here and there a man's lips moved as he chewed upon his quid of tobacco, an act of insolence in itself when fallen in before the Captain and his officers, but Halfhyde decided to ignore this and hoped fervently that Bassinghorn would ignore it also. He took the thick volume from the Clerk, opened it at the inserted marker, cleared his throat, looked down once more at the silent faces, then began reading in an unhurried voice, clear and strong, first the preamble, then each clause of the tacit agreement made by every man who served the Fleet at sea in the very moment of his enlistment, an agreement, backed by the Board of Admiralty, the Monarch, and the whole majesty of the law of England, from which there was no escape:

". . . every person subject to this Act . . . who shall commit . . . shall suffer death, or such other punishment as is hereinafter mentioned."

Death, aboard the Queen's ships, was still the required penalty for almost every seafaring crime from treason and mutiny downward, though mitigating circumstances and an easy-going Captain could scale down the punishment "hereinafter mentioned." Death, however, remained the operative word; death was ever at the Captain's command, the constant threat that kept men in obedience; or, by its very repetition as it was being repeated this morning, that lit a spark . . . as he read on in a level voice, Halfhyde dreaded the possibility of that spark igniting, dreaded it largely for personal reasons. As Mr Pinch had so rightly said, mutiny was a Jonah upon any officer's career. And if a First Lieutenant, in his first appointment as such, failed to satisfy Their Lordships in Whitehall, then the prospects for his future were bleak indeed. The spark that came, however, was not from any mere paper-written threat of death: it came from a sudden and terrible jet of superheated steam that blasted from the after funnel, slicing through the smoke, roaring, whining, to be followed by the screams of men running up from below.

Chapter 6

THERE WERE SHOUTS from the waist, shouts of fear and anger: men pressed towards the hatches. They were brought up short by a bellow from the quarterdeck: Bassinghorn himself, his eyes staring.

"All men on deck to stand fast, d'you hear me? Remain where you are until further orders. Captain Humphreys?"

The Captain of Marines hurried forward and saluted, "Sir?"

"Sentries on the hatchways, if you please, Captain Humphreys. No man is to go below without orders."

"Very good, sir."

"Mr Halfhyde, you and I shall go and look for ourselves, and take Mr Pinch and six men with us, no more."

Halfhyde nodded, and caught the eye of Mr Pinch. There was a look of horror in the Boatswain's face, a look that said imagination was painting shocking pictures: steam meant the boiler-room, and such an escape meant naked terror below. The screams were increasing, were heard clear above the blast of steam itself, as Mr Pinch dashed for the after hatch with his Captain and First Lieutenant, and six stokers picked haphazard from the ranks by the Master-at-Arms. They raced down the companion ladders behind Bassinghorn and entered the air-lock to the engine-room. The compartment was filled with vapour but there was not a moment's hesitation from Bassinghorn. He went straight down the spider's web of ladders into the depths, with Halfhyde and Mr Pinch behind him, forcing back the men coming up in panic; and on the starting-platform saw the pale face of Mr Bampton, eyes staring through the swirl of steam.

"Mr Bampton, what has happened?"

Bampton swallowed, passed a hand across his eyes and shook his head dully.

"Come on, man, your report, and quickly!"

Bassinghorn reached out, seized the Engineer and shook his body like a rat. Looking past Bampton he saw a Stoker Petty Officer coming from the direction of the stokehold, screaming like a baby, his left arm limp by his side, the flesh hanging in bloody strips, and his naked flanks swollen and coloured bright red. Bassinghorn ran for him, and the man collapsed into his arms.

"You'll be attended immediately," Bassinghorn said. The screams continued: Bassinghorn, drenched now with sweat, looked up as the Surgeon came running down the engine-room ladders with his sick-berth attendants. Thankfully the Captain passed over the burned body of the Stoker Petty Officer, and waved to Halfhyde. "The boiler-room, Mr Halfhyde. Come!"

They ran forward, bending through a dark tunnel between the great boilers themselves, a tunnel filled with searing steam. They were forced back, their exposed flesh tingling and red-dening fast. Bassinghorn lifted his voice to Bampton: "Shut off the steam, man, d'you hear? Pull yourself together and shut off!"

Bampton, clinging to the rail of the starting-platform, shook like a leaf. "I can't!"

"*Can't?* I'll—"

"Not from the affected boiler, sir. It must be left to discharge itself now. There is no alternative, sir." He covered his face with his hands. "My number two boiler, sir . . . has worked loose from its cradle, and severed the stop valve from the main steam pipe."

"And so?"

"Sir, the full head of steam . . . it's discharging directly into the stokehold!"

Bassinghorn stared at him, his face working in the dim engine-room lighting. "My God! Those poor devils, they'll be flayed alive! Mr Halfhyde, they must be got out at once—"

"No, sir. I'm sorry."

"You have my order, Mr Halfhyde—"

"Sir, it's already too late. It was too late in the very moment it happened." Halfhyde's face was yellow, ghastly in the electric lamps. "You can't risk more lives uselessly, sir."

"I shall go myself, if you see fit to disobey my order, Mr Halfhyde." Bassinghorn started forward, going back towards the boiler-room tunnel and the roaring steam: Halfhyde laid a hand on his shoulder, and caught the eye of Benjamin Pinch.

"I ask you not to go, sir."

There was no answer: Bassinghorn moved on. Halfhyde said, "All right, Mr Pinch, the responsibility's mine alone," and grabbed for the Captain's right arm. After a moment's hesitation, the Boatswain took the left arm. The Captain was brought forcibly to a halt. From the boiler-room and stokehold the screaming had stopped; the terrible roar of steam continued. Halfhyde could not shut out his imagination: as clear as day he saw the bodies, the men who had not managed to make their way out through the tunnel. Raw flesh, with all skin and underfat melted away, a revolting death. He staggered for a moment, got a grip upon his emotions and steadied. *Shall suffer death, or such other punishment as is hereinafter mentioned . . .* Bassinghorn would suffer his own punishment now: he could scarcely have chosen a worse moment in which to have the Articles of War read.

•   •   •

When the roar of steam had quietened, the dead were brought out. Back on the upper-deck, thankfully in God's free fresh air where a man could move nimbly out of death's path, Halfhyde spoke to the ship's company, telling them the facts before rushing rumour could make them even worse. The men were shocked; ordered to dismiss, they dispersed quickly and quietly. The Master-at-Arms remained behind, his face sombre.

"What d'you think, Master?"

"I think of trouble, sir."

"*Open* trouble?"

"Mutiny's a strong word, sir, a desperate act."

"They've not reached that point?"

The Master-at-Arms pursed his lips, looked away across the dark blue of the sea, then back to the First Lieutenant. "No, sir. I think not—I hope not. I hope there will be no more deaths, sir. I'm making the assumption the Captain will now return to Hong Kong."

Halfhyde gave the man a sharp look, but the face had closed up. However, the underlying meaning was clear enough to Halfhyde without further questioning. Dismissing the Master-at-Arms he became aware of Mr Midshipman Runcorn crossing the deck and looking grass green; he called to him, looked at him closely: the boy's face was pale, so pale that it was almost transparent, the bone structure visible beneath the bloodless flesh.

"Mr Runcorn, I remarked not so long ago that you appeared to have seen a ghost. You have a similar look again. There are things you must learn to look upon if you are to survive in the Service."

"Yes, sir. Sir, I—I saw the stokers being brought up." Runcorn swallowed, looked greener than ever. "Sir, they were like—"

"Meat for the beef screen, Mr Runcorn. I know. If ever we are in action, you'll see many sights like that." Halfhyde pointed towards the ship's side. "To the guardrail, Mr Runcorn. It's no disgrace and you'll feel better."

"Yes, sir." The Midshipman turned away, hurried towards the rail and bent his body over it. There were sounds of retching, epitaph for men dead in the Queen's service. The sea, Halfhyde thought grimly, was often a brutal life: the men who went down to the sea in ships had to adjust to it early in their careers, and adjust, if possible, without becoming brutalized themselves. Meanwhile, the reading of another committal service over the dead was not going to lift the spirits of the *Viceroy's* company. Halfhyde was pondering this when a sideboy saluted: the Captain's compliments and he wished words with the First Lieutenant. Halfhyde went down the ladder from the after hatchway and strode along the alley between the racked rifles under the guard of the marine sentry. Knocking on the Captain's day-cabin door, he was bidden to enter. He found Bassinghorn seated at his desk in a clean white uniform, his beard neatly brushed again, his face calm. Halfhyde felt some surprise: Post Captains in Her Majesty's Fleet were, certainly, by no means disposed to wear their hearts on their sleeves: but he would have expected so-recent events to show some mark. It was almost as though a hairbrush, a wash, and a change of clothing had been enough to obliterate memory. But when he looked into Bassinghorn's eyes he knew that this had been too harsh a judgment and too hasty: there was suffering in the depths of those seaman's blue eyes.

"You sent for me, sir?"

"Yes, Mr Halfhyde. Sit down."

Halfhyde sat.

"Let us clear one thing first: you were right to stop me. I bear no resentment towards you or Mr Pinch."

"Thank you, sir."

"A Captain has no right to endanger any life needlessly— even his own, for obvious reasons. I shall say no more about that." There was a sudden shake in the Captain's voice. "Those poor men . . . I am to blame, and—"

"No, sir. There's no blame attaching to yourself. A mechanical failure—"

"There will be a Board of Enquiry and they may blame my Engineer. I shall blame myself."

"Tradition is not always a good thing, sir. The Captain may be one with the ship. He is not one with a severed stop valve."

Bassinghorn gave a bleak smile. "You are kind to offer comfort, Mr Halfhyde, but my conscience is a matter for myself alone. Now I wish to discuss the future." He paused. "The Engineer has been confined temporarily to his cabin by the Surgeon—I understand there is a degree of shock. I have had words in his stead with the Assistant Engineer. I have given him orders to maintain such pressure as he can with his remaining three boilers—"

"But—"

"I am assured of two-thirds power, Mr Halfhyde. I shall have to be content with that, unless a repair to the damaged boiler and stop valve can be effected with our own resources. You have some comment to offer?"

"Yes, sir. The resources of the Hong Kong dockyard—"

"Will not be called upon."

"You are not returning to port, sir?"

Bassinghorn stared. "Mr Halfhyde, I have Admiralty orders to execute. Every minute brings Prince Gorsinski and his squadron closer to Parece Vela, and the island."

"Yes indeed, sir. But . . ."

"Pray go on, Mr Halfhyde."

"Sir, I was going to say . . . quite apart from steaming at reduced speed—a matter which the dockyard might be able to rectify without much delay—there is the matter of the ship's company."

"Yes?"

"You've already been concerned about possible trouble, sir. There are now more deaths. I would suggest a return to Hong Kong as a means of allaying trouble."

"You suggest, then, that I run for shelter beneath the Commodore's skirts, the skirts of a man who has already shown that he has no wish to become involved?" Bassinghorn gave a harsh laugh. "Oh, I think not, Mr Halfhyde! No, we continue into the Pacific in execution of our orders, and I shall expect you to keep the ship's company fully occupied—so that they don't dwell on their misfortunes, as perhaps they see them. The officers and petty officers are to be diligent and watchful, and are to report at once to you if they see any danger signals. I shall not be found wanting if trouble comes. I have always run a taut ship, Mr Halfhyde, and the *Viceroy* will be no exception."

"I would have a care, sir, if I were you. The men are not happy. There is . . . a curious feeling in the ship."

Bassinghorn raised an eyebrow. "I think we have changed our roles, Mr Halfhyde. Earlier it was I who spoke of a voodoo, you who dismissed the notion. But we shall see—we shall see! It will be the fulfillment of our duty that will turn the men's thoughts in a better direction."

The *Viceroy* steamed on, making good no more now than seven knots over the bottom as recorded by the patent log streamed clear of the wake on the starboard quarter. Halfhyde went below with the Assistant Engineer to take a look at the boiler-room, where the damaged boiler had now been isolated and left: there were not, it seemed, the resources aboard the ship to make a safe repair, and they must accept the slower speed. Halfhyde looked around in a degree of awe: here, so recently, men had died a horrible death. Now, there was no sign of tragedy: the enveloping, noisy steam had gone, was now decently contained within the three undamaged boilers for its power to be transmitted through the proper channels to the main shaft and the screw. There were no strips of flayed flesh. The boiler-room, the stokehold, had their normal aura, which to Halfhyde was far from pleasant, but that was all—except in the eyes of the stokers on watch as they delved the shining steel shovels into the piles of coal coming in clouds of dust down the chutes from the bunkers, and then dipped them like propitiatory offerings into the fiery mouths of the furnace-gods. The heat, beating in waves upon Halfhyde's face, was beyond description: the fires outlined everything in brilliant red, so that the awful compartment was a shifting picture in red and black, with the accusing eyes of the shovelling troglodytes eating into Halfhyde and the Assistant Engineer. Halfhyde, deafened, blinded, and melting, moved back through the tunnelway into the engine-room. Here there was much noise still but the heat was mild by comparison.

He raised an eyebrow at the Assistant Engineer. "Any trouble?"

"Trouble?"

"With the men."

"No, not really, sir. One or two looked a trifle scared when they came on watch and had to go in there." The Assistant Engineer jerked a hand towards the tunnelway. "But they know their duty—they'll be all right."

"More frightened of the Captain than they are of the enemy?"

"Enemy?"

Halfhyde laughed. "The boilers, then! It's a well-established principle: if you're more scared of your own commander than you are of the enemy, you'll not run in action. But those stokers of yours: their faces spoke to me, their faces and their eyes. Did they not to you?"

The Assistant Engineer shook his head and gave a short laugh. "If they did, I didn't notice."

"You are not a man of much imagination, Mr Pewsey. You must watch your stokers. I suggest you don't press them too hard. With one boiler less to feed, you can perhaps lengthen the rest periods?"

"That's my concern, sir, and Bampton's—"

"If trouble comes it'll be the concern of all of us," Halfhyde said. "I'm well enough aware that the Captain is asking for all possible power, but for the greater good, Mr Pewsey, I advise you to stand buffer between the cuddy and the stokehold!" Halfhyde smiled, put a hand briefly on the Assistant Engineer's shoulder, then left the starting-platform and climbed the labyrinth of steel ladders back to the air-lock and the freshness of the day. God, but he would hate to be an engineer! Thankfully, he climbed from the engine-room alleyway to the upper-deck, filling his lungs, listening to the sea sounds, the faint stir of a welcome breeze in the rigging, the hiss of water past the ship's side as the bow-waves were thrown back to tumble and caress and then stream away, bubbling, into the wake. Halfhyde paced the quarterdeck, kept an eye on the hands working in the after part of the ship. A little earlier the seamen divisions had been piped to Quarters Clean Guns. Halfhyde watched the crew of the after eight-inch. They depressed and elevated, trained to either side, greasing the moving parts, checking the firing mechanism. The Captain of the Gun, one Leading-Seaman Lockett, had an eagle eye and was immensely jealous of his gun's reputation. He kept his junior ratings hard at it. Like Bassinghorn, Lockett was a driver; also like Bassinghorn, he had a patent honesty of purpose and the hands responded to this . . . Halfhyde shrugged and turned his attention away from the gun. Perhaps he had been brooding too much, seeing spectres where none existed save in his own mind. Give them a clear run to the island, free of untoward incident, and very likely the ship's company would settle down again. With few exceptions, sailors were not the people to hold grudges or conduct running feuds. Halfhyde allowed his thoughts to wing ahead: by Bassinghorn's estimate they should reach this volcanic island, this unnamed and almost certainly useless base so far as Britain was concerned, in six days' steaming from their noon position.

And when they got there?

Halfhyde gave a sudden hollow laugh which caused the crew of the after gun to glance at him in surprise. A barren piece of rock, of solidified lava, with no vegetation, no soil, was to be seized in the Queen's name and planted with its only excrescence, the Union Flag—and all for what? To stop anyone else doing the same thing! Halfhyde pondered, as he had pondered many times since leaving Portsmouth, on dog-in-the-manger tactics. He could see—possibly—some basis for a Russian interest: the Czar was said to be feeling the need of a Pacific base for his fleet, a base that would be free all the year round of the ice that for so many months at a time blocked in his existing ports, imprisoning or shutting out his warships till the next season's sun. A tiresome incapacity, certainly; but as to this newly-emerged island, surely its possible use must depend upon its physical characteristics and proportions? Large it was said to be: permanent it was also said to be. But seismological instruments were things of very remote veracity: for his money, Halfhyde would need to see it all for himself, take a boat and a heaving-line right around it, inch by inch. Then he would be in a position to pronounce upon its suitability as a warship base . . . he shrugged; the jealousy of the great nations, the ceaseless quest for power, the shouldering aside of one another—suitable or not, somebody would decide they needed the island, like the British Admiralty!

Meanwhile orders had to be obeyed: seagoing officers did not, or should not, question them. They would reach the island— and then back to Hong Kong to report the flag planted and await orders for the backing-up of the small party that would have been landed to take possession, and the despatch of a token force to establish a base by usage.

Pacing in his deep thought, Halfhyde became aware of a pale round face like the moon in anaemia emerging from the quarterdeck hatch, and he halted.

"You're feeling better, Mr Mosscrop?"

"A little, thank you."

"Then welcome back to life." Halfhyde swept a hand around, cheerfully indicating the blue sea. "It's a nice day for it."

"Very nice." Mr Mosscrop, heavily wrapped in a blanket, moved gingerly towards the quarterdeck guardrail and stared down at the rushing sea. The *Viceroy* chose that very moment to lift a little to the swell, sagging back to starboard, and the sea came closer. Mr Mosscrop turned and lurched uphill, his face now like green cheese, then shot forward in an unsteady, short-paced run as the decks rolled the other way. He went back down the hatch groaning: Halfhyde grinned. Mr Mosscrop was bound back to his bunk. Well, the volcanic island was no doubt stationary enough. If it was not, if it was by some mischance rocking upon its underwater fixtures, then very little work would be done by the representative of the Director of Dockyards.

"Mr Halfhyde, we cannot be far ahead, if indeed we're ahead at all, of Prince Gorsinski's squadron." Bassinghorn stared into a freshening wind, stared towards low cloud darkening the southern and eastern horizons like a ribbon of black.

"True, sir."

"Mr Bampton's doing his best, I'm aware of that. I'll not ask for more revolutions."

For which the Lord make us truly thankful, Halfhyde thought. Aloud he said, "I've been thinking, sir, about Prince Gorsinski and his likely actions."

"We've considered that."

"Yes indeed, sir." Halfhyde narrowed his eyes ahead: the cloud-bank was increasing in height and intensity. "We've agreed he may be under orders to take the island by any method he finds appropriate, even to the point of action."

"Yes."

"Prince Gorsinski has the mind of a diplomat as well as that of a seaman, sir."

Bassinghorn frowned. "What, exactly, do you mean, Mr Halfhyde?"

"Sir, I mean this, quite simply: he will, I believe on reflection, prefer to use such methods as would not rebound against him . . . he will not, presumably, wish to start a war between Britain and Russia—or rather, his Czar will not."

"What, then, do you suppose these methods will be?"

Halfhyde didn't answer straight away: he continued staring ahead towards the rising bank of black cloud, as though peering through it into the intrigue-ridden mind of the Russian aristocrat. Then he asked a question in his turn: "Sir, do you suppose the Admiralty knew, when we were given our orders, that when the ice freed his ships, Prince Gorsinski would be sent to oppose us? Prince Gorsinski—rather than anyone else?"

Bassinghorn gave him a brief glance. "I can't answer that, Mr Halfhyde, since I don't know what the answer is. But tell me— why do you ask?"

"Because of me, sir."

"You, Halfhyde?"

"Sir, Russia has many ways of obtaining information about other countries' affairs. A system, one might say, of intelligence, something that our Government and Service departments lack. Prince Gorsinski would not find it hard to get a sight of the Admiralty's appointments lists. And—"

"And might know that you're aboard the *Viceroy?*"

"Precisely, sir, you have it! And he'd give his right hand to secure possession of me—that I know well!"

"But you don't know me, Mr Halfhyde," Bassinghorn said with anger in his voice, "if you imagine I would be a party to any such intrigue! Are you suggesting I might hand you over in some kind of deal, in exchange for the right to plant the flag?"

"No, sir. I know you would not. Nor would Prince Gorsinski ask that, since he must be under orders to take the island. What I suggest is this: Gorsinski may concentrate his energies, not on open action, but on seizure of my person, and then use me as a lever to secure the island for Russia."

"And after—"

"After the *Viceroy's* withdrawal, sir, should that be decided upon, Prince Gorsinski would move his ships in."

"And hand you back?"

Halfhyde gave a bitter laugh. "I think not, sir! Russians are not Britons. No, that would be promised, but in fact I would be held for eventual return to Russia. And in the circumstances of the past, and of my own history, I doubt if Whitehall would provoke a war in order to get me back!"

He was about to go on, to add the sardonic comment that he was in any case an embarrassment to the Board of Admiralty but an embarrassment that might be made good use of in the course of its disposal, when he was stopped by Bassinghorn's hand coming down smartly on his shoulder, and a shout in his ear: "Look south-easterly. Mr Halfhyde! The sea. There's a weight of wind coming out of that cloud. You must batten down for a blow and double-bank the strops on the anchors and cables promptly."

Halfhyde, looking through his telescope, saw the frothing tumult extending outwards from below the heavy cloud, which was now breaking at its top to wreathe and spiral into the sky, still blue above. Wasting no time, he ran for the ladder from the bridge, and slid down the rails on his hands, shouting for the watch. As he ran for the fo'c'sle-head he heard the shrill calls of the Boatswain's pipes, passing the order from the bridge for Both Watches of the Hands, a particularized pipe that called out all available seamen at the rush. Swiftly extra lashings and strops were passed to the stocks and shanks of the bower anchors to grip them hard to the catheads, more rope stoppers were passed on deck to prevent bumping and chafing of the great links of the cable; and the compressors were given a few more turns.

Throughout the ship, as she began to pitch to the first of a heavy sea, hatches were battened-down and watertight doors clipped shut, to be opened, until the coming storm was passed, only upon express permission from the bridge. Ports and deadlights were secured on their screws. Halfhyde, checking through the ship above and below, heard sounds of mortal torment coming from Mr Mosscrop's cabin. His tour of inspection complete, Halfhyde made his way to the bridge to report to the Captain, making use, when on the upper-deck, of the lifelines that had been rigged fore and aft, feet sliding and slithering on a deck already wet from a blinding rainstorm and from sea shipped green over the bows to fling down in breaking thunder below the bridge. Hauling himself up the starboard ladder, he saw an unusual consternation on three faces: the Captain, the Yeoman of the Watch, and Mr Midshipman Runcorn were all staring back towards the ship's port quarter.

Halfhyde turned and followed their intent looks: just for an instant he saw it, a fleeting glimpse before they were right into the cloud bank and the visibility came down like a blanket of driven wet: the great dark shape below the fighting-tops, the Russian naval ensign, almost the size and splendour of a battle ensign, streaming out from the mizzen peak, and the Admiral's flag of Prince Gorsinski hoisted to the main topmasthead, stiff in the wind above the muzzles of his great grey guns.

Chapter 7

"BEATEN TO IT, by God!"

Bassinghorn, his words torn away unheard on the rushing wings of the wind, fought his way along the bridge towards Halfhyde. He cupped one hand around his First Lieutenant's ear, used the other hand to cling fast to a stanchion. "The Russian squadron!" he shouted.

"I've seen the flagship, sir."

"The Admiralty—they'll never forgive this, Halfhyde!" Bassinghorn's eyes were staring, virtual mirrors of a kind of madness. "They have the speed—they'll go past us now like an express train!"

"Sir, I suggest we forget them for the time being."

"What?"

"The storm, sir. The *Viceroy* comes first now. When it's blown over—" Halfhyde broke off. Bassinghorn was taking no notice. He had turned away, was dragging himself forward against the tearing wind and rain and the almost solid spray crashing down on the stem. Halfhyde followed, caught a word here and there as the Captain, after ordering an alteration to starboard so as to bring the ship's head closer to the wind and sea, wrenched back the brass cover of the engine-room voice-pipe and bellowed down into it. "All possible revolutions . . . damn the discomfort . . . burns or not . . . God save me, Mr Bampton, if we lose the Russians I'll have you flogged at the gratings . . ."

Halfhyde, himself clinging to a stanchion, turned his face from the wind and drew a deep breath: it was impossible to breathe against that wind, it was of choking strength and men had muffled themselves against it with the upturned collars of oilskin coats. Bassinghorn slammed down the voice-pipe cover and turned to glance a trifle shame-facedly at Halfhyde . . . you couldn't flog engineers, or indeed anyone else in the modern Navy. Flogging had, for all practical purposes, been abolished in 1879. It was an empty threat that Bassinghorn might live to regret and it would certainly cause thoughts of mutiny to enter the soul of the already disgruntled Bampton . . . but as to the call for speed itself, the old *Viceroy* was making so little that she would scarcely be endangered by such small increase in revolutions as might be possible. Halfhyde, shouting into the Captain's ear, made the report he had not yet had an opportunity of passing.

"Ship secure for bad weather, sir, all watertight doors shut—"

"Yes, thank you, Mr Halfhyde. That damn Russian, now. What shall we do?"

"Put our trust in God, sir. It's all we can do." Halfhyde went aft, almost hurled by a gust of wind and a heavy lift of the bows. His duty now was to keep watch and ward over the old ship's watertightness and the safety of her deck gear, her boats and booms and guns, masts and rigging and cables. In foul weather at sea, a stitch in time saved nine more positively than ever it did ashore. On the bridge the Captain's duty was the overall one of preserving his command intact, of preventing the ever-present possibility of poor helmsmanship in heavy seas allowing her head to pay off into the possibly total catastrophe of broaching-to in the trough of the waves, when she would lie broadside to wind and sea, helpless, a thing to be held and battered by pounding water. But so long as her engines continued to give her steerage way, she should be able to keep her stem pointing into the wind. Halfhyde, at all events, was content enough to trust Bassinghorn's seamanship. Moving with difficulty along the decks, making constant use of the life-lines, keeping a critical eye on the weathertightness along the upper-deck, Halfhyde found his thoughts slipping away into the shrouded sector where Gorsinski's flagship had been so briefly seen. Once the information had been received from the Commodore in Hong Kong, a sight of the Russian had scarcely been unexpected: but it was still a shock to know that at this very moment Prince Gorsinski, kinsman of the Czar of all the Russias, was within gunshot of the *Viceroy*, storming along somewhere off the port beam and drawing ahead. Bassinghorn had been only too right: there was no hope now of overtaking the Russian squadron: when the weather moderated Gorsinski's ships would be well over the horizon.

As daylight faded from the sky the weight of the wind dropped, just a little. Men were able to relax; the galley fires, doused on an order from the bridge, were re-lit and somewhat later than usual the hands were piped to supper. At two bells in the first watch St Vincent Halfhyde, preceded by the Master-at-Arms bearing a storm lantern, and by a bugler of the Royal Marine Light Infantry, made his rounds of the mess decks and flats. As the single note from the bugler heralded the approach of the ship's Executive Officer, the men off-watch below straightened their night clothing and hid pipes in the palms of hands or shot black streams of tobacco juice from their mouths with unerring aim into the stinking spitkids provided for each broadside mess. The hectoring voice of the Master-at-Arms was raised from time to time.

"Attention for rounds . . . stand up, that man!"

Rolling with the ship, the small procession moved on: Halfhyde's face was wry. The atmosphere, always thick along the lowerdeck, was abominable following the battening-down. No air had circulated; the smells were heavy, all-pervading and legion, drawn in with every breath. Sweat, wet clothing, stale food, foul blankets and hammocks, lavatories, overlying the purely ship-smells of grease and oil, tar and rope, and the metallic emanations of the broadside guns whose great breeches pushed through into the gundeck messes, leaking water from the closed ports and forming a constant companionship with men eating, men sleeping, men dreaming of a run ashore in Pompey or of the beer and women of Waterport Street in Gibraltar when a ship's company was celebrating the last port for home after a long foreign commission . . . the guns, ever-present reminders of a warship's grim purpose, were as close to sailors as was a rifle to a soldier. As close as was his own sweaty body: Halfhyde, bending below the slung hammocks of sleeping men in the mess set aside for the permanent watchkeepers such as Quartermasters, Boatswain's Mates, and the like, wondered how in heaven's name the ratings could put up with that stench. It always increased appallingly along the lowerdeck, even in fair weather with the various vents open, the moment a ship sailed east of Suez or into the tropics. Basically it was due to that continual sweating, the melted body fat that dripped into clothes, blankets, hammocks—dripped and festered and stank like rotting meat. No doubt they became used to it; it was merely a different hardship from the hardships of civilian life ashore.

With the dangers and discomforts and smells of Service life went, hand-in-hand, the certainty of regular meals, of adequate clothing, of a slim financial security that at least allowed some indulgence when at liberty. It was a sad fact that simple poverty was the principal reason for enlisting in so many cases . . .

Rounds completed, Halfhyde returned the salute of the Master-at-Arms. "What d'you think, Master? How do they look to you?"

"As full of grouses, sir, as a dog has fleas."

Halfhyde steadied himself against the ship's movement, a nasty corkscrew motion of roll and pitch combined. "That's normal enough, Master. Grouses seldom fester. I'm always glad to see a deep poison surface by way of boils and pimples!"

"Yes, sir." The Master-at-Arms sucked a little at a hollow tooth. "Carry-on, sir, please?"

Halfhyde nodded; the Master-at-Arms jerked his head at the marine bugler: the carry-on was sounded. Rounds were over. Throughout the mess decks men chatted in low tones, or smoked to obliterate the other smells, or turned into their hammocks behind the naked gun-breeches. The ship plunged on, rolling, pitching, but riding more easily and no longer shipping the tons of water that had washed earlier along her open decks, isolating deckhouses, swirling men off their feet to put their whole trust in the life lines. During the night the weather moderated still further: when dawn crept up, hesitantly at first, then with its full Pacific splendour, the storm had blown itself out. Bassinghorn, who had remained at his station throughout, sustained by cocoa and sandwiches brought up by his servant, put the ship back on her proper course and went below to rest, leaving the bridge in the hands of his Navigating Officer, Lieutenant Puckridge. Halfhyde, up with the dawn, felt, as he always felt in a spectacular dawning, a strong sense of being close to God. He looked in awe at the spreading colours, green, crimson, yellow, purple, that lofted high over the sea's rim. The sea itself was like a dark velvet cloak dappled with the emerging sunlight as the great orb rose in fire above the horizon; an oiliness had replaced the rearing waves, and the ship lifted only to the swell left behind by the storm.

Halfhyde joined the Navigating Officer on the bridge. "The Russian squadron, Pilot. Were they sighted again in the night?"

"No."

"Did the Captain say anything about them?"

"He left orders that any sighting was to be reported to him immediately—that's all."

Halfhyde nodded absently, thinking his own thoughts. Below on the fo'c'sle Mr Pinch was checking the cable with a party of seamen. There seemed a fairly cheerful air. Halfhyde, ever sensitive to atmosphere, felt his own spirits rise: the storm itself, the spreading word about that sudden and dramatic sighting of the Russian warships, had possibly had a good effect. Real endeavour in an urgent cause had taken the place of dull routine, and the enemy—not too strong a word, Halfhyde felt—had been sighted and was set fair to beat the *Viceroy* to her destination. There was already a greater degree of cohesion, of one-ness, about the ship's company. But the Captain, when that forenoon he sent for Halfhyde, seemed in a state of acute despondency. His mission, he said, was finished before it had begun.

"I think not, sir. There's many a slip, remember."

"You imagine Gorsinski will suffer some engine-room tragedy such as ours, Mr Halfhyde? Why, he has three ships! He has merely to transfer his flag and leave the lame duck behind!"

"I think we must wait and see, sir." Halfhyde lifted his arms, let them drop again. "In all conscience, there's nothing else we can do!"

"Except consider fresh possibilities, Mr Halfhyde."

"Sir?"

"There has been a change, has there not? Until now—until last night—we have always assumed it would be us who reached the island first. My principal concern has been that of holding the island once possessed, the consideration of how to deal with Prince Gorsinski after his arrival. As matters now stand, we're going to find him already in possession, are we not?"

Halfhyde said, "That seems likely, sir, I agree. And I understand you have no orders, in that event?"

"No precise orders."

"The Admiralty," Halfhyde murmured, "is ever the Admiralty! Well, sir? Do you propose to strike the Russian flag, or accept its presence, for it comes down to that choice, does it not?"

Bassinghorn's tone was defiant, heated. "I shall remove it, Halfhyde, in the name of Her Majesty—"

"One ship, sir."

"What?"

"We are but one ship against three. We have three hundred men including marines. Prince Gorsinski will have upwards of twelve hundred. And we shall find ourselves much out-gunned."

Bassinghorn stared belligerently. "You would run, then?"

"I think it would be only prudent," Halfhyde said with a laugh, "but I'm not a prudent man. No, sir, I would *not* run, but neither, I think, would I invite action. There may be other means."

"What means do you suggest?"

Halfhyde shrugged. "I suggest no means at this point, sir. I must do some further cogitation. Some subterfuge is called for—

I believe Prince Gorsinski will expect this, and we mustn't disappoint him!"

Five days later, with the sea behaving kindly and the engines continuing to produce revolutions for a little more than seven knots, Mr Runcorn in the foretopmast crosstrees, his voice filled with excitement, hailed the bridge.

"Land in sight, sir, fine on the starboard bow!"

Lieutenant Campbell called back: "A description, Snotty?"

Runcorn levelled his telescope again, bracing his small body against the mast. "Flat, sir, and greyish. It's big, I think."

"Any ships visible?"

"No, sir."

Campbell bent to the Captain's voicepipe, and blew. "Bridge, sir. We've raised the island and there are no other ships in sight."

Bassinghorn's voice came up: "Thank you, Mr Campbell. Inform the First Lieutenant and Navigating Officer immediately, and maintain the lookout—I'll be on the bridge directly."

Campbell snapped the voice-pipe cover down and passed the orders. Bassinghorn and Halfhyde reached the bridge together. In a voice of excitement and triumph the Captain said, "We've beaten them to it after all, Mr Halfhyde!"

Halfhyde poured cold water. "I would doubt that, sir. The Russians are as well able as us to navigate! I would suggest they are there but not yet visible, and that is the way it should be, for by the same token we will be equally invisible to them at this moment." He coughed discreetly. "I suggest you stop the engines, sir."

"For what purpose, other than to delay?"

"An idea is taking shape, sir."

The Captain regarded him closely, eyes narrowed. "The sub-terfuge, Halfhyde?"

"Yes, sir. Meanwhile, every moment is precious, if we are to avoid being sighted by the Russian masthead lookouts. Will you stop the engines, sir?"

"First, Mr Halfhyde, some explanation."

Halfhyde held onto his temper. He said evenly, "As you wish, sir. I suggest we make the assumption that Prince Gorsinski will in fact have arrived—I see no reason whatsoever to assume he has not, and never mind his present invisibility. It's possible the island is high above the sea in places. Mr Runcorn has reported a sight of such high land, but Gorsinski's ships—"

"Being lower," Bassinghorn interrupted acidly, "are still hull down—yes, Mr Halfhyde, I follow you—"

"So much hull down that even their mastheads and tops are not visible. I say again—the same must apply to us."

The Captain frowned in some perplexity. "Then you suggest we remain here in obscurity?"

"I do, sir. But only until after sunset. We must use the dark-ness to approach the land, and then if the Russian squadron is there, we must make for the side of the island away from them."

"And then?"

Halfhyde gave a sudden laugh, a laugh with a touch of exul-tancy in it. "Then the subterfuge will begin, sir! And I'm beginning to understand why the Admiralty appointed me to your command."

"Why so, Mr Halfhyde, in particular?"

"Because, sir, with respect, you are an officer of very direct and honest mind, a seaman above all in a situation where sea-manship is needed as well as subterfuge. I, on the other hand, am a former half-pay officer . . . with all that that implies!"

"I fail to follow you now," Bassinghorn said with irritation in his voice. "This is—"

"There is a degree of the devil-may-care in me, sir. I am but poorly regarded by Their Lordships, and can accept a risk in the hope of being able to lift myself in their future regard, since I cannot sink lower. Also, I am a man of—"

"Of devious mind, Mr Halfhyde, if you ask me!"

"Precisely, sir, you have it admirably. You and I are foils, and an excellent combination. Together we shall plant the British flag, and may God forgive us for bending our efforts to so useless a task—"

"Mr Halfhyde, you forget yourself, sir—"

"I'm sorry, sir." Halfhyde met the Captain's stony eye, read in it a clear belief that he had taken leave of his senses. "I regret any insubordination in my manner of speech. I am far from mad, I assure you. Will you trust me, sir?"

Bassinghorn swung away, pacing the bridge back and forth, hands behind his back, the sun striking fire from the gold stripes on each of his shoulder-straps, shining white from the immaculate pipe-clay of his tropical helmet. After two minutes he halted in front of Halfhyde, feet apart, body square and powerful. He said, "I am in command, Mr Halfhyde. I have no liking for—"

He stopped, body swinging, head going back. There had been a shout from the foretopmast crosstrees. "Yes, Mr Runcorn, what is it?"

"I think it's the Russians, sir!"

"What d'you see, boy?"

"Mastheads, sir. Little more than the trucks and royals. Three ships, I think. It's difficult to be sure, sir, but they're in the lee of the island and possibly at anchor sir."

Bassinghorn blew out a long breath and looked at Halfhyde. Halfhyde said gently, "Sir, I suggest you put the engines astern, and creep away till nightfall. We haven't the means to mount a show of strength."

It was a long, long wait for excited men, men who had forgotten, or at any rate laid aside, their disgruntlement. Now they wished to strike a blow for England: the very thought of being beaten to it, outmanoeuvred, by the Russians was against their natures as British seamen conditioned by the glorious years of history to expect victory and nothing less: Halfhyde, as the silent ship, withdrawn out of sight of the Russian squadrons, waited all that day in the long Pacific swell, realized that his view of the operation was not shared by the lowerdeck or indeed by the ward-room. Neither Her Majesty nor Their Lordships despatched ships of war upon useless missions across the seas. Their orders had point, and the ship's company was going to drive that point home even if it had metaphorically to be rammed up the fundamental orifice of the Czar of all the Russias himself. Halfhyde, though still holding to his own sardonic view, was far from displeased at the obvious surge of patriotism that had swept the ship: such spirit was going to be needed at nightfall and more so thereafter. He himself was not keen to see Gorsinski get away with anything, and he meant to ensure that he did not. During the forenoon Halfhyde was closeted alone with Captain Bassinghorn, to whom he spoke forcibly and plainly, and at last secured agreement for a possibly dangerous proposition. As the slow hours wore away to sundown, he was very conscious that he was taking a lot upon himself and that any slip could spell his death or a lasting blight upon his career at sea. But there was that degree of recklessness—recklessness that he had taken pains not to identify as such to Bassinghorn—brought about by being held in that low regard for no real fault of his own. His face tight and hard from his inner thoughts and misgivings, Halfhyde, in the heat of the afternoon watch, sent for the Gunner.

"Cutlasses, Mr Portlock."

"Cutlasses, sir?"

"No less! And rifles, of course. I want twelve hand-picked seamen, gunnery rates, to be fallen in and ready when the ship anchors, which should be around five bells in the first watch. Have them standing by Number Five cutter, Mr Portlock."

"Aye, aye, sir—"

"And I'd like the Chief Gunner's Mate to exercise them at once in the use of the cutlass—an art some of them'll never have acquired—"

"Full cutlass drill, Mr Halfhyde?"

Halfhyde grinned, a tight stretch of lips against teeth. "You may forget the ceremonial drill, Mr Portlock. Teach them how to kill!" He turned and strode away along the deck, hands behind his back, leaving the Warrant Officer staring with his mouth open. Cutlasses—why, they belonged to Nelson's Navy, and never mind that they were still Service issue—they hadn't been used, virtually, since the days when the great wooden line-of-battle ships raked the enemy with cannon and then laid alongside for the boarding-parties to leap across and hack and chop like so many butchers . . . Mr Portlock, shaking his grey head in wonder, called up a sideboy and sent him scuttling for the Chief Gunner's Mate. And that afternoon the decks of the *Viceroy* rang to the shouts of men in close combat, and the angry clash of steel blades.

•   •   •

As the last dog-watch ended, merging into the first watch, full dark came down. Halfhyde knocked on the cuddy door, aware of the curious scrutiny of the marine sentry on duty outside. Entering, he reported: "It's dark enough to move in, sir. All men are closed up at their stations."

Bassinghorn nodded. "Very well, Mr Halfhyde. Are all the men in blue night clothing?"

"Yes, sir." Halfhyde himself, like all the other officers, was wearing a blue monkey-jacket and a cap without its white cover. Since sunset the ship had been darkened, the decks and alleyways hot behind closed deadlights and hatches; and she would steam without benefit of navigation lights, a slow dark ghost upon the waters creeping past Prince Gorsinski's ships, well clear to southward of the anchorage.

"On the bridge, if you please, Mr Halfhyde. You may ring for slow ahead. I'll be up directly."

"Aye, aye, sir." Halfhyde left the cuddy and climbed to the bridge. He passed the Captain's order to the Navigating Officer, who would con the ship in. A tremor ran though the decks as the *Viceroy* got under way. As her glide ahead began Bassinghorn mounted to the bridge, stood for a moment looking ahead past the bows, looking towards the hump of greater darkness that was the emerged volcanic island. As yet there was no moon, but a moon would show before long. The ship crept inwards, making a wide circle, the faintest of breezes murmuring through her rigging, around the ratlines and the shrouds and past the ears of Mr Runcorn, back in his high lookout position on the foretopmast. Apart from the small sigh of the wind, and the engine's beat, and the hiss of water past the hull, there was no sound.

Chapter 8

THE ISLAND changed its shape: as they came round, keeping well to the south still, they saw it from different angles. There appeared to be a central peak rising from a plain, if it could be called a plain. Even from a great distance, it looked an eerie place. Halfhyde, making his way aft towards his already-mustered landing-party, came upon a stout figure standing by the guardrail in the lee of Number Six cutter on the port side aft.

"Well, Mr Mosscrop, what do you make of our island, though it's not our island yet?"

Mosscrop's face was a pale circle in the darkness. "I can't possibly say yet, Mr Halfhyde, can I? I have to make a survey. After that, I'll send in a report—"

"Which will be lost in the Admiralty's files these next ten years, no doubt!"

"We don't rush things, Mr Halfhyde," the dockyard constructor said primly. "To some extent, you know, we do see ourselves as the guardians of the public purse." He stared towards the island for some moments in silence, then said, "I'm not impressed. Mr Pinch very kindly allowed me the use of his telescope while there was still light. It's not exactly Portsmouth, is it, Mr Halfhyde?"

"It's your job to make it so, I gather, Mr Mosscrop," Halfhyde said, and moved on, grinning into the darkness. He had no more liking for the prospect of making this odd island into a naval base than had poor Mosscrop: the place even smelled weird, a nasty sour emanation of soot and sulphur and ashes overhanging the Pacific; and he had noticed, whilst waiting around earlier, that the sea had appeared discoloured, a sort of metallic look. He had anticipated the Captain's order and had had soundings taken: the hand-cast lead had found no bottom to account for the shift from deep-sea blue, and Halfhyde could conclude only that the eruptions themselves were continuing to have some effect, some seepage into the water in the vicinity of the island. He crossed the deck towards the cutlass party, waiting under the Chief Gunner's Mate by Number Five cutter. He had a word with each man, quietly encouraging. The *Viceroy* moved on, coming up now on the northeasterly course she had taken after she had dropped some ten miles south of the island's nearest point. She was steering so as to leave the land five miles to port as she came abeam. From this position her course would be altered to due west and thereafter she would close the land on the opposite side from the anchorage where Prince Gorsinski's squadron lay.

Halfhyde pulled out his watch and made a quick calculation: another two hours, give or take a little. With rapid strides of his long legs he returned to the bridge. Bassinghorn was standing at the fore guardrail ahead of the standard compass, peering through his telescope at the distant island. Their progress through the water was painfully slow, and Halfhyde was consumed with an impatient desire to seize the engine-room voice-pipe and demand full revolutions from Mr Bampton and never mind the sharply contrasting phosphorescence that would be thrown up by too fast a movement through the sea, thereby signalling their approach to any watchers from the shore. If there were such watchers, the *Viceroy* was in any case going to be seen when she came closer in. And even as Halfhyde was visited by these thoughts, the moon sailed unkindly out from behind a bank of cloud and seemed to illuminate the whole Pacific Ocean.

There was an oath from Bassinghorn as silver light fell across the ship.

Halfhyde said, "This was not unexpected, sir. We must hope they're not watching on this side." He lifted his own telescope, scanned the island's still-distant fringe. "Sir, I suggest we increase speed now, and reduce the likely—"

"Yes, yes. Mr Puckridge!"

"Sir?"

"Telegraph to full ahead. Tell the Engineer I want maximum revolutions but he is to be ready to manoeuvre his engines ahead or astern upon my order, and at any speed required. And the leadsmen in the chains, if you please."

"Aye, aye, sir." The Navigating Officer passed the orders. Soon the increased thrust of the screw was felt throughout the ship: there was a faint singing noise, a vibrant hum, from the wire ropes of the standing rigging, the bow wave creamed up more sharply, and the water filled with phosphorescence as it tumbled aft along the sides to mingle with the wake. Bassinghorn turned to look: under the pall of black smoke from the funnels the wake stood out like a great green finger, a gigantic glow-worm pointing up their track.

"Touch and go, Mr Halfhyde!"

"Yes, sir." There seemed nothing more to say: Halfhyde ran over his plan as the *Viceroy* moved on. The landing should be simple enough, always provided they had not been seen. The whole essence of the plan hung upon anonymity . . . Halfhyde grinned privately as he stood waiting at Bassinghorn's side. The Captain had been slow to appreciate the finer points of subterfuge and his consent to the plan had been grudging at first. Even now, Halfhyde believed, he had his doubts. But such doubts would be kept to himself and not shown to the ship's company. Once the landing-party had been put ashore, Bassinghorn's part would be simply to wait. Halfhyde didn't envy him that task. For himself, he would be fully occupied, and that would be good. Nevertheless he felt a loosening of his bowels as he thought of Admiral Prince Gorsinski aboard his flagship, secure behind the many guns of his squadron and the slavish pamperings of his sailors. If indeed Gorsinski had the knowledge that Lieutenant St Vincent Halfhyde was aboard the *Viceroy,* then he would be licking his princely chops tonight!

In each of the small, projecting platforms known as the chains, one on either side of the ship before the bridge, a Leading-Seaman leaned his weight on the canvas apron and its chain rail, his body straight, his arm swinging stiffly in line with the cast of the eight-pound lead, tallow-armed to pick up samples of the bottom when bottom should be found. Time and again as the *Viceroy* approached the island the leads were swung in great circles, to be released at the point of the circle that would carry them ahead of the moving ship. Each time, as the lead-line came up-and-down in the water immediately beneath him, the leadsman hove in to read off the depth of water indicated by the particular marking that had been on a level with the surface: strips of leather, white or red rags of linen, bunting, serge, or flannel for the different depths, or short ends of marline for the deeps, indicators that spoke clearly to seamen as expert fingers, in dark or daylight, identified one from another. But so far the report, each time, had been the same: "No bottom, sir!"

The ship moved on, now on her westerly, inward-heading course, an anchor veered ready for letting go in any emergency.

The island loomed large, high and long: the telescopes found
no movement along the shore, only a small lap of wavelets.
Wavelets against rock: no surf, no waves washing a beach. It
was possible that there was no shelf, but deep water running
right up against the solid lava so that a ship could go alongside
as against a dockyard wall . . .

"By the mark, twenty!"

Bassinghorn turned his head. "Half speed, Mr Puckridge, and
the engine-room to stand by for manoeuvring."

"Aye, aye, sir."

"Tell the leadsmen to pass their reports more quietly—I have
good ears. Mr Halfhyde, I want complete silence from now,
along the upper-deck."

"I've already passed the order, sir."

"Then pass it again, Mr Halfhyde, if you please. There is to
be no mistake in any man's mind. The slightest unnecessary
sound will be punished by the cat."

In the shadows Halfhyde's lips formed an oath: again the stupid empty threat! Bassinghorn appeared to be allowing too much
play to his nerves. Halfhyde despatched a sideboy with whis-
pered orders to have deaf ears in regard to the cat lest worse
befall him at the hands of the First Lieutenant. They waited,
tensely now. Fathom by fathom the soundings shortened, seemed
to level out at around six fathoms of water below the ship's bottom. Bassinghorn said, "Well, we're not meeting shoaling water
at all events, but this is far enough, I think, Mr Halfhyde. Stop
engines, Mr Puckridge." The handle of the telegraph was pulled
over. "Slow astern, wheel amidships, belaying soundings," was the
next order. The sternway pulled the ship up, and Bassinghorn
again ordered his engines to stop. Silent, almost motionless, the
Viceroy lay peacefully on the water some half mile from the

island, stem pointed to what appeared to be a shallow bay below a peak of cooled lava. Bassinghorn nodded at Halfhyde.

"As soon as you like, Mr Halfhyde."

"I'm ready now, sir."

"Then good luck." The Captain held out a hand, gave Halfhyde's a firm shake. "I shall remain here until a little before dawn. You have until then."

Halfhyde turned away and went down the ladder. The cutter was already turned out, hanging from her falls over the water, with the landing-party embarked and the moonlight striking silver from the blades of the cutlasses and dull metallic gleams from the rifle barrels. In the stern-sheets was Mr Runcorn, relieved from the masthead lookout to accompany the landing-party as second-in-command. He saluted as Halfhyde approached.

"All ready, sir!"

"Then let's not delay, Mr Runcorn." Halfhyde stepped into the cutter, which swayed a little under his weight. He glanced across at the Lieutenant in charge on deck. "Lower away when you're ready, Mr Anstey."

The order was given to start the falls. With the ropes already married along the waist, the lowerers, found from the maintopmen, walked back to the davits: the cutter descended cleanly, the men handing themselves down the steadying lines as they went. The order came to slip; the Coxswain knocked away the disengaging gear and the boat took the water, free now of the falls, with a smack and a splash.

Halfhyde took over from there. "Bear off . . . out oars, give way together . . . hold water port . . . give way together. All right, Coxswain. Head her to approach below the peak."

"Aye, aye, sir." Stolid at the tiller, the Coxswain chewed on a quid of tobacco, staring towards the land. The cutter made little sound: the crutches had been muffled, so there was none of the rhythmic creak of oars as the boat's crew pulled strongly together. Halfhyde looked down at the Midshipman by his side, and smiled slightly.

"You look pensive, Mr Runcorn."

"Do I, sir?" Runcorn sounded startled.

"It's natural. I imply no criticism! It's a strange place, and a stranger business."

"Yes, sir. Sir, I'm afraid I don't really understand what we're trying to do, sir."

"You don't, Mr Runcorn? I thought I'd made it clear enough! But go on."

"Yes, sir." There was a pause. "Sir, could it not be construed as an act of war, sir?"

"It could indeed, Mr Runcorn!"

"Then, sir—"

"But if the Russians should strike first, then it is they who commit the act of war, is it not?"

"Yes, sir." Mr Runcorn pondered, his face screwed up. "But sir, if they do not—"

"Come, come, boy!" Halfhyde said testily, pulling his boat-cloak around his body. "Think! It's possible, isn't it, to provoke people into action? Use your imagination, and then you'll see."

"You mean, sir, we're to act as *agents provocateurs?*"

Halfhyde smiled. "Well done, Mr Runcorn!"

"But doesn't our very presence, in itself—"

"No, Mr Runcorn, it does not, since we come not in a spirit of aggression but in a spirit of peaceful interest, and to pay our respects to the Russian Admiral—"

"With cutlasses and rifles, sir?"

"Kindly don't interrupt, Snotty. To continue, if they should mistake our intentions, then that's their fault, not ours. Which explains, if you should be about to ask, why the *Viceroy* herself can't enter the anchorage on a similar mission. Her intentions would be somewhat too apparent for mistakes to occur!" He laid a hand on the Midshipman's shoulder. "It's all in the name of Admiralty, Mr Runcorn. And I shall seek no casualties on either side, you may be sure."

"But—"

"Contain your impatience, Mr Runcorn. It'll all come clear soon."

Already they were beginning to slide into the lee of the weird pile of lava, so much pumice-stone atop the upsurge of the sea-bed. In spite of the moonlight, the night seemed curiously darker, seemed to enfold them, and Halfhyde gave a sudden shiver, a prey now to his doubts. Perhaps it was a foolish mission: Britain and Russia were at peace. One rifle bullet could shatter that peace, a fact of which Halfhyde no less than Bassinghorn was fully aware: but for war-making that bullet would need to be a British one, and it was Halfhyde's concern that no British bullet should in fact be fired. If it should be, then the affair would pass beyond Bassinghorn's power to control. If on the other hand the Russians should react to the British approach with fire and sword, a touch of diplomacy and a knowledge of Prince Gorsinski on Halfhyde's part could ensure that the results were contained within the island. For the next few hours at least, Halfhyde would be walking a tightrope. He stared ahead as the cutter was pulled closer inshore, moving fast. When they were within a cable's-length of the inhospitable rock he slowed the stroke and they edged forward with a man in the bows taking soundings with the boat's lead. As he had suspected earlier, they had come in at a spot where there was no shelving. Moving ahead with caution still, Halfhyde brought the cutter alongside the bare volcanic rock ledge, as sheer as a dockyard jetty but rough with surface imperfections. The bowman and stern-sheetsman grappled in with their boathooks, finding their purchase easily enough in the jags and crevices, and Halfhyde jumped ashore.

"Landing-party out, if you please, Mr Runcorn."

"Aye, aye, sir!" His young voice sounding high and strained, the Midshipman gave the orders. The men scrambled ashore and were fallen in by a Gunner's Mate. Halfhyde told the cutter's Coxswain to wait until he saw the departure signal hoisted on the *Viceroy's* signal halliards. If the landing-party had not returned, he was to pull back to the ship. Similarly, if any Russians should appear, he was to make out to sea.

"Now, Mr Runcorn, we march due west—about three miles to the anchorage. I think we can take it Prince Gorsinski will have planted the Russian flag where he can gaze upon it from his sternwalk!"

It was an eerie business, a march into the unknown, the totally unexplored: it was a nightmare landscape, an artist's impression of what the surface of the moon itself might be like, and as remote from all civilization. The great deep valleys, the jagged peaks, the flat areas of plain and plateau—all this, Halfhyde reflected, had but recently been so much sea-bottom, or perhaps some deep-sea mountain range that had been lofted almost whole. Around it weird fish, strange semi-monsters of the Pacific deeps, had swum and fought, hunted, played, and lived. It was a cruel march too, over the jagged surface: the men, dressed for landing in boots and gaiters, needed the heavy metal-studded leather beneath their feet. They marched as quietly as possible, making all the speed they could. There was a steep climb, although Halfhyde, reconnoitring ahead, led them on a circuitous route round the heights. The march was a dangerous one: here and there they came upon deep chasms that had either to be passed by long deviations or cleared by jumping.

Runcorn was still in a questioning mood. "Sir, shall we have time to get there and return to the cutter by dawn?"

"I begin to doubt that, Mr Runcorn, but it was always on the cards that we would not."

"And if we don't, sir?"

"The Captain won't forget us, Snotty. He'll return with tomorrow's dark." They trudged on, their nostrils assailed by the lingering sulphurous smell. The moon was still bright, showing them the pitfalls in their track. And as they rounded the heights, and at last brought the western side of the island into full view, that moonlight showed them the great wide bay, almost like a lagoon with a long, wide spit of land reaching out in the protective manner of a ready-made breakwater. Inside this spit lay the three Russian warships, peacefully riding at their anchors, the *Ostrolenka,* the *Czarevitch,* and the *Gregoriev,* peaceful but immensely threatening, their great gun-turrets stark beneath the moon, their riding-lights like brilliant stars against the dark Pacific backcloth.

The party of British seamen halted, staring down at the scene. At Halfhyde's side Mr Midshipman Runcorn uttered, "At least they're human, sir."

"The ships, Mr Runcorn?"

"Oh no, sir. The men in them, sir. This place . . . it gives a man the creeps, sir."

"Did you expect to find it peopled by creatures with sixteen legs, or something, Mr Runcorn?"

"No, sir. But it does feel . . . well, sir, other-worldly."

Halfhyde snorted. "You speak like a wart, Mr Runcorn, not a Midshipman of middling seniority. You've as much reason as I to know that there's precious little other-worldliness about Prince Gorsinski's seamen and marines!" In spite of his words he shivered suddenly. That splendid squadron of newly-commissioned protected cruisers made the old *Viceroy* into a joke, a joke of Admiralty the point of which now came home to St Vincent Halfhyde with very sharp clarity indeed: he remembered, not for the first time since leaving England, Captain Bassinghorn's bitter remark about the expendability of worn-out ships and embarrassing officers. No Board of Admiralty in its right mind would despatch such as the *Viceroy* to take an island when there was any likelihood of opposition from first-rate, modern cruisers. The idea would be laughable: and the Admiralty, in apportioning its blame to exceeded orders, would laugh as heartily as the rest when Bassinghorn's name became mud.

Halfhyde stiffened his bearing: no Board of Admiralty was going to make a fool of Bassinghorn, or of himself. And, as he looked down upon the great natural harbour—as it appeared at first sight unmistakably to be—he began to realize for himself that, after all, this curious island could indeed be a useful base for whichever navy could seize it first. Fairly strategically placed to the south of the Japanese-held island of Parece Vela, it stood, a mid-Pacific sentinel, in the wastes between Hong Kong and San Francisco, between Vladivostock and Australasia, between the northland and the southland, the east and the west. Handy indeed, and no doubt capable of development. Fortifications, if the rock would take them—big guns lofted to the heights, commanding the whole island and the closer seas around it. It could prove one more star in the imperial crown of Russia . . .

"Or one more glittering gem of Empire," Halfhyde said softly, but loud enough to be heard.

"Sir?"

"Never mind, Mr Runcorn. We all know our duty. Now we shall go and do it as planned." He lifted an arm, and pointed down towards the anchorage. On a stretch of flat land about two or three hundred yards inshore from the water's edge, stood a flagpole, a thin affair and obviously hurriedly planted, but with the flag of Russia floating out on a light wind and two seamen armed with rifles and bayonets marching upon their sentry-posts. There was no apparent air of expectancy, or even of a simple watchfulness: had not the British warship last been sighted at sea in a storm, many days ago? Anything could have happened—but, clearly, she was not here! Why should the sentries, a merely token guard upon the flag, strain their senses in this desolate spot bereft of humankind?

Halfhyde's lips thinned into a tight smile. "Now listen to me carefully, all of you. We want no mistakes down there, no wild sweeps with the cutlasses. The rifles will be left here to be picked up on the return journey to the cutter." Concisely he passed the final orders; then the sailors slid like shadows down from the heights, their rifles piled behind a rock, their bodies lost against the dark background.

Chapter 9

THE SENTRIES continued pacing, seeing nothing, hearing nothing. The landing-party had closed to within fifty yards, still merged into the dark background, when Halfhyde lifted a hand free of his boat-cloak and checked the advance. As the sailors flattened to the ground he put his mouth close to the Midshipman's ear. "Six-legged creatures, Mr Runcorn!"

"Sir?"

"The time has come now. In full cry, and waving cutlasses, we appear in the role of devils out of hell. Ready?"

"This is scarcely paying our respects, sir—"

"Words, words! You are being prim, Mr Runcorn."

"But you said, sir—"

"I know what I said. There are various methods of paying respects, Mr Runcorn. The facts are that we have orders to plant the British flag and plant it we shall in due course, and defend it too. I ask again: are you ready?"

Runcorn nodded, his face white in the silvered dark. "I'm ready, sir."

"Good!" Halfhyde clapped him on the shoulder, then turned to look towards the rest of the landing-party. They knew the part they had to play. Halfhyde leapt to his feet with a loud cry, running swiftly away to the left of the Russian sentries; the British sailors, also uttering wild cries, scattered to the right under the orders of the Midshipman, waving their cutlasses around their heads. The sentries swung round, staring, taken completely off their guard and obviously terrified out of their wits. Running like the wind to come up behind them, Halfhyde grinned devilishly: Russian peasants always had a fearful respect for the supernatural, and the sudden emergence of wild men with cold steel on an uninhabited island would have all the appearance of the supernatural. A rifle shot rang out from one of the sentries, the bullet speeding harmlessly into the rock behind the yelling sailors. Halfhyde closed in, met the Russians as they backed towards the line of the shore. They halted, their rifles held across their bodies. Halfhyde addressed them admonishingly in their own language, his eyes showing amusement as he did so.

"Is this how you greet a British naval visit, using rifle fire against men armed only with cutlasses?"

They stared back at him wordlessly.

"Have you nothing to say, no excuse to offer?"

One of the Russians licked his lips and said in a shaking voice, "It is a strange visit. We did not know. Such cries are not usual."

Halfhyde waved a hand; the Russians cringed from him as though expecting to be struck. Halfhyde, flinging back his boat-cloak, displayed his uniform: the sentries stared at brass buttons and gold stripes, now recognizing an officer of the British Navy. "Your Admiral will be displeased, I think."

"I say again, we did not know. We thought you were attacking us with your noise."

"Mere enthusiasm, my friends," Halfhyde said, grinning. "And congratulation also," he added, indicating the Russian flag. "Though perhaps commiseration would be more appropriate! I don't envy your Navy, if it proposes to use this dreadful rock as

a base. However, let us not waste time. You have means of communication with your ship?"

The sentries exchanged glances: as they did so, Runcorn
approached and saluted Halfhyde.

"Sir, the flagship. There's a boat leaving her quarter-boom, sir."

Halfhyde swung round: the rifle shot had been heard and
was being investigated without the need of signal communication. "Thank you, Mr Runcorn. I shall wait. You have your
orders, have you not?"

"Yes, sir."

"Then carry on, and don't waste time."

"But sir, I—"

"You don't wish to leave me to the lion's mouth—I know,
and I appreciate your concern. But the cutter will not wait
beyond the dawn, Mr Runcorn, and you have the men to think
about now. If you don't leave on the instant, Mr Runcorn, I shall
see you mastheaded the moment I return aboard myself." He
grinned. "Don't worry too much. The plan, such as it is, shows
promise of working!"

"Aye, aye, sir." Runcorn saluted again, and turned away. The
Russians stared after him uncertainly. Under his orders, the
landing-party mustered and marched off towards the upward
slope to the heights behind, making back for the other side of
the island. Halfhyde watched them go, then turned his attention to the incoming boat from the Russian flagship. Its bows
cut a clean line of phosphorescence through the dark water as
it neared the shore. Halfhyde, now the die was finally cast, felt
a dryness in his mouth. The risk was enormous; much could go
wrong, and if it did, then his liberty and possibly his life were
ended. From now on, his one weapon would be his ability to
mount and maintain a gigantic bluff, to use his personal knowl-

edge of Prince Gorsinski to play the Russian like a whale upon the end of a harpoon line, and not be brought down himself by the flailing of the tail . . .

The flagship's boat, its oars now inboard, grounded gently on the shore. Halfhyde's professional mind registered that this anchorage had a shelving beach, or what would pass for a beach on a volcanic rock. The bowman jumped out, holding onto the bow line. Two seamen splashed ashore, bearing a gold-encrusted officer in their cradled arms. Carrying him clear of the water, they set him dry upon his feet and stood waiting for orders. The officer, a Lieutenant, fished out a lace-edged handkerchief and flicked at his uniform disdainfully, then called to the sentries, who pointed at Halfhyde and offered explanations.

In faultless English the officer addressed Halfhyde. "Who are you, why are you here, where have you come from? You are aware that this island is now a Russian possession?"

Halfhyde smiled, standing very straight drawn to his full height. "I am aware that a Russian flag has been planted, but it is a plant that will not grow. Your other questions I shall answer only to your Admiral, to whom I wish to be taken at once."

"You wish this? Your name, please?"

"Lieutenant St Vincent Halfhyde, Royal Navy."

There was a sharply indrawn breath from the Russian. "You are Lieutenant Halfhyde? This you admit?"

"I do."

"Do you know who my Admiral is, Lieutenant Halfhyde?"

"I have not that honour, but shall doubtless find out."

"Doubtless indeed!" The Russian smiled, showing a line of bad teeth. He gestured to the sentries, who closed in on Halfhyde. At the officer's order, he was seized and held fast, and pushed towards the waiting boat. More orders were given and from the boat a battery-operated lamp began signalling back to the flag-ship. As soon as Halfhyde had been embarked, the boat was pushed off and rowed fast from the shore. As they neared the flagship's quarterdeck ladder, Halfhyde saw another boat leaving the lower boom crammed to the gunwhales with armed men. It looked as though Prince Gorsinski was willing enough to risk an exchange of arms with the British Navy, but Halfhyde was satisfied that his landing-party had a good enough start upon the Russians.

Halfhyde was taken at once to the Admiral's quarters in the after part of the flagship. When he was brought into the great day-cabin, the Admiral was outside on his stern walk, gazing towards the island. He came in when the British Lieutenant was announced, bending his towering height through the entry port. Hands behind his back, in full uniform despite having been brought urgently from his bed, he stared at Halfhyde.

"So you have come back, Lieutenant Halfhyde."

"It would seem so, sir."

"I have dreamed of this . . . every night since you sailed out of the Bight of Benin!" Gorsinski brought his hands away from his back, lifted them, and stared at them. Big hands, as big as Bassinghorn's, covered on their backs with thick black hair, the hands of an ape. "Every night I have dreamed of the pleasure of strangling you, Lieutenant Halfhyde. Did you not know this?"

"How could I know it, sir?" Halfhyde shrugged, smiled inno-cently. "I dare say—had I thought about it—I would have suspected thoughts of revenge."

Gorsinski stared bleakly, jaws moving as though he were engaged in chewing Halfhyde's very flesh. "You are insolent, I think. You could scarcely not have thought about it! Yet you

come, of your own free will, and place yourself in my power!
Why, Lieutenant Halfhyde?"

"A mistake, sir, a mere mistake, such as anyone can make—"

"Mistake! Do not play the fool with me—"

"I did not know you commanded this squadron, sir. Not
until it was too late." Halfhyde gave a cough. "Hearing that a
Russian force had in the name of the Czar, whom God preserve—"

"Do not provoke—"

"Your pardon, sir. I was ordered by my Captain to land a
guard to pay his respects to Czar Nicholas. You've not been
informed?" There was a glint in Halfhyde's eye, a glint of tongue-
in-cheek amusement.

Gorsinski snapped, "I have heard, yes. Such stupid playacting . . . one learns to expect such of your wretched British Navy,
which is all playacting, a Navy in which paintwork and the
ruinous burnishing of cables and other metal is of more importance than gunnery." He made a gesture of fury. "You made fools
of my sentries, yes, this I readily admit, but you will not make
a fool of me, Lieutenant Halfhyde! You will tell me what the
purpose was of your ridiculous charade of screeching men—"

"Not a charade, sir. A peaceful guard—"

"A peaceful, ceremonial guard—in the middle of the night!"
Gorsinski smashed a fist into his palm. "Such stupid insolence,
that I should be expected to believe your rubbish!"

"Ah, well, we have our foibles," Halfhyde said demurely. "I
repeat, sir, a peaceful guard, armed only with cutlasses, with no
rifles. This peaceful guard was fired upon, by your Russian seamen, sir!" Halfhyde's tone was now a study in high indignation,
his eyes round with moral accusation. "We were met, sir, with
the force of arms. The world, when my Captain makes his report,

will think the worse of you, and you will not please your Czar."

"Fiddlesticks!"

"I think not sir. You have fired upon a British party—"

"A British party that had landed upon Russian territory without permission. I think the matter is two-sided, Lieutenant Halfhyde!"

Halfhyde shrugged. "I believe others than ourselves will judge that, sir. There is, however, a matter of rather more importance."

"And this is?"

"Myself, sir."

Halfhyde had been persuasive, talking easily and to the point: he was clearly Gorsinski's prisoner, but was Gorsinski wise to hold onto him? He had stated the facts baldly: Prince Gorsinski had taken prisoner a British naval officer who had landed personally unarmed upon the island and who had then asked to be brought aboard the flagship to pay his respects, not knowing into whose hands he was delivering himself. Should Gorsinski subsequently remove him to Russia as an act of revenge for past difficulties, did he imagine Her Majesty Queen Victoria, or Their Lordships of the Admiralty, or the British people, would accept this? Was Prince Gorsinski aware that he would involve his Czar in war?

With amusement, Halfhyde studied Gorsinski's reactions: Gorsinski, pacing the length of the day-cabin, was working things out and not liking the results. Much of what Halfhyde had said was nonsense, was mendacious, and Gorsinski was well aware of this; but much was true. In the rarified world of diplomacy and court intrigue, the lie was virtually the norm, the slanderous canard could be made to approach the truth. The secret of success was to justify the larger lie, never to be caught out, and never to give way to the temptation of revenge. But Gorsinski—and this Halfhyde knew and used as his weapon— was a man of naked passions, a man in whom the desire for revenge lay deep and raw. His humiliation off the Benin coast had been utter and catastrophic and had all been brought about by the man who now stood prisoner once again in his flagship. He could not let him go—but to keep him would be a clear embarrassment. Halfhyde continued his pricking of the Admiral's mental processes: his Captain, he said, was currently lying off the island with a heavily-gunned ship and would shortly be in possession of the report that his men had been fired upon and one of his Lieutenants taken prisoner. There was, Halfhyde added casually, an availability of strong reinforcements from the China Squadron based on Hong Kong. Captain Bassinghorn would doubtless decide to make all speed for Hong Kong and return with these powerful reinforcements: this would lead naturally to a confrontation of British and Russian naval power and it could scarcely be kept secret. There would be a world-wide reaction: Britain, though not needing allies, would probably find one in the Japanese should it become desirable; Russia would stand virtually alone in a war of her own making, and all for the sake of an isolated chunk of volcanically upthrust rock of doubtful value. Was it worth while?

"It can be avoided," Halfhyde said.

"By your death alone, I fancy," was Gorsinski's grim response. He had refused to listen further: he might well be reflecting upon his position in the meantime, but currently Halfhyde was nursing his own thoughts in the sordid loneliness of a tiny cell below-decks. Captain Bassinghorn had remained awake through the night, pacing the deck at intervals, sitting in a chair in his cabin from time to time until restlessness and anxiety sent him back again to the deck to resume his pacing and his telescopic watch of the shoreline. As the dawn came up he was on the bridge with his Navigating Officer and Lieutenant Campbell, acting as First Lieutenant in Halfhyde's absence, ready to proceed to sea. The landing-party was observed winding its way down from the heights just in time. Bassinghorn let out a great sigh of relief, and passed the word for the watch on deck to stand by to hoist the cutter when it came alongside.

Back aboard, the Midshipman reported at once to the bridge.

"Well, Mr Runcorn, how did it go?"

"Sir—it went as planned, sir! The Russians fired a shot, sir, but hit no one! They have shown their hand, sir—"

"More slowly, if you please, Mr Runcorn." The Captain looked down gravely at the youthful face. "Control your excitement. Mr Halfhyde?"

"Sir, Mr Halfhyde was taken aboard the flagship." Runcorn passed his full report, and was sent below to see to his breakfast and that of his men. The Captain paced the bridge in deep thought, his face troubled. A long career at sea had taught him to expect the unexpected and never to count any chickens . . . Halfhyde had appeared confident enough, had been persuasive, perhaps overly so. Having persuaded his Captain, he might well persuade the Russian Admiral—or he might not. The plan was a devious one, up to a point even a frivolous one, and it had its obvious pitfalls and loopholes. Bassinghorn paced on, watched by his senior officers, his next order awaited. Doubts had come to him during the long night, the hours of inactivity when all a man of action could do was to brood and ponder and sow in himself the seeds of a terrible fear. There was a nag in Bassinghorn's mind, a suspicion that events might have proceeded too smoothly, too much to plan. The landing-party had been allowed back unscathed . . . of course, that had been planned for, had been expected by the smooth tongue of Mr Halfhyde, had been explained by young Runcorn, but . . . Bassinghorn pushed his doubts down: one thing was sure, and dictated his actions for the coming day: when a plan had been agreed upon, it must never be altered in mid-stream when another depended, perhaps for his life, upon its due execution.

Bassinghorn swung round on his Navigator. "Mr Puckridge, we shall proceed in accordance with my previous decision, and lie off out at sea. I trust Mr Halfhyde will rejoin when we close the island again at sunset."

"Aye, aye, sir."

"Carry on, if you please, Mr Puckridge."

The orders for sea were passed; the *Viceroy's* engines were rung to half ahead and she moved outwards, trailing smoke.

Halfhyde knew he was being left to stew, to fall a prey to doubt; but his intent was firm and he had a strong desire to succeed in his self-set mission. He was left entirely alone and without food, peered at now and again by a sentry through a small spy-hole in the cell door. He was left until the following evening, when once again he was brought before the Admiral. Gorsinski, hands behind his back, stared at him disdainfully.

"You have considered the possibility of your death, Lieutenant Halfhyde?"

"I believe that can be avoided," Halfhyde answered easily, "and with it the possibility of your wrecking yourself upon the rocks of an unsought war."

Gorsinski gave a loud laugh, a scornful one. "Explain how," he said sneeringly.

"That I shall do, sir." Halfhyde proceeded carefully, choosing

his words, using his knowledge of Prince Gorsinski, his aware-
ness of the Russian aristocrat's intriguing mind and his personal
vanity. He was, he said, under no illusions as to Prince Gorsinski's connections and his undoubted ability to acquire useful
knowledge concerning his potential enemies: thus,
taking into account his long preoccupation with thoughts of
revenge upon Halfhyde, he must have taken some pains to
acquaint himself with Halfhyde's career and physical movements
and would very likely be aware of Halfhyde's standing or lack
of it inside the British Admiralty and the reasons for the same.
This point Gorsinski neither confirmed nor denied. Halfhyde
went on to say that, for its part, the Admiralty was also not without its own intelligence system: they could be assumed to have
known that Admiral Prince Gorsinski was in the Pacific with his
squadron and that there was always the possibility that he might
move upon the island.

"And that you might fall into my hands, Lieutenant
Halfhyde?"

Halfhyde inclined his head. "Just so. They would not, of
course, have informed me."

"An intentional sacrifice?"

"Not a sacrifice. A jettisoning of an embarrassment—but at
the same time, sir, something very much more."

"Well?"

Halfhyde said, "An excuse for attack upon your ships, leading to British sovereignty over the island."

Gorsinski frowned. "Why are you telling me this? Are you a
traitor, Lieutenant Halfhyde?"

"By no means. I—"

"But what you have said, it smacks of disloyalty."

"I frequently feel disloyal to the landlubbers of the Admiralty, sir, but never to my country. I am not disloyal to my country now. What I am suggesting is this: I would not be unwilling to see the Admiralty hoist with its own petard, as our saying is. In short, your Highness, remove your flag and leave the island— then there will be no excuse for war."

"But for your presence aboard my ship."

Halfhyde shrugged, said casually, almost lightly, "Then let me go! I shall have done you a favour by interpreting to you the British Admiralty's likely way of thinking. I am entitled to ask you a favour in return, I think."

"And if I refuse this?"

"Sir, I am accustomed to looking out for myself, come what may. I've escaped from you twice, and each time to your discomfiture. There is a saying that things tend to go in threes, is there not?"

"This time it will be different, Lieutenant Halfhyde," Gorsinski said in a strangely soft tone. He moved to the door and snapped an order to the sentry on guard outside. There was the crash of a rifle butt on the deck as the man saluted, and as he did so, Halfhyde's escort came into the Admiral's cabin and were ordered by Gorsinski to remove the prisoner. At bayonet-point Halfhyde was marched out, back along the steel-lined alleyways to his cell, his mind racing. He had a strong feeling that events were not proceeding well, not moving after all in his direction: this feeling worsened his temper, as did the continual prick of the Russian seaman's bayonet in his back. He halted in his tracks: the nagging bayonet pressed harder.

Halfhyde looked over his shoulder. "Take that damned thing away. I am, after all, a British officer!"

In Russian, he was told to move on. Ahead of him, the Petty Officer of the escort had also turned, and was coming back towards him. A hand fell upon his shoulder; he shook it off furiously, his basic fighting instincts gaining precedence over his diplomacy: this was not the way old Daniel Halfhyde, Gunner's Mate in the *Temeraire,* would have allowed himself to be treated by Napoleon's men had they ever taken him! Halfhyde shook a fist in the Petty Officer's face: saw the sudden reaction, the unspoken order to the armed seaman. Turning fast, Halfhyde saw the rifle's aim, the finger tightening on the trigger: only afterwards did he ponder on an act that was, no doubt, nothing more than a threat. Once again he acted from instinct: with both hands he seized the rifle barrel behind the shining bayonet, lifted it so that its aim was clear above his head and, as the weapon was fired, rammed it with all his strength back into the seaman's neck, sending the butt hard into the man's throat so that the head slammed cruelly against an angle-iron supporting the steel-lined deckhead. The man fell, limp and silent: from behind Halfhyde the Petty Officer gave a single short cry. The richochet of the rifle had penetrated his head: he was as dead as a doornail, as was the armed seaman, whose neck was broken. Halfhyde stared in horror, his fury, his foul temper gone. By this time the alleyway was filling with other Russian sailors. There was nothing he could do but face the music and curse his own impetuosity that had brought failure both to himself and the aspirations of the British Admiralty: and to Captain Henry Bassinghorn. Seized and brought once more before the Admiral, he found Gorsinski pale with anger and hate.

"You spoke of events moving in threes, Lieutenant Halfhyde. Not this time, my friend! Your presence as a prisoner might well have disturbed your Admiralty as you said . . . but death is a very final attitude—"

"And equally an excuse for reprisals, Prince Gorsinski. You as a man of diplomacy will surely not—"

"Silence!" A hand lashed across Halfhyde's cheeks. "All you have said since you were brought aboard has been nonsense, and defiant nonsense—and now you kill my seamen!" Gorsinski stared at him with red-flecked eyes, face working with almost insane rage, then turned to his Flag Captain standing by his side. "Captain Angelov, you will prepare your starboard main upper yard for an execution at noon tomorrow. All men of the flagship and ships in company will muster to watch the Englishman hang as a common murderer."

Halfhyde, back in his cell, sitting on the bare wooden bench, scowled bleakly as from time to time the sentry's beady eye could be seen, pressed close to the spy-hole. Failure had been total, even the initial bluff had not been good enough—and now, this! Halfhyde was immensely sorry: he would sooner he had killed an officer. Those Russian seamen had simply been obeying the orders of a tyrant. There was no excuse for what he had done: Great Britain and the Czar were not at war, even if unfriendly enough. Failure was hard to take, though it had always been on the cards. Bad enough—but death was death. He stirred himself, tried to find hope. Somewhere, events could be shaping up towards help, although he had asked for none, had bargained for none beyond the making of the appointed rendezvous at sunset. At this moment Captain Bassinghorn would in fact be approaching the other side of the island, and his movements when Halfhyde failed to appear could not be forecast.

Earlier Halfhyde had said to Gorsinski that the *Viceroy* would for a certainty be making for Hong Kong for reinforcements . . . now, he was forced to ponder frustratedly on what, in fact, Bassinghorn was really likely to do. Imaginings produced no hard result: this was still an unknown quantity, and the other unknown quantity in what yet remained of Halfhyde's future was Prince Gorsinski himself: Gorsinski, as Halfhyde had plenty of cause to know from past experience, was a hothead; a man who—like Halfhyde himself—let his temper run away with his prudence, a man who ordered things that, when his temper had cooled, he was capable of regretting. An eye for an eye was all very well; but at least revenge should be preceded by a trial. Gorsinski, however—and this was the real point—never went back upon a decision once that decision had been uttered in the hearing of any of his subordinates. At noon the men of the Russian squadron would be expecting the sight of a yardarm hanging: Halfhyde had a sinking feeling that Prince Gorsinski would not disappoint them. Gorsinski, with his close links with the Czar, could within his ship do virtually as he pleased. And in Halfhyde's case, the case of a man who had killed two Russian seamen not in any act of war, Gorsinski was very likely to get away with it even before the weight of public opinion in the British Empire; in short, Gorsinski would most probably not by his act be exacerbating the situation to the point of war: Halfhyde—and he knew it now—had played directly into Gorsinski's hands.

In the early hours of next morning, after the Russian bugles had blown and the ship's company had turned out to clean up the decks and prepare breakfast, strangely alarming sounds came down to Halfhyde in his narrow prison—the sounds of heavy gear being hauled along the upper-deck, the drag of blocks and tackles and purchases, rope being flaked down in readiness for running a noose aloft, and the rush of barefoot seamen, comrades of the dead men, seamen whose willing hands would within the next few hours be hauling his bound body to the yard, swaying it out across the water of the anchorage for the long farewell of the Pacific Ocean.

Bitterly, Halfhyde met the stare of the probing, invading eye through the spy-hole: he had been every kind of fool from the start, placing his initial reliance too heavily upon the persuasiveness of his tongue. At least, it was a belated lesson in humility!

Chapter 10

THERE WERE FOOTSTEPS outside, the crash of a rifle, then voices, orders: keys rattled, the door of the cell was opened, and a seaman in a white canvas suit thrust a tin plate through to Halfhyde. For the condemned man, breakfast. Halfhyde looked at it with repugnance: a filthy mess resembling porridge, porridge with big black beans floating in it like half-submerged slugs. It would need considerable forcing, but a British naval officer did not appear faint-hearted at the last. Halfhyde prepared to show the Russians that the prospect of death had not diminished his appetite: but fortunately was spared the ordeal. Behind the plate-bearing seaman was an officer of lieutenant's rank, gilded and splendid and haughty, staring at Halfhyde as though he were of an even lower order than his own peasant dogs.

"Eat," the Lieutenant ordered.

Halfhyde, with the plate in his hands, looked up. "Who tells me to eat?"

"I do, Lieutenant Parranadin."

"I see. You order me to eat this filth?"

"It is what our men eat—and enjoy. Yes, you are ordered by me to eat. You will eat."

Halfhyde's stomach settled down: honour had been satisfied. He need not, would not, eat to order. He smiled up at Lieutenant Parranadin. "You will have to feed me, my dear sir, or I shall not eat."

The Russian made a gesture of annoyance and, thrusting the seaman from his path, advanced threateningly into the cell. Halfhyde, smiling still, brought up the plate and sent the mess slamming into the Lieutenant's startled face. Sticky unpleasantness drooled down his chops, spattered the gilded epaulettes, fouled the brass buttons and the gleaming starched white sharkskin of the uniform tunic. The sentry and the other man look petrified: Halfhyde continued smiling. Honour had been more than satisfied now. He endured stoically the rain of blows from the sentry's rifle butt: it had been well worth while.

Other sounds came down later: more bugle calls, taken up by the ships in company. There was a rush of feet as the *Ostrolenka's* sailors made at the double for their stations, then more controlled shuffles as they were fallen in by divisions. Distant shouted orders reached Halfhyde, then there was a silence. In this silence he heard the approach of his gaolers, the precise footsteps coming along the alleyways to halt outside his cell, left, right, left—crash, crash, bang. Once again, keys jangled. The door came open. Outside was an escort of four seamen armed with rifles, and another Lieutenant, this time with gilded tassels hanging from his left shoulder: the Flag Lieutenant, Gorsinski's tame popinjay, whose face Halfhyde remembered from the ill-fated *Romanov* in the Bight of Benin. "I thought you had died in the mutiny," he said. "Perhaps God is keeping something better up his sleeve for you."

"Which in any case you shall not live to see, Lieutenant Halfhyde." The Russian gestured with his scabbarded sword, held loosely in his left hand as it drooped from the sword-belt. "Come now, out of your cell, and quickly. The Admiral is waiting."

Halfhyde moved out, was at once seized by the guards and

marched along the alleyways, going aft through the mess decks ahead of the Flag Lieutenant. He was taken up a steel ladder and through a door in the after screen: he stepped into brilliant sunlight. The Pacific stretched, deep dark blue, to the distant horizons beneath a cloudless sky that shone like burnished metal. To port lay the island, its lava-peaks high and jagged, a threatening and awesome dull grey overshadowing the Russian cruisers. There was a curious silence everywhere, broken only by the marching footsteps of Halfhyde and his armed escort. The decks were crammed with men, the seaman and stoker divisions fallen in under their officers and petty officers, grim-faced men, mostly with a lean and hungry look, mostly bearded and none too clean. Here there was not the look of British sailor-men: these men looked dangerous, dangerous in a very different kind of way, and also cowed, with quick shifting glances flashed at the Flag Lieutenant as that gilded demi-god stalked past behind the prisoner; glances that dared not linger too long on aristocratic faces lest the slicing cuts of the cat-o'-nine-tails, each thong lead-weighted, should follow at the gratings.

Halfhyde was taken up another ladder leading from the quarterdeck, where stood Prince Gorsinski with his Flag Captain and secretary and the *Ostrolenka's* Commander. They watched in silence as Halfhyde moved on to where, between the ship's boats griped-in to the davits, the great mainmast drove down through the decks and double-bottoms to its seating in the keelson. Halted on the Flag Lieutenant's order, Halfhyde looked aloft towards the starboard main upper yard: at the yardarm a hemp line had been rove through the sheave of an iron snatch-block, its two ends trailing down to the foot of the mast. Outboard of the snatch-block hung a noose with a hangman's knot, seized back in a loop to the yard itself, gently swinging. Halfhyde gave an involuntary shudder, quickly controlled. The drill was simple, yet so final. Tied to one end of the hemp line, with two seamen hauling upon the other end, he would be sent aloft, willy-nilly, to the yardarm, where his body would be lowered again until his neck took the noose. Then the seizing would be cut away by a man on the yard, and he would drop, his own weight tautening the noose and the hangman's knot breaking his neck as surely as his escort's neck had snapped against the angle-iron.

Halfhyde stiffened his body and composed his face, feeling his lips tremble now. He bit down hard, his jaw setting, as from aft the Commander called the ship's company to attention. A bugle sounded out, loud and clear and strident. The call was taken up by the two ships in company, the notes echoing back savagely from the island's heights. As those echoes died and the squadron waited, the Admiral spoke. Blood drummed through Halfhyde's ears; through it he picked up and interpreted something of an impassioned speech: to an approving response from his men Gorsinski was ranting about murder, about crimes against Czar and State. Halfhyde gave a savage grin, a tight baring of his teeth: he had been at least partially instrumental in causing the blowing up of Gorsinski's last flagship, and the smashing together of his remaining cruisers. Revenge must be sweet for Gorsinski now! Sweat streamed down Halfhyde's face as Gorsinski's voice stopped. An order was given and Halfhyde was pushed towards the foot of the mast. His hands were roped behind his back, then his body was bound with codline to the heavier hemp. On a signal from the quarterdeck as bells struck the noon hour, a party of seamen tailed onto the rope's-end and walked away with it. Halfhyde felt the pull on his body as the hemp started around the sheave in the snatch-block, felt his feet leave the deck. Smoothly he was hauled aloft, smoothly and slowly so as to prolong the moment, to give a decent view to the hundreds of upturned eyes. He stared upwards, lifting his own eyes to heaven, moving his lips in prayer as the sweat poured. He found no heaven: only the slowly but inexorably approaching starboard main yard, tapering towards the noose at its arm.

"What the devil has gone wrong, Mr Bampton?" Bassinghorn stood upon his bridge, a dawn breeze tugging at his white uniform and blowing the deep blue sea into small wavelets. "Of all the times for your confounded engine to stop, this is the worst— and you shall answer for it, possibly in irons, Mr Bampton!"

"I'm sorry, sir—"

"Sorry!" The Captain took several turns up and down the bridge, muttering to himself, then once again faced the shaking Engineer. "Is there nothing you can do, man? Nothing?"

"Given time, sir—"

"Time is what we may not have. Damn your blasted mechanical contrivances!" Bassinghorn seethed: the night had been an anxious one and he was much troubled. No one had turned up at the rendezvous, though he had waited until midnight before taking his ship out again to sea. After some deliberation he had made the decision, well knowing the risks involved, to steam south around the island and come up towards the Russians' anchorage, keeping, so far as might prove possible, out of sight until the situation had clarified. There was, he had felt, and felt still, a strong possibility that Halfhyde might have need of the *Viceroy*'s guns; and now he was stopped in mid-ocean, helpless, at the mercy of wind and sea and engineers. He was filled with anger at failure and inefficiency; nevertheless, there was a silver lining and one that found much favour with Captain Bassinghorn, who for some while had been eyeing the black smoke that poured from his funnels: eyeing it with distaste, not only for its inherent filth and poisonous fumes, but because, visible in daylight for many miles, it was as good as a signal to the enemy.

"Very well, Mr Bampton, take yourself below and do your best." He swung round on the Officer of the Watch. "Mr Anstey!"

"Sir?"

"Both watches of the hands, Mr Anstey, at the double. I intend making sail—"

"*Sail,* sir?"

"Sail, Mr Anstey. There are certain items stowed in number four store-room. The key is in the bureau in my cabin. Have it fetched, and have the stores broken out. You will find a partial suit of canvas, the last suit made for the old *Warrior*—it will fit our yards, and though it is old and incomplete, it will still do its job. This is to be treated as an evolution, Mr Anstey, and carried out with the utmost despatch."

Men stared up at the bridge, as though the Captain had taken leave of his senses. The Boatswain, Mr Pinch, came along the upper-deck, shouting them into action: Ben Pinch was a sail man himself, as much as the Captain, and he received the order with pleasure. Moreover, he knew the ship, had handled her sails before. Not many of the *Viceroy's* company had sail experience, but there were enough to provide a competent nucleus of skill and knowledge: the Master-at-Arms, the Chief Gunner's Mate, the Chief Boatswain's Mate, the Carpenter, and four seaman Petty Officers, plus a score of Leading Rates and below. Lieutenants Campbell and Puckridge had each, as Midshipmen, served a commission in the *Inconstant,* flagship of the Flying Squadron under Rear-Admiral the Earl of Clanwilliam. All this was enough for Bassinghorn: as the bulky canvas was manhandled up from number four store-room—which on the *Viceroy's* last commission at sea had in fact been the sail locker—a fresh buoyancy came into his step.

"Mr Pinch!"

"Sir?"

"Courses and tops'ls—upper and lower. It's all we have."

"Aye, aye, sir." Mr Pinch, dashing sweat from his fringe of grey whiskers, made haste along the upper-deck to sort out what threatened to be a pandemonium of lifts, braces, tacks, and downhauls as the hundreds of ropes required to control the sails were brought on deck for reaving to the yards. Men swarmed like monkeys up the ratlines and moved out on the footropes to secure the blocks in readiness, then the braces were sent up. Other men prepared the great sails themselves, threading the halliards into the cringles for hoisting to the yards, dropped ready on their lifts to take them. Even before a single sail had been shaken out, the ship seemed different, seemed to come alive, began already to smell of rope and canvas rather than of coal-dust and smoke. From the after screen emerged the sweating face and dirty overalls of Mr Bampton: his look was sour, the look of a man made redundant by something far older than himself.

Bassinghorn leaned over the bridge rail. "You have done well, Mr Pinch, and I'm grateful."

"Thank you, sir."

"We are not far off the anchorage now, and thanks to you, Mr Pinch, are unlikely to be seen yet." The Captain stared aloft at the courses and the upper and lower topsails straining out from their cringles, bowling the ship along nicely before a fresh breeze. The patent log was showing a speed of five knots through the water, and Bassinghorn was smiling his pleasure in so closely approaching his three-quarters-power engine speed even without a full press of canvas above his head. He was sniffing the good, clean, smoke-free air when there was a hail from the fore-topmast crosstrees.

"Anchorage in sight, sir!"

Bassinghorn lifted a strong, carrying voice in response: "What sight of the Russian squadron?"

"Trucks and royal masts, sir."

Bassinghorn lifted a hand in acknowledgement, then turned to the Officer of the Watch. "I shall approach a little closer, then lie off and wait. We'll not be seen from the decks."

"Masthead lookouts may be posted, sir."

Bassinghorn nodded but made no answer: what Anstey had said was true. But those doubts were still nagging at Bassinghorn's mind. One of his officers was aboard the Russian flagship . . . it was possible that Prince Gorsinski might detach a ship to sea, perhaps to carry Halfhyde back to Russia if the plan had gone awry. A risk must be taken, the very risk that he had seen receding when the filthy smoke had stopped coming from the funnels—and by virtue of that, the risk was now undoubtedly smaller than would have been the case had he approached as a smoking beacon! If Gorsinski should go to sea, then he, Bassinghorn, would remain in company: the British flag had a right to sail the open sea without interference, and it would at least be interesting to observe Prince Gorsinski's reaction. Bassinghorn again looked aloft at his taut canvas, booming out above the decks. To keep up with the Russians at sea he would of course need to put his engines back into commission the moment they were reported ready, but for now he was closing the distance satisfactorily enough.

"Decks in view, sir!"

Near enough now: Bassinghorn passed his orders to lay the topsails aback. As the yards were hauled round on the braces, the wind came out of them. The courses were let go; the *Viceroy* drifted, her way coming off sharply. A moment later there was another shout, an urgent one, from the foretopmast head:

"Sir, the flagship's hoisting something to her main upper yard. It looks like a man, sir!"

Chapter 11

EVERY EYE in the anchored squadron was on the British officer: a torpedo-boat could have crept in unremarked, and sent her warheads speeding for the Russian hulls. Halfhyde, as his body reached the yard and his shoulders bumped against the wood, was conscious of nothing but the terrible surge of blood in his ears—that, and the blinding sun right overhead. A moment later he was but dimly aware of the yard receding, of his body being lowered a little, and of a man reaching down from the yard above him, one hand beginning to pull up the noose. His body turned a little with the rope, and he became vaguely aware of a ship . . . distant, but approaching under bellying sails. He scarcely registered; this sudden arrival meant nothing to him. Then, while the Russian sailor on the yard still fiddled with the noose, trying to settle it neatly above Halfhyde's neck for the final act to follow, a red blob of flame appeared from below the oncoming vessel's canvas, followed by a puff of smoke. A roar of gunfire came, and a whistling wind ruffled Halfhyde's hair. There was a scream above his head: the Russian toppled headlong from the yard, startled out of his handhold on the wire stay, to take the deck in a spread of blood and burst flesh. The shell exploded in a shattering roar on the island behind the flagship, sending chunks of rock flying into the air. Halfhyde uttered an exultant cry as he realized it was the *Viceroy* coming in. He looked down at the deck below to see Gorsinski shaking a fist in rage towards the

British ship. A bugle sounded, and the ranks of men broke as the gunners moved at the double to their stations for action. Halfhyde's momentary exultation faded: the old *Viceroy* would stand no chance, would be hammered to pieces by the guns of Gorsinski's heavy squadron. He watched in mounting horror as the *Viceroy* came on, as the guns in their turrets below him swung to bear on her. After that one shot she had fired no more. Seconds passed, became minutes: no guns opened. Halfhyde, looking down, saw Gorsinski in impassioned argument with his Flag Captain, his arms waving ferociously in the latter's face. Gorsinski was literally hopping up and down upon his quarterdeck: if the moment had not been desperately serious, potentially, for many hundreds of men, it would have been hilarious.

Halfhyde saw Gorsinski look aloft, and stare towards him. An order was shouted, and a man at the foot of the mast began to cast off the end of the hemp line from a belaying-pin: swiftly, uncomfortably, Halfhyde came down. He was landed on his feet with a jerk that sent shafts of pain up his spine. Knives cut away the codline binding him to the rope and he was marched aft to the quarterdeck where Gorsinski was waiting.

Halfhyde grinned in the furious face. "You have had second and wiser thoughts, sir, it appears."

"Do not build too much on that, Lieutenant Halfhyde!"

"I think your chance has gone, sir, and you realize it. You have not returned the fire, at all events." Halfhyde's eyes glittered. "Has the Flag Captain more wisdom than his Admiral?"

Gorsinski's hand came out, striking like a snake, the hard bony back of it taking Halfhyde across each cheek in succession. Halfhyde's head rocked, but he kept cool, kept a smile on his lips. The Admiral was about to speak again when a Midshipman approached, saluting, and Gorsinski turned to him impatiently.

"Well?"

"A signal, Your Highness, from the British warship. Her Captain presents his compliments—"

There was an explosive sound from the Admiral.

"—and intends coming aboard, Your Highness, immediately."

For a moment Gorsinski looked furious; then, controlling himself, he laughed and made a gesture of disdain. "Then let him come! He knows well enough that his puerile command can be blown out of the water at any moment I choose to give the order . . . let him come, and see my muscle at close quarters! Flag Captain?"

"Your Highness?" The Flag Captain gave a formal bow from the waist.

"The British Captain is not to be piped aboard nor accorded any other honour. He is to be met by a common seaman, and brought before me." As the Flag Captain seemed to hesitate, Gorsinski stormed at him. "Do you hear me, Flag Captain Angelov, or must I shout your eardrums out through a megaphone?"

"Your Highness, I hear you. Your orders will be obeyed, of course. But—"

Pointedly, the Admiral turned his back and walked across to the starboard guardrail. Captain Angelov shrugged, briefly met Halfhyde's eye and looked away, but not before Halfhyde had seen, and noted, the look of baffled helplessness: as ever, Admiral Prince Gorsinski was not beloved by the officers under his command, and for a certainty was hated by those he always termed his common seamen, the men whom he treated as what in his view they were—mere dogs, to be whipped and shouted at and starved into instant obedience. Halfhyde, still under guard, looked across at the Admiral's back. Gorsinski was standing tall and straight, his head held imperiously back, the beard jutting. Beyond him the *Viceroy* was visible, lying with her sails loosed outside the narrow spit of land projecting across the anchorage. A few minutes later, minutes of a tense silence aboard the Russian flagship, a cutter was seen coming around the spit, pulled strongly, with a bulky figure seated in the stern-sheets. As soon as the cutter began to close the starboard side, Prince Gorsinski rudely turned his back once again and strode over to the port guardrail, where he stood with his hands clasped behind his back, staring out towards the island. The *Viceroy's* cutter came alongside the bottom platform of the starboard accommodation-ladder; soon the head of Captain Bassinghorn appeared and he stepped, still in that tense silence, to the upper platform, where he stood for a moment at the salute. Halfhyde noted his punctilious formality: he was wearing full-dress uniform of home service blue, with cocked hat, epaulettes, cut-away coat, and sword, such as had not been worn in hot climates since 1885. He must have been sweating like a pig; but he made an impressive figure and one clearly angered at the cavalier fashion in which the representative of Her Britannic Majesty was being received aboard.

He stared at the seaman detailed to greet him. "Captain Henry Bassinghorn," he said abruptly, "commanding Her Majesty's Ship *Viceroy*."

The seaman, not understanding, saluted, said something in Russian, and turned away. Bassinghorn followed him across the deck, stopping for a word with Halfhyde. "It was you at the yardarm, Mr Halfhyde, was it not?"

"It was, sir."

"Why?"

Halfhyde explained. "I regret killing the men, sir, but it was not intentional, and would not have happened had I not been on my way to the cells."

"A British officer, in the cells?" Bassinghorn's tone was acid. "Nevertheless, you acted impetuously, like an idiot without thought for the future. I condemn your action utterly."

"I'm sorry, sir."

Bassinghorn swung away without further words. He went on behind the Russian seaman, stared at by officers and men. He planted himself firmly behind Gorsinski, who remained with his back turned and one hand now resting on the guardrail. He began, "Your Highness, I have the honour to make certain representations to you, concerning the manner of treatment accorded one of my officers." There was no response; Bassinghorn waited, then said tartly, "Sir, you have the manners of a guttersnipe, or of a pig. And I think you are a coward, that you will not face me."

Suddenly Gorsinski swung on his heel, his face flushed. "Perhaps you imagine I have no English, Captain!"

Bassinghorn shook his head. "On the contrary, I knew your command of it was excellent. That is why I spoke as I did. And now, sir, in the name of Her Majesty Queen Victoria, I protest at murder almost done—"

"Ask your Lieutenant Halfhyde who murdered first, Captain!"

"I have. A breach of conduct that I shall deal with as I think fit. I do not condone what has been done, but I demand that my Lieutenant be returned to my ship immediately."

Gorsinski sneered. "You have an Admiral aboard your puny ship, Captain?" he asked.

"My ship carries no flag, as I think you are well aware."

"I speak only to my equals," Gorsinski said insolently, "not to my inferiors. In the absence of an Admiral I will say this to you, then no more: you have fired upon my squadron, one of your officers has committed murder as I regard it, and you must take the consequences. You are now my prisoner, Captain Bassinghorn, as well as your Lieutenant. So is your ship. Captain Angelov!"

"Your Highness?"

"The squadron is to raise steam for immediate notice and prepare for sea. A boarding-party is to be put aboard the British ship and will steam her in company with us. As soon as the squadron is ready, we sail for Okhotsk and the jurisdiction of Russian courts."

Gorsinski stalked off the quarterdeck.

An insane temper was largely responsible: passion and an auto-cratic temperament inflamed on this occasion, admittedly, by the ill result that had attended Halfhyde's attack upon the escort. And Gorsinski could not bear to be bested ever, would go to great lengths to crush those who dared oppose him. Bassinghorn's outraged protests had proved so much wasted breath. Halfhyde's thoughts were bitter as the cell door was once again locked on him: Gorsinski would have his pound of flesh; he would without a doubt find a way of justifying his actions to the aristocrats at St Petersburg; he had his contacts and his relationships where they counted the most . . . and to a point his hands were clean anyway. He had killed no one, had fired upon no ship! It was only too true that Halfhyde had killed, that Bassinghorn had opened fire and in so doing had caused the death of another Russian sailor. In all the circumstances the British Government might find it impossible to establish a case; events had played most cruelly into Gorsinski's hands, and Halfhyde admitted to himself his own share in that. One thing alone was certain now: once they reached Okhotsk, they could say goodbye to freedom, perhaps even to their lives. Yet to get away must surely be impossible. Halfhyde sat on his wooden bench, listening to the many sounds of a ship being prepared for sea. The rushing feet on deck, the banging from the cable locker as cable was shortened-in preparatory to weighing anchor; the thump and clash of blocks and tackles; the shouts of Petty Officers as the boats that had been lying at the booms were hoisted and secured to the davits, with their griping-bands hauled flat and taut; the engine sounds as the boilers were stoked to give a full head of steam; the whirr and grind from the aux-iliary machinery spaces. From somewhere close by his cell there was a smack and a rattle as another boat took the water—the boarding-party, no doubt, making across the anchorage to take over the *Viceroy,* held under the guns of the squadron with a signalled threat, made just before Halfhyde and Bassinghorn had been taken below, that any indiscretion would lead to pulveriz-ing broadsides from the heavy Russian cruisers. It was a *fait accompli.* Nothing could be done. Halfhyde gave a groan; his tongue, his overweening ideas that had persuaded Bassinghorn, had so far cut no ice with Prince Gorsinski and never would again. The time for that was past. Soon Halfhyde felt a shudder run through the cell and then more banging as the centre-line capstan on the fo'c'sle heaved in the remaining links of the cable. Then a heavy crash against the side told him that the anchor was coming home for hoisting to the cathead. The shudder increased, changed its character, became the shudder of revolv-ing screws, stopped, started again with a deeper shudder that spoke of engines moving astern: Gorsinski's Flag Captain was turning his ship short round on his engines to head her for the narrows past the land-spit and out into open water.

Chapter 12

THE BREEZE that had brought Bassinghorn up from the southward continued through the afternoon and night, and freshened:
as dark came down the following evening, the ships were over-
taken by worsening weather. Gorsinski, pacing the bridge of his
flagship, cursed the wallowing *Viceroy* still under her sail power.
The engineers he had put aboard with the steaming-party had
not, it seemed, been able to effect a repair. The speed of the fleet
being, as ever, that of the slowest ship, Prince Gorsinski wal-
lowed with the *Viceroy* and watched his cruisers shipping water
heavily over their sterns from the following wind and sea: at
times the quarterdecks had seemed, while there had still been
light enough to see, to be submerged, sliding beneath the wind-
blown swell and vanishing until the next plunge of the stem
lifted them, and the sea drained away in torrents through the
wash-ports or clear below the open guardrails down the heaving sides. Gorsinski frowned: the weather-pattern was merging
curiously early into that of the typhoon season, which was an
unwelcome thought, and currently a worrying one. But perhaps
not so curiously after all: experience had taught Gorsinski that
in the general vicinity of Japanese waters literally anything could
be expected of the weather and never mind the set seasons.
Using his telescope he gazed ahead towards the *Viceroy*'s stern
light, clear on his port bow. He scowled: the British ship was

down to her lower topsails and making heavy weather of the passage as she ran before the gathering storm. Gorsinski turned and caught the eye of the Flag Captain.

"How is the steering, Captain Angelov?"

"Not easy, Your Highness. The slow speed is against us."

Gorsinski nodded. "As I thought. You must watch your helmsmen constantly, Captain. If the head should pay off and allow a heavy sea to take the quarter on either side . . ." He had no need to finish: Angelov was well enough aware of the dangers inherent in broaching-to, and well enough aware of the difficulty in keeping the head before the sea when the speed was so low as barely to give steerage way. A reminder that his Admiral was also aware, and was taking note, was all that was required. Gorsinski, scowling again through the night towards the British warship, went below, followed by his Flag Lieutenant, leaving word with the Flag Captain that he would be in his quarters and was to be informed immediately of any change in the weather or shift of wind, and of the sighting of any shipping. Making his way down the bridge ladder, he was almost blown off his feet: his oilskin billowed out behind him, its front flattened to his chest as though by pressure of a human hand. Walking aft, leaning his weight against the wind, he waited impatiently while the Flag Lieutenant struggled to knock away the clips of the entry into the superstructure. The door was clipped down hard again once the Admiral had passed through, and the Flag Lieutenant followed in an uphill stagger as the stern lifted to a surge of water passing below the keel. Inside the ship there was a thick, cold fug that made Gorsinski's aristocratic nostrils curl. Returning the salute of the sentry outside his cabin, Gorsinski swung round on the Flag Lieutenant.

"The British prisoners. They are, after all, officers—not common seamen. They have had time enough to reflect in the cells. I wish them accommodated in spare cabins—" He broke off: he had been standing just inside his open doorway, and now heard the shrill whistle coming from the speaking tube in his day-cabin. "Answer that at once."

"Your Highness . . ." The Flag Lieutenant brushed past deferentially, and lifted the flexible shank of the speaking tube, putting the shining brass end to his ear. He looked up at Gorsinski. "Your Highness, a signal from the British ship—"

"All right, I'll speak." Gorsinski crossed the cabin with long strides, and took the tube from the Flag Lieutenant. "This is the Admiral. What is it, Captain Angelov?"

"Your Highness, there is trouble aboard the *Viceroy*—"

"What trouble—quickly!"

"The British have taken some rifles, Your Highness, and have turned on our boarding-party. They are refusing to help sail the ship."

There was an oath from Gorsinski, and his eyes blazed across the cabin at his Flag Lieutenant. "Who is the signal from, Captain Angelov? Our men—or theirs?"

"Ours, Your Highness—from Lieutenant Parranadin, who is still in charge."

"I see." Gorsinski's voice was low, ominous. "If the British wish for trouble, they shall have it. You will send for the Gunnery Lieutenant, Captain Angelov, and inform him that the forward turrets and the casemate batteries will prepare for action. I shall come myself to the bridge, at once."

He rammed the speaking tube back into its clip, his face black with anger.

• • •

"Are you all right, lad?"

"Yes, thank you, Mr Pinch." Runcorn was shivering uncontrollably, teeth rattling together as he tried manfully to clench them tight. The cold was appalling, and he was wet through from the racing seas, but so were they all and he would not complain. Mr Pinch, his face concerned, had thrown a tarpaulin around the Midshipman's shoulders, and it helped a little, but not much, as the seas surged over the after rail of the quarterdeck and the wind lifted it like a tent. They huddled together behind the four rifles they had snatched from the Russian guard. Every now and again a bullet sang down from forward, sending chips off woodwork or scoring metal, but failing to find the British sailors crouched in the cover of the after eight-inch gun. The fighting, when Runcorn himself had led a dozen angry seamen against a detached section of the boarding-party in the waist, had been short but sharp: no Russian casualties, but Captain Humphreys of the Royal Marine Light Infantry lay dead, his body sliding to the surge of the decks, over to starboard, back again to port. An Able-Seaman, flinging himself down from aloft onto a Russian about to attack Mr Pinch, had laid the man out with a blow from his flailing legs, but had gone over the side to drown. Two more Able-Seamen had had their heads stove in by belaying-pins. The seas sweeping over the quarterdeck and waist had washed away the blood, but Runcorn could see it all vividly still, and felt himself to blame. Little had been achieved, though others of the ship's company had taken advantage of the mêlée and joined the Midshipman: Mr Runcorn was currently in command of 24 men, a mixed bag of Petty Officers and junior ratings, plus Mr Pinch. None of the Lieutenants had managed to break out: the Russian officer-in-charge, reacting quickly, had ordered guns in their individual backs before they could make a move.

Mr Pinch, flinging seawater from his eyes, asked, "What do you intend to do, young sir?"

"What do you advise, Mr Pinch?"

The Boatswain hesitated. "Are you asking for me to be presumptuous, Mr Runcorn?"

"Oh no, Mr Pinch, not presumptuous. It wouldn't be that. But you've been at sea longer than I, haven't you?"

Mr Pinch smiled. "Aye, I reckon I have that by a year or two!"

"Well, then! I'm in command, of course, and I'll take the responsibility—naturally." The voice was young and it shook just a little: but there was an underlying firmness and an unquestioning acceptance of his status. "But I'd like some help, Mr Pinch, if you don't mind."

The Boatswain put a fatherly hand on the Midshipman's shoulder. "And you shall have it, Mr Runcorn, sir." He lifted a horny hand and scratched his whiskery fringe. "For a start, we know the Russians number some forty-odd men. I'd not advise an attack, not with just the four rifles."

"Not an all out attack—perhaps not, I agree."

"What have you in mind, Mr Runcorn?"

"Just a peppering, Mr Pinch, a shot from time to time to keep them off—and keep them on the hop. We're nicely placed, I think, to pick them off when they go aloft, for one thing." Runcorn hesitated. "Do you know much about the law, Mr Pinch, regarding hostilities?"

The Boatswain shook his head. "No, Mr Runcorn, not much. But I'd not worry about that if I were you. We're fully entitled to get the ship back, and assist the Captain and Mr Halfhyde, and I don't doubt the Admiralty will see it that way too. We're by way of being at war, Mr Runcorn—us and that Prince Gorsinski at all events!"

Mr Runcorn nodded, seeming satisfied. He said, "I think we'll parley first, Mr Pinch."

"With Gorsinski?"

"No. With the Russian officer of the boarding-party. I've had the Captain and Mr Halfhyde in mind . . . we don't know what's happened to them or what may happen. They'd be better off here, and if they were here, we'd fight better."

"So—"

"For a start, Mr Pinch, I shall demand their return aboard as soon as the weather moderates. If the Russians don't agree, we'll open on the boarding-party every time they show themselves and gradually rid ourselves of them!" Runcorn grinned happily. "How's that, Mr Pinch?"

"Makes sense," the Boatswain answered.

"And we'll do the same to any boat's crew that approaches, unless the Captain and Mr Halfhyde are aboard." Runcorn scrambled up to a kneeling position, and lifted his head from the cover of the ready-use ammunition racks behind the gun. At once there was a flash of fire and a bullet snicked along the top of the breech, ricochetting out over the sea's wildness; Runcorn dodged down again. Just as he did so, there was a sudden sharp exclamation from Mr Pinch.

"Sir, the flagship!"

Runcorn turned and looked: he saw nothing, but heard a sound like thunder above the wind. Shouting, the Boatswain ordered all hands to flatten to the deck. A moment later a high screaming sound came from overhead as a shell flew across the plunging ship. It took the water some two cables'-lengths off the *Viceroy*'s starboard quarter, sending up a huge spout of sea. Closely following, another shell screamed across: this time, a better shot. It took the mizzen-mast a few feet below the crosstrees, exploding with a shatter of noise and fire and smoke. Flames licked greedily aloft and then the mizzen topmast and royal came down with their yards in a tangle of rigging, falling heavily across the after gun-shield, smashing through the bulwarks. The Boatswain was up in a flash, hacking with his knife at the bird's-nest of ropes, working like a demon to clear away the heavy mast, reacting with a seaman's instinct to jettison irreparable damage. Mr Runcorn, his face white, stared at shambles and death: one man lay with his stomach open, drooling entrails, slit like a rabbit by a shell splinter. Another's head was smashed like an egg, shattered by the end of a yard that still stood up-and-down in spilt brain matter. As shouts came down from forward Runcorn saw more horror: a man staggering like a drunk, pouring blood from an empty arm socket, the arm itself standing up some feet away, like an uprooted tree-stump, from a bight in the parted wire stay that, whipping back with immense force, had torn it out. Just then there was a shout from Mr Pinch: "Stand clear, she's going!"

The shattered section of mast fell away over the stern, trailing on the end of some uncut ropes. These parted under the weight of wood, and the mass was seen for an instant on the crest of a wave before it sank down the other side. Then an astonishing thing happened: as a group of Russians ran onto the quarterdeck to attack, a surge of the following sea lifted the great mast high above their heads and sent it crashing down, back aboard the wallowing ship, to settle with one huge end across the broken bulwarks and the other, the jagged end, smashing into and mangling the bodies of the attacking Russians. Runcorn swung away from the sight and the screams, and called to the Boatswain.

"Gunnery rates, Mr Pinch! Sort them out and close them up,

if you please, and load. We'll answer back at least, before they sink us!"

"Your Highness, we must cease firing. Our own men are in danger now."

"I am concerned with the British, Captain Angelov. Our men must take their chance in the name of the Czar. Had the weather been fair, then I might have dealt with the matter differently." Gorsinski was looking through his telescope, his oilskins flapping about his tall body, water pouring down his face. "As it is, my hand has been forced."

"You will sink them," the Flag Captain said.

"That is what I intend to do, Captain Angelov." Gorsinski closed his telescope with a snap. Angelov gave a small shrug: though he might command a first-class armoured cruiser of the Russian Fleet, the responsibility was not his but Admiral Prince Gorsinski's, and Gorsinski had the personal authority, authority beyond his seagoing rank, to carry it; and never mind his Flag Captain's disapproval. Staring across the raging seas towards the *Viceroy*, Angelov turned as he became aware of a commotion on the ladder behind him and made his way towards it, sliding and slithering on the unsteady platform of the bridge. He heard an angry shout:

"Out of my way, damn you—damn you to hell, get down!"

Angelov stared in astonishment: a British voice, clear above the thunder of the guns, but not yet heard, apparently, by the intent Gorsinski. A moment later a bull-like figure appeared at the head of the ladder—the British Captain, by some ill chance, it seemed, set free.

"What is the meaning of this?" Angelov demanded in Russian. Behind the British Captain he now saw the other man, Halfhyde, and behind again, crowding up the ladder, four of his own armed sailors. He stormed at them. "Why have the prisoners been released? Why—"

"Sir, it was ordered by the Flag Lieutenant that they were to be taken to proper cabins—"

Bassinghorn broke in, "The Russian Navy, it seems, is hide-bound in its reactions. An order was given, an order was therefore obeyed in spite of obviously changed circumstances, but I am not complaining. Why are you firing upon my ship?"

"I—" The Flag Captain broke off. Gorsinski was coming across the bridge, his face like thunder.

"Captain Bassinghorn, you may like to know that the men responsible for allowing you your freedom will go to Siberia when we reach Okhotsk. Explanations can wait. For now, you—"

"You will kindly order the cease-fire, Prince Gorsinski, and at once!" Bassinghorn faced the Russian threateningly, his beard thrust forward, his arms lifted, his fingers spread wide. Halfhyde came round from behind him, stood at his side. Gorsinski's eyes blazed and he shouted into the wind at the guards, ordering them to seize and remove the prisoners. For an instant, as the Flag Captain hovered uncertainly, everything seemed to stand still, to be in suspension: the next instant there was confusion. Halfhyde, blood pounding past his eardrums, thrust his Captain aside, took Gorsinski by the throat, and squeezed. A scream did no more than rattle in Gorsinski's throat as Halfhyde, swinging him round bodily, hurled him ferociously at the armed guards. Helped by a lift of the ship from forward as a heavy sea crashed down on the quarterdeck and drove the stern under, the rear-most file of guards fell backwards and toppled down the ladder. In a flash Halfhyde had thrown himself on the other two, who were still on their feet but staggering. He smashed a fist into the face of the nearer one, who went clean over the bridge rail to hit the deck below and lie still. From the last man he snatched a rifle and, under the astonished eye of Captain Bassinghorn, aimed it at the Officer of the Watch who was moving towards his collapsed Admiral lying in a heap by the head of the ladder.

"Get away from him!" Halfhyde shouted. "He deserves all he gets—*move!*" He jabbed with the shining bayonet on the rifle's end, and the Russian yelped as steel nicked through his oilskin. "Now, order your guns to cease firing, or I'll spit you like a pig!"

"You—"

"Do as I say!" Halfhyde jabbed again, hard: there was a spurt of blood, a brief reddening of the oilskin until the flying spray washed it off. The officer passed the order down a voice-pipe; within seconds a bugle call sounded out above the wind. The guns fell silent. Halfhyde looked around, breathing hard. Of the Flag Captain there was no sign: Halfhyde had a feeling he had slipped on the wet bridge planking and slid helplessly below the guardrail during the fighting. From the corner of his eye Halfhyde saw two more happenings: there was an organized crowd of seamen under a Lieutenant running with difficulty along the port side of the upper-deck, heading for the bridge ladder; and the helmsman, leaving his place at the wheel, was coming for Halfhyde with a knife in his hand—but was intercepted by Bassinghorn. A huge hand, bunched into a fist, smashed into the man's mouth: the knife spun away and the seaman fell, rolling as the ship itself rolled, away under the guardrail of the starboard wing and straight into the sea. As both Halfhyde and Bassinghorn prepared to deal with the oncoming party below, the *Ostrolenka* gave a terrifying lurch, and there were ominous sounds from below her upper-deck, crashing and bangings of shifted stores, of coal flying around in the bunkers. Halfhyde ran for the wheel, which was spinning like a top, first this way then the other, as the rudder took charge. Water came over in a solid mass, poured down the very funnels as the ship rolled over, over more, bringing her masts nearly parallel with the sea. There was a sustained roar from below, followed by clouds of steam.

"She's broaching-to, sir!" Halfhyde yelled at Bassinghorn. "Look out for Gorsinski, if you please." He gestured to where the Admiral was lying. Bassinghorn grabbed for Gorsinski, seizing the inert figure just before it slid away, and tying it to a stanchion with a couple of tacklines from the flag locker at the after end of the bridge. Halfhyde looked around, summing up their situation. There was no sign now of the revenge party below. The sudden terrible lift of the decks had disposed of them all in the shortest possible time.

Bassinghorn, breathing hard, joined him at the wheel and shouted in his ear: "You are a damn fool and a dangerous one, Mr Halfhyde! To attack a Russian Admiral—"

"My apologies for a breach of diplomacy, sir, but I was facing a murder charge inside Russia. As someone more erudite than I once said, sir—nothing concentrates a man's mind so much as to be under sentence of death." He seized the Captain's arm. "Meanwhile, sir—the ship. She's almost on her beam ends!"

Bassinghorn turned, stared into the elements: the *Ostrolenka* was swinging wildly, a dead mass of metal at the mercy of the wind and sea, battered and storm-wracked—and she was bearing down fast upon the *Viceroy,* nearer and nearer, with her immense ram lifted from the water and seeming to hang over the British ship's quarter as though to smash her bodily to the deeps.

Chapter 13

"SHE'S GOING to hit, Mr Pinch—"

"No, lad, she'll not do that." The Boatswain spoke with reassurance, managing to put into his voice more conviction than he felt as he watched the wild swing of the *Ostrolenka's* massive steel ram. It seemed in his fancy to tick round like the second hand of a pocket-watch, to hang above the *Viceroy's* quarterdeck and blot out both sea and sky in an immensity of storm-tossed metal. Despite the wet and the cold, Mr Pinch was sweating. There was nothing anybody could do at this stage—anybody, that was, of the *Viceroy's* legitimate company: from both angles they were in Russian hands. Mr Pinch shut his eyes and prayed, and felt a sudden touch of peace: if they had to go, then the Pacific Ocean deeps in the grip of natural forces was as good as anywhere on God's earth for sailormen . . .

"Mr Pinch, she's away!"

The Boatswain opened his eyes as Runcorn's shout came down to him on the tearing wind. He stared round-eyed: away she was—but only just, only by the thickness of a man's thumb. Mr Pinch, as the huge ram lifted sideways and started its plunge just clear of the *Viceroy's* rails, saw the Russian's port bower anchor right above his head, could virtually stare right up the hawse-pipe, could almost hear the beat of her engines. As the great armoured cruiser lurched round, heeling right over with her funnel-stays parted and the funnels themselves, Mr Pinch

fancied, about to shake clear out of their seating, a body, sliding helplessly on the slope of her upper-deck, fell from under
the guardrail, screaming into the wind, arms and legs whirling.
The head took the muzzle of the *Viceroy*'s after gun, and shattered: the body dropped out of sight below the counter. Slowly
they began to draw away from the reeling Russian cruiser, which
remained broadside to the wind and sea, with solid water sweeping her from stem to stern, pouring over her and into her
wherever it could gain access, making her almost one with the
sea itself.

Mr Pinch dashed water from his eyes. "All clear, Mr Runcorn.
And it's put a stop to the gunfire, thank God!" He stared in awe
at the great hull, now vanishing into the night. "Let's hope no
harm has come to the Captain and Mr Halfhyde—that's all! As
for me I'd not like to be aboard that ship tonight."

Gorsinski had struggled up to a sitting position, awkwardly since
his body was still lashed to the stanchion by the tack-lines. He
shouted at Bassinghorn: "You fool, you have put my ship in
peril. For that you shall hang!"

Neither Bassinghorn nor Halfhyde heeded the Russian: their
own lives apart, they were seamen, and reacted instinctively to
save the ship. They were both at the wheel now, fighting the
racing seas, waiting their moment to bring her back on her
course so that once again she could run before the storm in
comparative safety. The helm was answering still, as if by a miracle; and there was still power, though badly reduced, in the
engine-room. The ingress of the sea down the funnels would
have doused some of the furnaces, Halfhyde knew; it was a wonder it had not doused them all! As it was, there must be a
shambles below, a shambles turned into very hell by the scalding

steam and the glowing chunks of coal that would have been hurled from the furnace-mouths when the ship was thrown onto her beam ends earlier. His face streaming water, he stared ahead into the night. He still had a mental image of the *Viceroy*, helpless below the *Ostrolenka's* swinging bow. For an instant he had seen the men crouched in the lee of the after gun, had spotted Runcorn's white face staring upwards as the thousands of tons of metal had grazed by the ship's quarter. Now, he shuddered at the thought of what might have happened had the swing been different by a single inch. Without humour, he bared his teeth in a grin: a miss, they said, was as good as a mile. No doubt it was; but it left its mark on a man's mind all the same. And they were not out of the wood yet: far from it. The ship was still totally at the mercy of the elements: the waves dropped and pounded, forcing her under, smashing boats at the davits, parting stays, forcing the gun-turret on the fo'c'sle from its mounting so that it took a drunk's lean to starboard with one of its great gun-barrels dipped massively into the deck. Over it all was the tremendous screaming of the wind like a devil's orchestra playing some demented medley of death and destruction, aided by the maddened whip of parted wires flailing against metal and the singing of such stays as yet remained intact. From time to time there came the high whistle of the voice-pipe from the engine-room: this remained unanswered. Whatever the message, there was nothing any man could do now but try to ease the ship round with what power there was, not to allow the pounding waves to take her as their prey. From time to time Halfhyde threw a glance at the ships in company, the other two cruisers of Gorsinski's squadron, and their own wallowing *Viceroy* whose stern light could be seen occasionally, dipping and lifting to the seas. There was no signalling from the Russian cruisers: they could not help, and their Captains would not bother their Admiral with useless messages. Unheeded by Bassinghorn and Halfhyde, Gorsinski shouted on, clutching at his stanchion, hanging on for his life, the tack-lines taut about his waist. On the upper-deck, not a man was seen: there was no help for Prince Gorsinski. To come out on deck now would have been suicide, and useless also. All salvation lay in the two things, steering and power. The ship had to be coaxed round, any tendency for her to take charge had to be checked, every advantage taken of the lift of the seas, every disadvantage resulting from the sea's movement avoided so far as possible. Bassinghorn was a skilful seaman, a man born to sail and thus to the instinctive use of natural forces, the right man to command in such a situation: Halfhyde was content to follow in the wake of a long experience and was ready for each small shift of the wheel as Bassinghorn bellowed in his ear.

"Up a little now . . . easy!" They came up a fraction, bringing the pounding seas a fraction abaft the beam.

"Down . . . let her give, let her give, Halfhyde, then hold her steady. *Now*—hard up!" Together they brought the wheel back, up into the wind, to shoulder a rearing crest. Inch by inch, fighting against any sudden rush that might result in a catastrophic pounding on the quarter, they eased the ship round, bodies braced against the heave of the deck, braced against the constant, almost permanent, list. As a big wave rushed below the forefoot, the *Ostrolenka* lifted, the bow swinging hard to starboard, and there came a sudden grinding, tearing sound from aft of the bridge. Turning his head briefly, Halfhyde saw the forward funnel take off into the night, all stays parted long since, the unremitting shaking at last shearing it away from its seating.

It went like a grey ghost, spinning, careering, lifting on the wind, leaving behind it a gaping hole wide open to the surging sea. Then, though painfully slowly, the gained inches of safety told: as the ship lay better, the angle of list began to ease slightly. Hope returned; their spirits lifted. As the head came round further, Bassinghorn let out a long sigh.

"All right, Mr Halfhyde. The sea's where we want it, now."

Halfhyde nodded, every bone in his body aching with the sheer effort of remaining upright. He looked astern: the weather was foul enough, there was no improvement, no drop in the wind's terrible strength. But the quarter was laid cleanly before the waves, before the onrushing lines of crests, rank upon rank like soldiers on parade, taking them at ninety degrees in safety, though the ship was still listing from the shift of stores and bunker coal below-decks. Soon the signalling, not unexpectedly, began from the *Czarevitch* and *Gregoriev*, asking if the Admiral required assistance. Halfhyde himself, with his knowledge of Russian, sent back the replies after consultation with Bassinghorn. "Thank you. No assistance required. Am in full control and can make running repairs to superficial damage when weather moderates." The signals made, Halfhyde looked along the bridge at Prince Gorsinski, a half-drowned Admiral and a bitter one, a furious man with staring, red-rimmed eyes.

Halfhyde gave a tired smile. "As my signals indicate, sir, your ship's intact. More or less . . ."

Gorsinski glowered, but gave a nod. "The seamanship was good," he said, sounding reluctant about it. "For that, you have my thanks, you and your Captain. I now ask, please, to be untied."

Halfhyde lifted an eyebrow at Bassinghorn. Bassinghorn's

response was immediate and forceful, to Halfhyde's immense relief: "My humble apologies, Prince Gorsinski. There will be no release—"

"You cannot—"

"I can and I will!" Bassinghorn snapped. "My First Lieutenant still has one of your rifles, and will use it in the event of trouble." He indicated the rifle, lashed securely to another stanchion in the lee of a canvas dodger. "I regret the discomfort, but you will remain upon the bridge with us, and you will obey my orders." Bassinghorn drew himself up, hands behind his back, head lifted, body braced against the sea's lift and scend. Thanks to his impetuous First Lieutenant, the die, however dangerously, was now cast, and Bassinghorn, in accepting present facts, had with much inner conflict decided that he had no alternative but to bow to the inevitable and conduct matters as best he could. "I have assumed the command. I regard the *Ostrolenka* as—as a prize of war. Remember that you yourself seized my ship in the first place, Prince Gorsinski. When the weather moderates enough to make the turn, I shall steam the *Ostrolenka* back for the island pending contact with Her Majesty's China Squadron in Hong Kong."

The air, for the next few minutes, was blue: Gorsinski threatened reprisals of every kind, but Bassinghorn was not now to be moved: there was a stubborn obstinacy about him that impressed Halfhyde if not Gorsinski. The drenched and shivering Admiral was untethered from his crouching position at the guardrail to be resecured with a loose oilskin-hidden bight to the standard compass. Bassinghorn said, "I propose to make use of you as a hostage, Prince Gorsinski, to secure obedience on the part of your men. Whilst on passage all hands are to remain below-decks and steam is to be maintained to the best of your engineers' ability. You will pass these orders by voice-pipe at once, if you please, sir, and bear in mind that Mr Halfhyde has a full command of the Russian tongue."

White with fury, Gorsinski did as he was told. A little later as the sky began to respond to a leaden dawn he obeyed more: the Russian signal book was sent for and duly delivered, its bearer being ordered to throw it up to the bridge from the foot of the ladder and then make himself scarce. With Halfhyde acting as signalman, the orders went by light to the cruisers plunging along astern: "Flag to ships in company. Intend to return to island with *Viceroy* as soon as weather moderates. *Czarevitch* and *Gregoriev* will maintain present course to Okhotsk." This message passed, Gorsinski was ordered to send down for an Able Seaman to take the wheel: the flagship, as seen from what would obviously be a close telescopic scrutiny from the other ships as the sky lightened, must appear as normal as possible. "And have a care to keep it so, Prince Gorsinski," Bassinghorn said, "for I give you my word, there will be much trouble if you do not!"

Late that afternoon there was a drop in the wind's strength that led to a gradual flattening-out of the spume-blown crests. Bassinghorn, after a careful study of the weather and a word with Halfhyde, spoke to the Admiral. "I shall now make the executive signal," he said formally. "Your Captains will salute you, sir. You will be ready to return their respects. Send for a bugler, if you please."

Fuming, Gorsinski used the voice-pipe again. When a bugler appeared upon the midship superstructure, Bassinghorn nodded at Halfhyde, who again used the signalling lamp. When the executive signal to detach was acknowledged, Bassinghorn started to turn the flagship away. The *Viceroy,* also obeying the executive, followed suit. Faintly across the tumbling waters the bugle notes were heard from the onward-heading cruisers. From the *Ostrolenka* the bugler sounded off in return. Gorsinski, as the flagship's head came round slowly, lifting and falling to the remaining weight of the sea, watched in helpless rage, watched his ships vanish into the poor visibility of flung spray and lowering cloud, their great sides pouring water as they rolled and pitched to the seas passing under their counters, their ensigns whipping a long farewell to their Admiral. Gorsinski had a lonely look. Bassinghorn, rubbing his hands with gleeful pleasure now that it was one ship against another, and both up to a point under his own command, forebore to ram the point home to the sick-looking Russian aristocrat.

They talked together in a corner of the bridge, in low tones, and away from Gorsinski though they kept him in constant view.

"We shall need a fortnight in our bunks after this, Mr Halfhyde. It'll take us forty-eight hours and more to reach the island against the weather."

"Yes, sir. We could do with some relief in the meantime, I fancy." Halfhyde gave a cough. "I've been thinking about the *Viceroy*, sir."

"What about her, Mr Halfhyde?" Bassinghorn looked across to starboard: the *Viceroy*, a little ahead of their beam, was riding the seas with apparent confidence, but slowly under her sail power.

Halfhyde answered, "Two things, sir, two aspects: we need more of our men aboard with us—we don't know what's brewing below these decks, and we're but two, with one rifle and no spare ammunition. Also, we must consider the position of those of our men who turned on the Russian boarding-party."

"You suggest we try to go alongside?"

"I do, sir."

Bassinghorn shook his head. "A manoeuvre of doubtful value but undoubted danger, Mr Halfhyde, and not from the weather alone. The Russians have eyes. If we should approach, they would be ready for us." He gave a hard laugh. "And, as you said, we are but two!"

"Plus the others aboard the *Viceroy*."

Bassinghorn pondered, but shook his head. "Our situation is at least—and at present—stable. We should not upset it."

"And when we reach the island, sir, what then?"

"We'll not cross our bridges, Mr Halfhyde. We must act according to events as they occur."

"With no plan, sir?"

Bassinghorn looked at him. "Have you a plan? If so—"

"No, sir, I haven't. Not yet."

Bassinghorn stared ahead, watching the seas. They were still restless, even turbulent, but the weight had gone out of the wind as the storm center flowed well north of them. Though listing badly still, and making a much reduced speed, the *Ostrolenka* was seaworthy and Bassinghorn anticipated no more trouble in that direction. His anxieties now were other ones and in a sense more pressing ones: the weather could be fought by a seaman, but the diplomats and the Board of Admiralty were enemies of a very different sort . . . thinking his uneasy thoughts, Bassinghorn gave a sigh of frustration: hearing it, Halfhyde asked, "You're worried, sir? For my part, I believe the outlook is fair. If we can keep our feet without falling asleep, we're heading for success, I think?"

"A kind of success, Mr Halfhyde, yes. But failure also."

"In regard to our particular orders, sir?"

Bassinghorn gave a low laugh without humour. "You are a man of easy optimism but also of understanding, my dear fellow!

Our particular orders—yes—our orders not to provoke! By God, we have provoked—and that is failure, is it not?"

"Perhaps. But it was an inevitable failure, sir."

"And made no less a failure by its inevitability. Does the Admiralty ever admit inevitability as an excuse, do you suppose?"

The question was rhetorical, and since Halfhyde knew the answer, in any event, to be a negative, he attempted no response. The situation *vis-à-vis* the Admiralty was, undeniably, not good. For the man on the spot and in command, it seldom was. Instant decisions did not normally allow diplomacy and delicacy; when freed at an opportune moment from a prison cell, a serving officer tended naturally to seek out and take his advantage in action. The politicians and the Sea Lords of the Admiralty, had they been present aboard the Russian flagship during the night and in Bassinghorn's position, might perhaps have bowed and scraped with due solemnity and politeness and sent a diplomatic note to Prince Gorsinski, observing all the proper protocol . . . Halfhyde gave a gesture of impatience at his own thoughts. The men of Government had their own job to do, of course they had; but part of their job, it seemed to him, was ever to cast the blame upon the simple serving officer who, usually untrained in the ways of Whitehall, was left with no defence against minds that twisted and turned like scheming serpents . . . again, Halfhyde checked himself. It was bad for the mind of an officer to dwell thus mutinously upon his betters! Excusing himself, he walked back along the navigating bridge towards the standard compass and its princely prisoner. Gorsinski was looking sick and tired, drooping like a lily, a very gilded one, upon the stalk of the binnacle. His face was white and drawn and he was having difficulty in keeping his eyelids open. Behind his Admiral, the helmsman was looking stolidly ahead, his gaze going now and again to the compass-card as he checked the course. The man was looking half scared, half defiant: a natural mixture, no doubt—but Halfhyde suddenly didn't care for the atmosphere. There was a curious tension—again, a natural thing to feel in the circumstances, a feeling that they were standing upon a volcano, a coming eruption from below that would be very different from the volcanic forces that had produced that contentious and damnable island . . . in all truth, there would be below hatches a seething of men anxious to avenge what had happened to their ship, if not to their Admiral. Halfhyde pursed his lips, felt all at once highly insecure: Prince Gorsinski was not merely the trump card, he was the only one in the British pack at this moment. What if a meeting of the men below-decks should decide the Admiral could be jettisoned? Officers versus men—who would win? The threat of Siberia and death, or the inflammable insidious thoughts about admirals and princes that could run like very lightning through the lowerdeck of a ship at sea, a lowerdeck crammed with men who could decide this was a fine moment to respond in action to the new ideas that were already said to be sweeping the great Russian land mass straddled across Europe? Prince Gorsinski had faced mutiny before, and to the considerable advantage of Lieutenant Halfhyde; but if it should happen again, the result was unlikely to be so favourable. The result, indeed, was likely to be overwhelming. And, since Bassinghorn and Halfhyde had captured Prince Gorsinski, it would be their undoubted duty not to sacrifice their prisoner but to preserve him.

Halfhyde took a turn up and down the bridge, considering the prisoner in a fresh light, seeing ever more urgently the need to seek assistance from their own men aboard the *Viceroy*.

Chapter 14

MR MIDSHIPMAN RUNCORN tried to avoid looking down at death, more death, by staring across the water towards the *Ostrolenka*, upon whose bridge Captain Bassinghorn was plainly to be seen. Mr Runcorn tried to concentrate on Post Captains and their majesty, but death was too present and too recent: even four gold rings failed to obliterate what had happened, what was still there in the waist. One of his seamen had broken out, unarmed and against orders, and had raced forward from the quarterdeck on a crazy attack of his own. Shouted back by Mr Pinch, he had turned deaf ears. He had gone no more than half a dozen yards before a Russian bullet stopped him. The bullet went into his throat. He had fallen with a gargling cry, there had been a lot of blood, and he had not died quickly. Rescue had been pointless and impossible, and the body was still there, like that of a swatted fly that no one had bothered to remove. Mr Runcorn, brooding darkly, had felt to blame. Mr Pinch, studying the Midshipman's face, philosophized whilst keeping a sharp look-out for the Russian rifles.

"It's nasty, Mr Runcorn, that I don't deny, but it's to be expected."

Runcorn glanced at the Boatswain's weather-beaten face with its fringe of grey whiskers, at the many deep-cut lines running from the corners of his eyes. He stiffened himself. "You've seen death many times, I suppose, Mr Pinch?"

"I have. All kinds, sir. Death from gunshot, both rifle and cannon fire. Death from falling from aloft. Death from fever, from festering wounds, from poisonous bites received whilst landed in tropic parts. Nasty were them, sir, and no doctor closer'n a hundred miles, back aboard the ship." Mr Pinch paused; when he went on again there was a difference in his tone, a note that sounded a warning. "Keep talking Mr Runcorn, and don't look forward."

"What is it, Mr Pinch?"

"The bloody Russkies, that's what." The Boatswain was breathing heavily. "Looks to me like they're mustering for an attack in strength. They have the advantage o' fair weather now—their feet won't slide from under! And something else."

"What?"

"The flagship's bridge. The Captain has his glass on us."

"It's hardly been off us, Mr Pinch—"

"True, sir, true. But this time he may see something that'll send him to our assistance."

"Before we're wiped out to a man?"

"Never say die, Mr Runcorn. We'll give a good account of ourselves. I have a corner-of-the-eye view, sir. I'll not shift my head, nor you yours. I'll give the word." He raised his voice just a little, speaking cautiously to the ratings huddled around the gun, telling them to remain in cover until he gave them a shout. Runcorn waited, his back turned to what was taking place: he found waiting for unknown unpleasantness a most terrifyingly uncomfortable feeling, but one that his cadet years in the *Britannia,* and his year at sea as a lowly Midshipman hounded by Sub-Lieutenants, had well prepared him to endure.

"There is trouble coming, I fear," Bassinghorn said, looking

towards the *Viceroy.* Since the weather had moderated the previous afternoon into a blue sky and a flat sea, a sea now lifting
only to the swell left behind by the storm, he had feared trouble and had searched his mind as to what should be his course
of action when it came. "The Russians are moving aft towards
Mr Runcorn, and there are men handy in the ratlines."

"Then we must move in, sir." Halfhyde joined his Captain at
the starboard bridge rail. "When a full-scale attack comes, they'll
be mown down like rabbits."

"There's little we can do, Mr Halfhyde—"

"Then that little, sir, must be done!"

"I'm sorry," Bassinghorn closed his telescope with a snap.
"You cannot regret it more than I, but my first duty lies to my
orders from the Admiralty—"

"But—"

"There are no buts, Mr Halfhyde."

"For God's sake, sir, we can put the flagship alongside—"

"I have thought much from every angle, Mr Halfhyde, but I
fail to see the engine-room responding to manoeuvring orders
from the bridge."

"It's worth trying, sir. We still have Gorsinski, remember!"
Halfhyde had had his doubts as to Gorsinski's value, but it could
still be considered fifty-fifty. "We must make the best use of
him—"

"To do what? If we try to board the *Viceroy,* we shall be pul-
verized by the rifles before we can set foot on deck—and there
are only two of us, Mr Halfhyde—"

"Three with Prince Gorsinski—"

"Who is scarcely likely to fight with us!" Bassinghorn snapped.

"But a very useful hostage, for ensuring—"

Bassinghorn, who had once again been watching the *Viceroy's* decks through his telescope, broke in. "It is already too late, Mr Halfhyde. Look there!"

Halfhyde looked: men were running along the deck, making aft; rifle fire could be heard plainly, a fusillade of shots from the deck and from the tops and ratlines. At once firing came from aft as well, shots few in number but remarkably accurate. As the two officers watched from the flagship's bridge, a couple of men fell from the maintop and crashed to the deck. Halfhyde, giving an exclamation of anger at his own helplessness to assist his ship's company, turned from the rail and made with long, rapid strides for the wheel.

Bassinghorn swung round. "Mr Halfhyde, what are you doing?"

"Creating a diversion, since you will not do anything!" Halfhyde answered rudely, his long face flushed. He seized the helmsman, and, pulling him from the wheel, sent him staggering with a heavy shove towards Bassinghorn. "Look after him, if you please, sir, while I take the ship in." Bassinghorn gaped, but made no further protest; he took a grip on the helmsman, holding him still with his big hands. Halfhyde put the wheel over hard to bring the ship's head round to starboard, grinned into Gorsinski's face as the Admiral twisted in the ropes binding him to the binnacle, ropes in which he was sagging and looking not far from death by exhaustion. The *Ostrolenka* began to swing, her deck heeling to increase the list a fraction as the rudder took charge. When she was headed straight for the *Viceroy* Halfhyde eased the wheel and she steadied on course. Bassinghorn held tight to the rail, staring. Blood was drumming in Halfhyde's ears, his face was alight as he sent the Russian flagship cutting through the blue water, traveling fast with her bow wave creaming and tumbling along her sides. He laughed aloud with exultancy, and Bassinghorn called to him. "Halfhyde, you shall not run my ship down. You risk court martial if you try to do that!"

"I'll not run her down, sir." Now, as they approached, Halfhyde's eyes were narrowed in concentration. "I'll just put the fear of God into them that I'm about to do so—that's all!" He stared ahead: his manoeuvre was having a clear effect. The Russians who had been aloft were sliding down the shrouds, letting the ropes run through their hands in their haste. Everywhere men were running; Halfhyde, heading the *Ostrolenka* towards the *Viceroy*'s stern, sent them flying into the eyes of the ship, crowding along the fo'c'sle in a mad dash to find such safety as they could. He swept past the stern, right below the counter with feet to spare, almost as close as when the flagship had borne down out of control during the worst of the storm. The surge of their wash lifted the British ship aft, sending her head plunging down: Halfhyde, with a clear view down the slope of the Russian's list to port, saw the faces staring up, recognized Runcorn and the Boatswain, gave them a wave and a shout of encouragement, and in the next instant was past and clear and putting the helm over to close the *Viceroy* once more. As they came past the stem, shots came up, wild firing that Halfhyde treated with contempt. Using the bridge megaphone he shouted down in Russian.

"If you molest the British crew, your Admiral suffers. Have a care for the vengeance of Prince Gorsinski, kinsman of your Czar!" He was briefly aware of the faces, even of the mixed expressions—fear, bewilderment, anger—as at close quarters they were given a sight of their helpless Admiral, hanging sideways with the list, secured to the binnacle. With a sudden abandon, Halfhyde shook a fist down at the Russians; and then, as he brought the wheel over again to steam at speed down the *Viceroy*'s port beam, he saw the upsurge of British bluejackets, some with rifles, some with cutlasses, pouring like a vengeful tide from the after entry port in the midship deckhouse, running, yelling like devils, making for the fo'c'sle, seamen, stokers, and marines, with Runcorn and the Boatswain coming up from the quarterdeck. The exchange of fire was no more than a token: the bluejackets rushed the fo'c'sle and carried it without trouble, overwhelming the already shaken Russians by sheer weight of numbers.

Halfhyde called to Bassinghorn. "If you please, sir, the telegraph to stop."

"What do you propose, Mr Halfhyde? You appear to have taken charge—"

"I apologize humbly, sir. I was insubordinate, which I regret is a habit of mine, but I plead a good cause, a good result, and a dangerous lack of time once the Russians began their attack on Mr Runcorn. What I propose now, sir, is that we rejoin the *Viceroy*—with Prince Gorsinski still our prisoner to ensure that there is no attack from the flag."

Bassinghorn opened his mouth, then shut it again with a snap. He stalked across to the engine-room telegraph and pulled the handle over. Halfhyde, half expectant of disobedience below, gave a sigh of relief when the indicator from the engine-room followed the bridge pointer in acknowledgement of the order. The engines died, the creaming bow wave slackened. Halfhyde steered the *Ostrolenka* in, bringing her alongside in an ocean swell that sent her hard against the *Viceroy*'s side to smash away two sets of davits before the British ship's company had run to the fenders. He looked down to see the side lined with rifles pointing up at the Russian's listing decks. After a word with

Bassinghorn, he passed a message down the voice-pipe for the Flag Captain to report at once to the bridge, alone. It was the *Ostrolenka's* Commander who came up with one arm in a sling. The Flag Captain, he said, had been seriously injured when flung across the bridge at the height of the storm.

"Then you shall listen in his place," Halfhyde said. "You will steam your ship in company with the *Viceroy,* bearing in mind that your Admiral will be aboard with us, and will be the first to suffer in the event of trouble." There was no answer from the Commander, whose eye Gorsinski was refusing to meet: Gorsinski's silence, his obvious reluctance to commit himself, gave the implicit consent to Halfhyde's order. Stiff-faced, the Commander nodded in acceptance, waiting now to take over the ship. Halfhyde, remembering his earlier thoughts about incipient mutiny when officers and men had been confined together below-decks in ignominious helplessness, felt that the Commander, back again in authority aboard, could be relied upon to hold down his lowerdeck.

"You have done well, Mr Runcorn, very well indeed." The Captain looked along his decks, now freed of the Russian boarding-party who had taken their dead with them when they were put back aboard the *Ostrolenka;* the British dead had been washed clear overboard by the seas during the storm; only the most recent casualty in the waist remained. Bassinghorn laid a hand on the Midshipman's shoulder. "You have my congratulations, Mr Runcorn, and my thanks."

"Sir, it was Mr Pinch—"

Bassinghorn held up his hand, smiling. "Mr Pinch was a tower of strength, I don't doubt, but you were in charge upon the quarterdeck. I shall stress your adherence to your duty in my report to Their Lordships, and yours also, Mr Pinch."

"Thank you, sir." The Boatswain cleared his throat noisily. "We're all glad you're back aboard and safe, sir."

"All, Mr Pinch?"

Mr Pinch met his eye. "All, sir. The lowerdeck's happy, sir. They've had a scrap and it's cleared the air."

Bassinghorn nodded, keeping his face stiff and formal, but Halfhyde noted the glad look in his eye: the Captain currently had more than enough to worry him without the addition of a semi-mutinous ship's company to his problems. "Very well, Mr Pinch. Mr Halfhyde, you will splice the mainbrace, if you please."

"Aye, aye, sir." Halfhyde nodded at the Master-at-Arms, who acknowledged the order with a salute and went off to pass the word and then go below to the spirit room to break out the rum-casks for the extra issue to the mess decks. Bassinghorn said abruptly, "To my cabin, gentlemen. We, too, shall splice the mainbrace."

Turning, he led the way aft to his quarters. The marine sentry crashed to attention, face expressionless. Bassinghorn entered the cuddy, where his servant was waiting. Nothing seemed to have changed in his temporary absence.

"A whisky each for the officers, Briggs, small ones. For me also."

"Aye, aye, sir." Petty Officer Briggs, small and alert, brought glasses and a decanter on a silver tray. Bassinghorn, standing straight before his fireplace, gave a gruff toast when the whisky had been poured and handed round.

"Gentlemen, Her Majesty the Queen. God bless her."

"God bless her . . ." The toast was gravely drunk. Mr Runcorn choked a little over his glass. Mr Pinch's dram was downed in a gulp, and a horny hand used to wipe lips and whiskers.

"If you'll excuse me, sir?" Mr Pinch, though a Warrant Officer these last five years, was still a touch awkward in the presence of his betters.

"Work to do, Mr Pinch? Then off you go. Mr Runcorn?"

"Er . . . no, thank you, sir—"

"Mr Runcorn, I was not about to suggest another glass of whisky. I was suggesting that you, also, had work to attend to, perhaps?"

"Oh—sorry, sir!" Mr Runcorn, blushing scarlet, followed the Boatswain from the cuddy. Bassinghorn dismissed his servant, then sat before his opened desk, tapping his fingers on the polished wood. He looked dead on his feet, Halfhyde thought: Bassinghorn was on the elderly side for long physical endurance.

"We need sleep, Mr Halfhyde," Bassinghorn said as though reading his First Lieutenant's thoughts. "We shall have it when we have eaten—food is the first thing now." He sighed, and rubbed at his eyes. "Then we shall talk about the future."

"Are you still feeling a sense of failure, sir?"

Bassinghorn stared without seeming to see, as though looking either forward or back but not at the present. "There is still that feeling. I shall shortly be preparing reports, which in due course will decide the way the Admiralty views our efforts. In the meantime, we should reach the island and the anchorage in twelve hours, perhaps a little less. I understand Mr Bampton is making some progress with his engine repair."

"Yes, sir, that is the case."

Bassinghorn stood up. "Very well, Mr Halfhyde, I suggest you take yourself to the ward-room for a meal, then." He hesitated, frowning a little and looking down at his desk. Then he met Halfhyde's eye. "Thank you for all you've done," he said simply. "You've proved an admirable First Lieutenant in adversity."

•   •   •

In the ward-room, where none of the officers had eaten since the seizure of the ship by the Russians, Halfhyde was monosyllabic and preoccupied, failing to satisfy a natural curiosity. Like Bassinghorn, he had much on his mind. He had no fear that the Captain would report adversely upon him or that the episode of his blatant disregard of orders aboard the Russian flagship would be raised again: in his report, Bassinghorn would pass over that. His anxieties were wider ones. Bassinghorn had spoken of failure, and though Halfhyde had discounted this to his Captain, he knew very well that the pitfalls were legion and the progress made was so slight as to be negligible: true, they were back aboard the *Viceroy* with a distinguished prisoner; but the Russian flag would be found, when they arrived, still floating over the disputed island. In their efforts to carry out their orders to ensure the planting of the British flag they had brought about a state of war, none the less serious potentially for being so far localized. For this, Halfhyde knew he must shoulder the major part of the blame.

It had been his scheme from the start, now seen in all its blackness and bleakness to have been ill conceived. Halfhyde, hungry as he was, ate without appetite, going through the motions merely to appease his stomach. After he had thus eaten he went on deck before going to his cabin. The *Ostrolenka,* shorn of her Admiral currently locked in a spare cabin under a marine sentry, was steaming two points on the *Viceroy's* bow, nicely in sight of the Officer of the Watch, nicely placed for the *Viceroy's* forward guns and her port broadside which could rake the Russian decks at immediate notice if and when necessary: the ship was now steaming with half her guns' crews closed up, and would remain so for an indefinite period after anchoring.

Suddenly feeling the full weight of his weariness, Halfhyde turned away from the rail and went below. Throwing himself into his bunk without bothering to undress, he was dead asleep within seconds.

"Island in sight, sir!"

The Officer of the Watch, Lieutenant Campbell, acknowledged the shout from the crosstrees and sent his Midshipman down to report to the Captain. Bassinghorn went at once to the bridge. Another dawn was stealing up the sky in splendid colours: the raising of the island's peaks had come rather later than originally expected. Mr Bampton had been over-optimistic in his report to the Captain, and sail had been necessary for a while longer before the Engineer had announced that he was in a position to use his steam power. Bassinghorn's reception of the news had been mixed. Now, climbing to the bridge, he stared bleakly at his bared masts and yards and angrily at the streaming trail of thick black smoke that spoiled the Pacific morning.

"Good morning, Mr Campbell. How long to the anchorage?"

"Two hours, sir."

"Hm." Bassinghorn stared all round the horizon: the seas were empty of all but the two ships. Bassinghorn nevertheless felt a distinct unease. After a turn or two along the bridge he halted, frowning. "Mr Campbell, my compliments to the First Lieutenant. I'd be obliged if he'd come to my cabin."

"Aye, aye, sir."

"Inform me again when the anchorage is in sight, or at once if any ship should be seen. In the meantime, the guns' crews are not to relax their vigilance, Mr Campbell. And make a signal to the *Ostrolenka,* if you please. She is to proceed to the same ground as before, and she is to be ready to let go before me. After anchoring, all hands are to go below-decks—I want her upper-deck empty."

Bassinghorn turned and clattered down the ladder again. Within five minutes Halfhyde had reported to the cuddy, fully dressed in white uniform.

"You sent for me, sir?"

"Yes, Mr Halfhyde, we are due to anchor in two hours. First, I think we should have further words with Prince Gorsinski."

"To what end, sir?"

"I am uneasy, Mr Halfhyde, most uneasy."

Halfhyde waited; Bassinghorn moved across to a port and stared out of it at the flat blue water aglint with the dawn's rising gold. He spoke with his back towards Halfhyde. "Gorsinski has appeared confident throughout, I think. Do you agree?"

"Not throughout, sir. He was far from confident when we took over his flagship, and after—"

"Yes, yes." Bassinghorn swung round, crossed the cabin with heavy steps. "I mean since then, since he has been aboard my ship. I find it worrying."

"I think he's simply more comfortable now. Good food and clean sheets make a world of difference to a man's outlook."

"He can be deprived of them," Bassinghorn said sharply. "No, it's not that. There was an air about the man when last we spoke . . . as though he's in possession of some information not known to us."

"Fresh information, sir?" Halfhyde paused, searching the Captain's face. "That can scarcely be the case, can it? He's had no opportunity for that."

"Perhaps not fresh information. Earlier intelligence— even perhaps received by him during his winter stay in Vladivostock . . . intelligence that he knows is shortly to come to its fulfillment, Mr Halfhyde!" Bassinghorn smashed a fist into the palm of his hand. "Now do you understand me? I feel it is not unlikely that other Russian ships may be in the vicinity, and under orders to rendezvous with Prince Gorsinski's squadron at the island—"

"I think, sir, he would not have sailed away in that event."

Bassinghorn waved a hand. "Then they may be under orders to relieve him to take over his watch upon the island—the point makes little difference. What is important is the possibility of other ships being in the vicinity, and this is something we must try to establish by questioning Gorsinski again."

Halfhyde pursed his lips doubtfully. "He'll not tell us, sir, I believe we can be sure of that. And suppose he did? How does it help? Would the knowledge affect your decision, sir?"

Bassinghorn said, "It might, Mr Halfhyde, it might. I can always alter course for Hong Kong—"

"And Sir John Willard, who wishes not to be disturbed?"

"He'd not deny the support of the China Squadron in the circumstances."

Halfhyde gave a harsh laugh. "If you believe that, sir, you'll believe anything! With great respect, sir—Commodore Willard struck me as determined not to become involved, which was precisely why he sent for you—to make the point in person and with emphasis! You'll get no help from that quarter, believe me, and if you enter the anchorage off Hong Kong with Admiral Prince Gorsinski as a gift to Commodore Willard . . . why, then, sir, a pound to a penny the one distinguished officer would be returned to his country with humble apologies by the other distinguished officer and—and you'd find yourself charged with something not far short of treason as like as not!"

Bassinghorn stared coldly. "A long speech, Mr Halfhyde."

"But a true one as I believe. If I were you, sir, I'd steer well clear of Hong Kong and Commodore Willard until you have better things to offer—whether or no Gorsinski is joined by other ships. And as to that, I'd not question him again either."

"Why so?"

"Why not keep him guessing, rather than let him see he's doing precisely that to us?" Halfhyde's expression was almost devilish as the sunlight, coming through one of the ports, threw his nose into relief, its shadow darkening one side of his long face. "Ignorance, sir, is not always bliss to a man of imagination!"

The Captain appeared undecided, pulling at his beard and shaking his head. He was about to say something further when there was a knock at his cabin door. The Midshipman of the Watch entered, his white helmet held beneath his arm and his eyes wide with self-importance.

"Captain, sir—"

"Yes, Mr Parsons, what is it?" Bassinghorn stood with his feet apart, braced against the ship's movement.

"Sir, there are ships ahead—"

"Ships!" The Captain met Halfhyde's eye. "Talk of the devil, Mr Halfhyde!"

Halfhyde gave a mock bow. "I congratulate you, sir—"

Disregarding Halfhyde, the Captain swung round again on the Midshipman. "What ships, Mr Parsons, and how many?"

"They're hull down as yet, sir, fine on the starboard bow—but six trails of smoke have been sighted, sir, on a closing course."

Chapter 15

BASSINGHORN ran for the navigating bridge as though pursued by the devil, and lifted his telescope to the southern horizon. He brought up a line of royal mastheads, and the smoke: six ships without a doubt, and, by the spacing of the trucks, big ships.

"Mr Campbell!"

"Sir?"

"General quarters, if you please."

"Aye, aye, sir!" A bugler of the Royal Marine Light Infantry, already summoned to stand by for the expected order, lifted his bugle and sounded out, sending the ship's company at the double to their action stations. Moving aft, the bugler repeated his call, then ducked down into the superstructure to pass the order below. The decks swarmed with running men, the other half of the guns' crews closing up with the action lookouts and the ammunition parties. Halfhyde, going about his duty to supervise the preparation of the ship to withstand action, passed by the cabin where Gorsinski was confined; the marine sentry outside slammed to attention and saluted.

"Beg pardon, sir—"

"Well?"

"Sir! The Russian gentleman, sir. He's been banging, sir, on his door."

Halfhyde grinned unfeelingly. "Much?"

"Something awful, sir."

"I'll have a word. Open up, and keep your rifle pointed."

"Sir!" With a crash of boot-leather on the wooden deck, the sentry turned about and unbolted the cabin door, swinging it open for the First Lieutenant's inspection of the occupant. A furious Gorsinski stood facing Halfhyde.

"Good morning, sir—"

"Lieutenant Halfhyde, I heard your bugles blow for action. Are you meaning to fire upon my flagship, Lieutenant Halfhyde, you and your Captain Bassinghorn?"

"Certainly not—"

"Then why?"

Halfhyde narrowed his eyes. "You don't know, Prince Gorsinski?"

"I do not know—no! If I did, I would not ask!"

Halfhyde studied the angry face, the reaction that looked entirely natural, the fury of any man confined aboard a ship that he suspected of being about to engage his own vessel. Halfhyde said, "I'm sorry, but I'll not enlighten you at this moment, sir. But be easy. We are not attacking the *Ostrolenka*." Gorsinski began shouting, but Halfhyde ordered the door shut and locked again, and proceeded on his rounds of the lowerdecks, checking that all deadlights were clamped down hard before the watertight doors were clipped shut, that the mess decks running behind the breeches of the broadside guns were cleared so far as possible of inflammable material, observing the hundred and one duties of an Executive Officer prior to action. When he returned to the bridge to report he found Bassinghorn with an eye still glued to his telescope. There was as yet no clearer image of the ships ahead: seemingly they had altered course a little to the south of east, and, drawing across the *Viceroy*'s own course so that they were now on the port bow, still showed only their royals and trucks and, as ever, the filthy streaming clouds of smoke. A few minutes later, however, when Bassinghorn had muttered something about their having closed a fraction, a shout came from Mr Midshipman Runcorn at the foretopmast cross-trees, also with telescope:

"Bridge, sir! I have them in good view, sir!"

"Can you identify, Mr Runcorn?" Bassinghorn called back.

"Yes, sir. Six battleships, sir." The youthful voice cracked with excitement and wonder. "Sir, the ensigns . . . the Rising Sun, sir —it's the Japanese battle fleet!"

Bassinghorn said harshly, "Prince Gorsinski, Mr Halfhyde. You're certain he had no knowledge of this?"

"Certain enough, sir, for my money. Why should he know— and if he did, would he see any comfort in the Japanese fleet?"

"I don't know." Bassinghorn paced the bridge, casting continual glances towards the distant line of ships, now in full view. The anchorage and its breakwater-like arm of land were also in view now, and it had become clear from an appraisal of the Japanese course that their ships were steaming for the anchorage as well. So far there had been no exchange of signals: each side, it seemed, was awaiting the other's move. Bassinghorn, who had had enquiries made as to whether any of his officers understood Japanese, had met with a negative response. In the meantime, not wishful to approach, with his guns manned for action, a Power considered friendly enough to be an ally in time of need, he had ordered the Secure. The *Viceroy* was now moving ahead at cruising stations, a peaceful degree of readiness that could alarm no one. As Bassinghorn paced, another shout came from Mr Runcorn aloft: "Captain, sir! They're hoisting their pennant numbers, I believe."

"You believe, Mr Runcorn?"

"Sir, it appears to be a *Japanese* hoist, sir!"

Bassinghorn gave a short laugh. "Very natural, if to be deplored!" His telescope went up to his eye again and he called for the Chief Yeoman of Signals. "The flagship's signalling, Chief Yeoman."

"Reading, sir," the Chief Yeoman answered. Then, "She's calling the *Ostrolenka*, I think, sir."

Bassinghorn looked towards the Russian flagship and the large St Andrew's Cross, blue on a white ground, flying out from its staff. He said, "Make in English, 'kindly address your signals to me.'"

"Aye, aye, sir." The Chief Yeoman took up a signalling lamp and began flashing towards the Japanese flagship: a light twinkled in acknowledgement. The Chief Yeoman manipulated his shutters slowly and deliberately, then reported, "Message passed, sir."

Bassinghorn nodded. "Thank you. Now we can only wait." He looked towards the *Ostrolenka;* the Japanese flagship had continued sending to her while Bassinghorn's signal was in transmission, but she seemed to be making no reply. Halfhyde, grinning to himself, concluded that she also had her language problems . . . then the Japanese flagship's light was seen again, directed towards themselves. The message came slowly, hesitantly, was received by the Chief Yeoman with much tongue-clicking and written down at his dictation by a signalman poised with pad and pencil. At last the Chief Yeoman flicked his final acknowledgement and read off the signal to the Captain.

"From the Japanese flagship, sir, the *Shimonoseki,* Vice-Admiral Fukunaga." The Chief Yeoman of Signals scratched his head and regarded his Captain with a grin.

"The message!" Bassinghorn snapped.

"Yessir. 'Good morning English Captain and Russian Admiral,' sir."

Bassinghorn gaped. "That's all?"

"That's all, sir."

"After all that—that damned cufuffle?"

"Yessir."

Bassinghorn glared towards Halfhyde, who shrugged, smiled, and said, "I expect it's the best they can do in English, sir. And at least they put us first. That's a happy first step—isn't it?"

The attempt at levity failed to find a response in the Captain. He swung round on the Officer of the Watch and the Navigator. "I intend to anchor as planned. Pipe for the cable and side party and special sea dutymen. Hands will fall in wearing clean white uniforms in fifteen minutes time. Chief Yeoman!"

"Sir?"

"Make to the *Ostrolenka,* 'proceed ahead of me now and anchor. You will disregard the Japanese.' Mr Halfhyde, a word in your ear, if you please." Bassinghorn, followed by Halfhyde, moved into the starboard wing of the bridge. "We are presented with a problem, Mr Halfhyde—"

"Another one!"

"Another one. Now—you're aware, of course, of what I was told at the Admiralty as to the Japanese view of this island: that the Emperor and his advisers have no need of it as a base and are not averse to British occupation and use. That was clear enough."

"Yes, indeed. And the problem, sir?"

Bassinghorn snapped, "Why are they here, Mr Halfhyde, that is the problem!"

"Perhaps to assist us, sir?"

Bassinghorn gave a hard laugh. "That I doubt! Why should they assist us?"

"A friendly Power, sir—"

"Even friends don't give military assistance unasked."

"True." Halfhyde reflected, eyes narrowed over the water towards the great battleships adorned with the Rising Sun of Japan, now drawing aft of the *Viceroy,* down her starboard side, as they slowed their engines to allow the British ship first entry, polite as ever. "It's unlikely, no doubt, that the Admiralty would have asked them to assist. I suppose it's possible there's been a change of mind in Tokyo—"

"And they want the island after all—exactly! That's how I read the situation myself, Halfhyde. Well, they shan't have it! I'll not give way at this stage."

"Six ships of the line, sir, with heavy guns, will make mince-meat of both ourselves and Prince Gorsinski."

"We shall give a good account of ourselves, Mr Halfhyde, when the need arises, and as to what you say, we can't count on Gorsinski's support, whatever the enmity of his Czar towards the Japanese. The Russians are intriguing scoundrels, as we well know. With three nationalities here, one can be played off against another."

Halfhyde nodded his agreement and asked, "What's our course of action to be, then, after anchoring?"

Bassinghorn frowned. "It's all in the melting pot now, of course, but all I can do is to honour my plan and my orders. That is to say, we shall disregard the Japanese presence for as long as may be, and in the interval a landing-party will be put ashore with orders to remove the Russian flag and substitute the British. Before they land I'll signal the *Ostrolenka* and remind them that their Admiral suffers if they interfere—"

"And the possibilities of worsening the diplomatic outlook, sir?"

"My hand has been forced," Bassinghorn said, "and the diplomatists must now look out for themselves. I must obey such of my orders as I still can. Once we've anchored, Mr Halfhyde, you will go ashore with the landing-party and take personal charge."

"Aye, aye, sir."

"You may take Mr Runcorn again, since he has knowledge of the island already. And also as soon as we've anchored, send Mr Mosscrop to me together with the other civilians."

Bassinghorn looked around from the bridge: eight sizeable ships, six of them among the world's biggest, and they were virtually lost below the peaks and between the wide arms of the anchorage. This was without a doubt a place to be reckoned with, a potential naval station that must not fall into other hands. But how was he to hold it, with his overwhelmingly outgunned command? Something, somewhere in the world's chancelleries, in the courts of power, had gone sadly wrong! Sir John Willard, keeping out of it all in the fleshpots of Hong Kong, might yet live to regret his attitude. He alone had the ships handy, he alone . . . yet he did not know the need, and could not be told. Bassinghorn gave a sigh of frustration: one day, but not yet, ships at sea might well have communication with distant shores by means of the new-fangled wireless telegraphy that was beginning to stir men's imaginations. Deplorable in a sense, for it would pre-empt every Captain's, every Admiral's command of his own ships; no move would be made until reported by

Marconi's magic to some distant Commander-in-Chief or some even more distant Admiralty for approval. But it would go a long way, Bassinghorn knew, helping a situation such as this . . .

He clamped down on his pointless thoughts and turned to face the civilians assembled before him. Putting his hands behind his back, he cleared his throat and loomed large and important before the group. "Well, gentlemen, I think you know why you are here." He coughed, floundered a little. He was unused to dealing with civilians, didn't like them very much, distrusted them a great deal, for they had not the serving officer's concept of duty, of dedication, nor—yes—of honour. His mind thus attuned, he tended towards pomposity. "I must apologize for not having spoken much to any of you whilst on passage from Portsmouth. I have had other matters to attend to, as you are aware. I trust you have been comfortable—as comfortable as possible in the unfamiliar surroundings of shipboard life, which is a hard life. Mr Mosscrop, I trust you have not been too ill."

Mosscrop's pale face hung before him, so washed-out with its terrible experiences as to appear altogether disembodied. "I'm better now, thank you, Captain, much better now—"

"The ship is motionless, Mr Mosscrop, and I would expect you to be better—"

"—but during the storm I was prostrate, Captain, and—"

"Yes, yes, yes." Irritation with the pitiful appearance of the dockyard constructor brought back Bassinghorn's command tones. "Now, gentlemen: my First Lieutenant, as I dare say you know, is about to land upon the island and remove the flag that you see there." He pointed across the water towards the Russian flag still flying from its makeshift staff, unguarded and, so far at any rate, unapproached by any of the *Ostrolenka's* personnel, who were evidently still acting with due circumspection in case they should seal the fate of their Admiral. Bassinghorn reflected momentarily and with satisfaction upon the Russian temperament and training: accustomed themselves to harsh measures and a lack of humanity, they expected the same in others. He continued, "When Mr Halfhyde has removed that flag and put the Union Flag in its place, and mounted a guard, then this island becomes a British possession, occupied by me in the name of Her Majesty the Queen. From that moment, your duties will commence, gentlemen. Botanical specimens may grow in lava or they may not. Geological interest may be present in plenty or it may not—I cannot say and it is not my job to do so. I shall not interfere with any of you. I shall play my part, which is to provide a secure base for your work and also to conduct the hydrographical survey of the coasts and anchorages and their approaches, a task I shall arrange to start upon at the first opportunity. I—" He broke off suddenly, his attention caught by movement at the quarterdeck ladder of the Japanese flagship: there was a full muster of white-uniformed officers and men by the head of the ladder, and as Bassinghorn watched a gilded figure started down from the platform. The notes of a bugle were heard, and the shrilling of the Boatswain's calls. Bassinghorn swung round on his Officer of the Watch. "Mr Campbell, the Japanese Admiral may be coming aboard. He must be received with proper respects."

"And if he passes towards the shore or the *Ostrolenka,* sir?"

"You will sound off, Mr Campbell, in the customary manner. After that, we shall see. Quickly, if you please!"

"Aye, aye, sir." Lieutenant Campbell called up a seaman boy with messages for the acting Captain of Marines who would provide the guard. Bassinghorn, catching sight of Halfhyde on deck by Number Three cutter, called down from the bridge.

"Mr Halfhyde!"

Halfhyde looked round. "Sir?"

"The Japanese Admiral is on his way, Mr Halfhyde. I don't know what in heaven's name is going on, but whatever happens he's not to plant any Rising Suns upon Her Majesty's territory, is that clear?"

"Very clear, sir—"

"Then make haste, Mr Halfhyde! Get yourself and your party ashore before Admiral whatisname arrives!" Bassinghorn's voice carried loudly along the deck and across the anchorage, expressing urgency and anxiety.

Chapter 16

"HE'S HEADING for us, sir."

Bassinghorn, now standing by the quarterdeck ladder aft, nodded. "Thank you, Mr Campbell. Fall in the guard and band, if you please." He waited. The Royal Marine Light Infantry guard mustered on the quarterdeck, their boots clumping as they doubled up, followed by the drums and fifes, and the Captain moved out onto the upper platform of the ladder, his telescope beneath his left arm, his helmet's brim keeping the high sun out of his eyes. Below him another sun, red-rayed on white, sped across the Pacific's blue towards the *Viceroy's* starboard ladder. To port, Halfhyde was being pulled fast for the shore with a Leading-Signalman and the Chief Yeoman, the latter bearing the Union Flag. Dead astern as the *Viceroy* was currently swung at her anchor, lay the Russian flagship, her decks deserted in obedience to Bassinghorn's order.

The boat from the *Shimonoseki* was coming now under the *Viceroy's* lee. Bassinghorn stepped back from the platform and took up a position facing the ship's side. As the boat came alongside and Campbell gave the word, a bugle sounded the Still from the after end of the waist, and the marine guard and band crashed to attention. As the guard presented arms, the drums and fifes played the General Salute, all men on the upper-deck came to attention and the Captain and his officers saluted. The Boatswain's calls shrilled into the palms of the piping party, and a diminutive man, gold-encrusted, came up the ladder and stepped onto the upper platform, clutching a sword the size of which seemed out of all proportion to its bearer.

Bassinghorn, as the notes of the General Salute and the piping of the side ended, stepped forward. "Welcome aboard my ship, sir," he said, giving a stiff bow.

The Japanese bowed in return, more elaborately than had Bassinghorn. "You are kind, Captain. I am Vice-Admiral Fukunaga, commanding the Second Battle Squadron in the name of Nihon-koku Tenno, and I am at your service."

"Ah yes, yes." Bassinghorn coughed. The title, he believed, was that of the Emperor of Japan: only foreigners referred to him as the Mikado. Some personal memorandum was indicated from himself, he felt. "I am Captain Henry Bassinghorn, Royal Navy, commanding Her Majesty's ship *Viceroy*."

"I am aware." Beady black eyes in an oval yellow face studied Bassinghorn from beneath a vast feathered cocked hat. "I wish to express humble felicitations to Her Most Honourable Majesty, Queen Victoria."

Somewhat desperately Bassinghorn bowed again, seeking words. "I am obliged on Her Majesty's behalf, Admiral Fukunaga . . . and wish to reciprocate."

The beady eyes narrowed. "Rec—ip—rocate?"

"Oh, never mind," Bassinghorn said, his weathered face going a shade red. "I simply meant, Her Majesty would wish to send her greetings to your Emperor . . . as a friendly Power, indeed an ally." He hesitated, his mind upon the doings of Lieutenant Halfhyde, his thoughts speeding the First Lieutenant upon his mission. It was, he felt, a matter of some urgency that the Union Flag be planted, a *fait accompli*, before the Emperor's representative began to talk business and reveal the reason behind his battleships' visit. "You will inspect the guard, sir?"

Admiral Fukunaga bowed again and, followed by Bassinghorn, his own Flag Lieutenant, the marine officer commanding the guard, and the Master-at-Arms, he moved along the ranks of the burly Royal Marine Light Infantry, stoic men wearing white helmets and red tunics, mightily sweating in the strong sunlight over the island. "Very good men," he said, smiling, when the inspection was over.

"Thank you, sir. Now if you'd like to come to my quarters, I shall be delighted to entertain you."

"I come, yes, thank you, Captain."

Bassinghorn ushered his guest below, casting a quick glance from the lip of the hatch towards the shore: Halfhyde's boat had almost beached, and barefoot seamen were jumping out to ease her in and secure her. Bassinghorn sighed inwardly with relief and hastened the passage of Admiral Fukunaga down the ladder. In his day-cabin Petty Officer Briggs hovered: Fukunaga was offered, and accepted, whisky. Briggs poured a small one for Bassinghorn, and toasts were drunk with due solemnity and a leisure proper to the occasion. Queen Victoria, Bassinghorn often reflected without any intent of disloyalty, was a world-wide boon to the distillers. Ceremonial thus duly honoured, the two officers sat, Fukunaga's heavy sword dangling between his stumpy little legs. The face held an enigmatic look; Bassinghorn, scenting duplicity of some sort as yet undivulged, broke the silence.

"Your squadron, sir. May I know the purpose of its visit?"

"For our manoeuvres, Captain."

"Ah. Then you have other ships in the vicinity—a fleet exercise?"

Fukunaga nodded. "Just so. Many ships. The Imperial Navy is immense, is strong."

"Yes, indeed. A fine Navy."

"We have been compared with Great Britain."

"I'm aware of that, sir."

"We are more strong than the Russian Fleet. Much more strong."

"Quite so."

"Which is now reduced to one ship here, when there were three."

Bassinghorn felt a hint of danger, not liking Admiral Fukunaga's tone. "You have received word of that?" he asked.

"Our intelligence is excellent, Captain. Very good intelligence. It is known in Tokyo that Prince Gorsinski was here with three ships—yes. Now there is one only, Prince Gorsinki's flagship." There was a glitter in the black eyes of Admiral Fukunaga. "The reason, Captain?"

"Prince Gorsinski ordered the *Czarevitch* and the *Gregoriev* to detach to Okhotsk."

"Why, Captain?"

Bassinghorn shrugged, temporizing still. "You must ask Prince Gorsinski that, Admiral Fukunaga."

"Yes, I shall do so. Your ship was at sea with the *Ostrolenka,* Captain. Why was this?"

Bassinghorn's mouth hardened. "Your pardon, sir. I have my orders, and they are between the British Admiralty and myself."

"And between Prince Gorsinski also, I think," Fukunaga murmured, half to himself. "It is known to me why *you* have come to the island, Captain—"

"That doesn't surprise me," Bassinghorn broke in. "It is understood in London that your Emperor had no use for the island as a base for the Imperial Japanese Navy, and I assume you to know this too. Thus it follows that you must know I have come to take possession in the name of Her Majesty. That is why I am here, Admiral Fukunaga, and if you will look out from my ports you will, I think, see the British flag. I have carried out my orders."

Fukunaga waved a hand. "I accept that your flag is there without looking. And now, Captain?"

"Now? Now I shall make a survey, both of the land and the waters, and report fully to the Admiralty on my return to the United Kingdom."

"And your flag, in your absence?"

Bassinghorn shrugged. This was a question to which he himself had not yet found the answer. On the face of it he could do no less, and no more, than leave behind an armed party with plenty of ammunition and provisions while he steamed for Hong Kong in the hope that, with success to report in the actual taking of the island if not in the proper execution of the political content of his orders, Sir John Willard would detach a vessel from the China Squadron to act as guard-ship until permanent forces were sent to garrison and prepare the base. But in point of fact, it was obvious enough that the moment the *Viceroy* left, the Russians, with or without their Admiral, would land a party strong enough to overpower any British force. Bassinghorn was only too painfully aware that his own actions, however inevitable they had been, had given the Russians the excuse to act as they pleased. No doubt it would be possible, via the hostage-threat of Prince Gorsinski's presence aboard the *Viceroy,* to force the *Ostrolenka* to proceed to sea in company; but Bassinghorn was reluctant to push too far his cocking of snooks at international diplomacy and knew that the *Ostrolenka's* arrival under escort in Hong Kong would be far from acceptable to Sir John Willard, while to detach the Russian flagship earlier would simply be asking for her to return to the island . . . Looking now at the smiling face of Admiral Fukunaga, Bassinghorn realized that the Japanese was wily enough to have guessed a good deal of what was running through his mind. The answer he gave to the last question was lame. He said, "I have yet to make my dispositions."

"Against Gorsinski?"

Bassinghorn nodded.

Fukunaga was smiling more broadly than ever. "For this you will need help, Captain. Who can help you?"

Bassinghorn spread his hands. "If I could get word to Hong Kong, then help might be forthcoming."

"But you cannot send word without going yourself, and you cannot go yourself without sending word for the help you need—this is a difficult problem, Captain!"

"I know that," Bassinghorn said with a touch of asperity.

Fukunaga said, "I can help you, Captain."

"You? How, may I ask, sir?"

Fukunaga laughed gently, studying Bassinghorn's anxious, bearded face with amusement. "You do not think my Emperor wishes the Russians to establish a base for their ships, do you? There has been no friendliness between us for some years, Captain!"

"I understand that, of course. But why, then, didn't you occupy the island yourselves, and stop the Russians making their attempt?"

"We did not need the base," Fukunaga said simply, "and we have nothing to fear from the British who do need it. Also much is to be gained from our friendship with your country, by treaties leading to mutual trade—"

"Trade!" Bassinghorn was scornful.

"Trade is now important, Captain. Nations live more by trade than by wars today. Do you not see? We allow you a free hand with this island from our part. Your Queen will respond, perhaps."

"A tit for tat?"

"Please?"

Bassinghorn waved a hand. "A British expression, sir. A blow for a blow . . . but never mind! I understand you. You are offering help—is this in fact why you have come here?"

Fukunaga gave a small bow. "Yes, Captain. That is why. You have but to ask, and I will give. The Russian flagship will not land her armed men, because my squadron's batteries will be pointing at her."

"Your Emperor . . . is he willing to risk a war, Admiral?"

"My Emperor is willing. He does not wish the Czar to extend into the Pacific. He considers the risk must be accepted now, to protect the future." Fukunaga got to his feet and went across to one of Bassinghorn's ports, He waved a hand towards the shore. "There is your British flag, Captain, waving over your island. We are glad of this, for reasons already given. Now make your dispositions in safety. When I return to my own flagship, I shall signal to the Russian, telling him to go away and not to come back!" The mouth split into a wide grin, a grin with more than a hint of sadism in it. "One person will remain, one only."

Bassinghorn stared. "One person? Who is that person, Admiral?"

"Prince Gorsinski. I shall order him to be brought to my flagship."

"And then?"

Fukunaga grinned once more. "When first steaming to this island, this British island, Captain, his flagship rammed and sank a fishing boat from Kanazawa on Honshu, in the Sea of

Nippon, and steamed on, not stopping for survivors, two of whom were found by another fishing boat."

"You mean—"

"He is to be punished, Captain." There was a curious finality in the Admiral's voice, a clear death warrant for Prince Gorsinski, risk of war or no. There was a vicious cold-bloodedness about it that made Bassinghorn shiver, notwithstanding Gorsinski's own undoubted cold-bloodedness: set a thief to catch a thief, he thought, they're each as bad as the other! Escorting Admiral Fukunaga shortly afterwards to the quarterdeck, Bassinghorn said nothing about the presence aboard his ship of the Russian: he could not quite fathom his own reasons for this reticence other than that he wished for time for thought. The reticence was pointless, really; Fukunaga would find out Gorsinski's whereabouts as soon as he made contact by signal with the *Ostrolenka* . . .

"Mr Halfhyde, I congratulate you. You have set wider the bounds of Empire."

Halfhyde gave a sardonic laugh. "For how long, sir?"

"For eternity!"

"Indeed?"

"Well, let us hope so at all events," Bassinghorn said. "How are the civilians doing?"

"I've not seen them since they were put ashore, sir. Mr Mosscrop took the journey badly. He was seasick."

"In an anchorage?" Bassinghorn was incredulous.

"Anchorage-sick, sir. Mr Mosscrop would be sick upon a puddle, I fancy." Halfhyde raised a hand, shielding his eyes from the sun and looking towards the *Ostrolenka*. "No sign of life there. By the look of it—so long as we have Gorsinski—the return trip in the cutter will be Mr Mosscrop's only anxiety."

"So long as we have Gorsinski," Bassinghorn repeated, and laid a hand on Halfhyde's shoulder. "Come below. I've matters to discuss, and urgent ones."

In his cabin he gave Halfhyde a résumé of his conversation with Admiral Fukunaga. The help, he said, was ready to hand; all problems could be said to have faded away, if somewhat unexpectedly, by virtue of Nihon-koku Tenno having despatched a battle squadron to their assistance. "I believe even the diplomatic considerations are taken care of now," he said.

"In what way, sir?"

"Why, insofar as the Japanese will take upon themselves the mantle of aggression!"

"A let-out for us?"

"Exactly!" Bassinghorn, all at once not meeting Halfhyde's eye, looked down at his hands. "I leave aside the question of— honour. I'd have wished it otherwise. I dislike the suspicion of being carried upon the back of the Japanese, but I see no alternative."

Halfhyde gave a grim laugh. "No more do I, sir, but is this one acceptable to you? I note you leave out the question of honour—this I consider wise, for of honour there will be none! There is a clear snag, sir, one that cannot be compromised with."

"Gorsinski?"

"Gorsinski, sir. Oh, the man's a braggart and a sadist, and he's been responsible for too many deaths among our own men recently—I know all this—"

"And left a fishing boat's crew to drown, Mr Halfhyde, which is the very worst thing any seaman can do."

"Aye, sir—except one."

Bassinghorn looked up. "What's that?"

"To hand over to Oriental beastliness a man who once saved one's life, sir." Halfhyde leaned forward. "Prince Gorsinski saved me from Siberia. I can't forget that. I'll fight him all right if my duty leads that way, and in action perhaps I'd kill him—I don't know. What I do know is this, sir: I'll not be a party to handing him over in cold blood to go to his death."

"And if it becomes your duty to do that?"

"The same applies, sir."

"You would refuse an order, Mr Halfhyde?"

"I think, sir, that I would be forced to. You spoke of honour. In a sense, Prince Gorsinski is not our prisoner—since we are not at war—but our enforced guest, and—"

"Words, Halfhyde, mere words!"

"Words nevertheless have meanings. We have no strict right to hold Prince Gorsinski because—I repeat—we are not at war. It follows from that, I think, that we have no right to present him for slaughter to Admiral Fukunaga. If you do that, then I would prophesy a far greater degree of diplomatic difficulty to await us upon our return to Portsmouth!" Halfhyde sat back, arms folded, face pale with anger, staring at his Captain. "I give you fair warning, sir, that I shall refuse any such order."

"If you refuse any order of mine, Mr Halfhyde, you will at once be placed in arrest, and—"

"Arrest me if you wish," Halfhyde broke in, shrugging. "I think you will find such an arrest hard to justify to Their Lordships, whatever my reputation at the Admiralty may be. I have spoken sense, sir—*sense,* as well as honour! It is not for us to act as international policemen, to make choices between Powers not at war. Admiral Fukunaga must be his own policeman, and we must not become his cat's-paw. I trust that you will reflect further upon this, sir, for there is an alternative and a much better one."

"Then kindly present it to Admiral Fukunaga!" Bassinghorn said passionately, his face suffused. "He left me with no alternative that I could find—"

"Then we shall put the ball back in the Japanese court, sir."

"How, Halfhyde, how?"

Halfhyde smiled. "With the greatest of ease, sir! We return Prince Gorsinski to his flagship—not now, but under cover of night, and secretly. After that, the affair lies between others than ourselves, does it not? We become the onlookers. You will know, I think, what is said about onlookers? They see most of the game."

"You mean—"

"I mean, sir, that with Nihon-koku Tenno occupying the mind and actions of the Czar of all the Russias, and vice versa, Her Majesty will be very adequately served in her wish to secure a Pacific island base for her Navy. Whilst onlooking, we shall survey . . . and in the meantime, sir, I suggest we have words with Prince Gorsinski and secure a measure of agreement for his own good."

Bassinghorn was about to answer when a knock came at the door of his cabin and Midshipman Runcorn entered. Bassinghorn looked round in annoyance. "Yes, Mr Runcorn, what is it?"

"A signal from the flag, sir, the Japanese flag, sir." Runcorn was breathing hard and his face shone with sweat: he had been moving at the double, and his voice was high with news unspilt. "Admiral Fukunaga is aware that you hold Prince Gorsinski aboard, sir, and demands his immediate surrender."

"Demands, Mr Runcorn?"

"Yes, sir. Demands, sir. And he indicates that he's prepared to seize Prince Gorsinski if necessary, sir."

"He does, does he?" Bassinghorn's face was hard; his big hands clenched and unclenched. "Very well, Mr Runcorn. There will be no reply to the Japanese signal for the time being, but you will give my compliments to the Officer of the Watch and ask him to pass the word, quietly, for all seamen and marines to be ready with their arms and remain below until ordered to muster on the upper-deck—but stand fast the port and starboard broadside guns' crews, who will man their armament. You understand, Mr Runcorn?"

"Yes, sir—"

"Then carry on, if you please."

The Midshipman, his eyes alight with anticipation, left the Captain's cabin. Halfhyde raised an eyebrow, his long face sardonic. "No hand-over, then, I take it?"

Bassinghorn glared stonily. "I have an intense distaste for being presented with demands. In the meantime, Mr Halfhyde, you will have Prince Gorsinski brought to me, under guard."

Chapter 17

A SILENCE HUNG over the anchorage: there was a curious and pregnant atmosphere of waiting for something to happen. The *Ostrolenka's* decks were still deserted in accordance with Bassinghorn's earlier orders; those of the *Viceroy* were almost as deserted, only the gangway staff of Officer of the Watch, Midshipman of the Watch, Corporal of the Gangway, Quartermaster, Boatswain's Mates, and sideboys being visible at the head of the starboard accommodation ladder. Below-decks there was now full readiness: the mess decks had been cleared for action as the broadside guns' crews mustered, invisible to outside eyes, at the breeches of the side-armament the barrels of which protruded through the gun-ports in the ship's iron plating. Here below-decks there was an atmosphere as curious as that over the anchorage itself: there was a grim understanding, a realization that duty must be done, but a full knowledge of the odds against the *Viceroy* if action should come. There would be a holocaust and the decks would run with blood before the magazines blew up under the thunder of the Japanese guns. They would, in fact, have literally no chance; and there were many mutters into beards along the mess decks, mutinous comment cast into the fug of a ship half battened-down for action. The Petty Officers and the ship's police, moving among the men, cracked down hard upon such comment when they happened to overhear it, but they too were in split minds: the word had spread throughout the ship that the Japanese Admiral had made a demand and a threat, and this was resented strongly enough; but was scarcely seen as sufficient to send a whole ship's company to their deaths in a battle that they could not, by any stretch of the imagination, win. The consensus of mess deck opinion was that the Captain was bluffing and in the end would be forced to climb down. There was mixed feeling about this as well. No one was inclined to relish the idea of Prince Gorsinski getting away with it, but all held high the reputation of the British Navy for straight and honourable dealing, even the mutterers and the malcontents who earlier had resented the reading of the Articles of War. They were not the pressed men of the old days: they were volunteers and they valued their self-respect when the enemy was in sight at the ends of their gun-barrels.

In the cuddy Prince Gorsinski, fully and accurately informed of the situation closing around his person, was angry but grateful to Bassinghorn.

"You must thank Lieutenant Halfhyde, not me," Bassinghorn said.

"Then I do so." Gorsinski gave a tight formal bow towards Halfhyde. "You remember past favours, I think. It is late to do so, but I am appreciative, and perhaps it is not too late. I think I can assist you."

Bassinghorn asked, "How can you do that?"

"I can surrender myself to Admiral Fukunaga."

"Are you willing to do that?"

Gorsinski smiled coldly. "Most unwilling, Captain, unwilling to the point of not doing it—"

"Then why suggest it at all?" Bassinghorn snapped.

"As a blind only, my dear Captain. This is a time for subterfuge, not for action, and you know this as well as I do."

Gorsinski snapped his fingers disdainfully in the Captain's face. "Your ship—pouf! Mine also, both of us together, we would have no chance before the guns of a battle squadron! You are bluffing, Fukunaga is bluffing also!"

"You think so?" Halfhyde asked.

"I know so," Gorsinski answered flatly. "The Emperor of Japan has no love for us Russians, but he would never support his Admirals in firing upon our ships, or upon me—which is your salvation, Lieutenant Halfhyde, for so long as I am aboard your ship."

"Then you wish to stay? Is this how you'll help us?"

Gorsinski smiled again, and flicked dust from his uniform. "Precisely so, my friend!"

"A battle of wills, a battle of bluff?"

"And a battle of time. Stand fast, give not an inch, and Admiral Fukunaga will sail away."

"With his tail between his legs?" Halfhyde gave a sardonic laugh. "I think not, Prince Gorsinski!" He turned to Bassinghorn. "Sir, I'd advise sticking to my earlier suggestion: that we return Prince Gorsinski to his flagship tonight—"

"One moment," Bassinghorn said, staring at Gorsinski. "Admiral, you spoke just now of a blind, of a handing-over that would, in fact, not be what it seemed. Do you wish to elaborate?"

Gorsinski shrugged. "If you wish me to. What I suggest is this: you signal Fukunaga that you accede to his demands, and will hand me over, but that first you wish to question me . . . I have been unwilling to answer your questions and you need time. I think he will understand my unwillingness and also your need to find things out about Russian intentions for the future, in regard to sovereignty over this island. Are you disposed favourably so far?"

Bassinghorn caught Halfhyde's eye, and nodded. "Perhaps."

"Good! That, then, provides the delaying tactic. In the meantime, you will prepare your ship for sea, but secretly—"

"Secretly!" Bassinghorn made a gesture of impatience. "Secretly, when my funnels will belch smoke as the fires are stoked to give steam!"

"Really, my dear Captain, must I teach you your job? In such an anchorage, with uncertain weather around us, is it not prudent to maintain steam at all times, and are you not in fact doing so at this moment?"

Bassinghorn said grudgingly, "Yes, I am."

"Then a little extra smoke will arouse no suspicions. Now: after full dark, and not before, you will signal the Japanese flag that you are sending a boat away with me in it, but you will not tell him that you are yourself going to sea. The boat will be sent, but will not contain my person. It will be pulled past the flagship and hoisted to your davits as you steam out. Admiral Fukunaga will be unready, and you will have a clear exit."

"For what purpose?" Bassinghorn asked blankly. "I fail to understand—"

"Come, come, Captain! You will sail for your base at Hong Kong—you will have some little start if Fukunaga should decide to give chase, enough I fancy to be out of sight in the darkness before dawn, before he can close you in daylight. I believe he would not follow far in any case—he'll have no wish to risk confronting your China Squadron if they should be at sea."

"And the island?"

Gorsinski said, "Upon your arrival in Hong Kong, you can

make your own arrangements as you wish. Already your Union Flag is flying over the island. I shall be in no position to interfere."

"But your flagship, Prince Gorsinski—"

"The *Ostrolenka* sails with us, Captain Bassinghorn. You will pass my orders, which I shall sign, by boat—also after dark. Those orders will be obeyed. And I shall be transferred back to my flagship at sea. This, I think, satisfies all parties except Admiral Fukunaga."

Bassinghorn said, "I ask again, what about the island?"

Gorsinski swept his right arm down across his body in an exaggerated bow, and smiled broadly. "It is the property of your Queen Victoria. I give it to you with my blessing, in return for your favour, Captain!"

"In return for your life? What will be your Czar's reaction, may I ask?"

"Approval. I am a Prince of the Blood. I must not fall victim or hostage to the Emperor of Japan. I am more important than an island in the Pacific wastes, Captain Bassinghorn!"

"He has an overweening sense of his own importance," Bassinghorn said with bitterness when Gorsinski had been taken back to his guarded quarters. "By God, I'd give my pension to see him hoist with his own petard!"

"We have the island, sir," Halfhyde reminded him. "We shall have carried out our orders."

"If Gorsinski can be trusted, yes!" Restlessly, the Captain stalked up and down the cabin, hands grasped together behind his back, a worried man. The preliminary signal had been sent to Admiral Fukunaga, and so far remained unanswered; but there had been no positive action from the Japanese to secure an earlier-than-after-dark hand-over, and so far as it went, the plan was holding water. The pitfalls, however, were many: Gorsinski, once returned aboard his flagship, could swing round and steam back on his tracks. Was he likely to do so? Would he not fear the actions of Admiral Fukunaga, who might still attack the *Ostrolenka* if she should return to the island? And might Fukunaga not, in fact, attack the *Viceroy* in any case, despite Gorsinski's apparent certainty that he was merely bluffing? Undoubtedly it could be a bluff; war was war, and not to be provoked . . . yet, with a sinking heart, Bassinghorn acknowledged that he himself had not shrunk from possible provocation when faced with a decision: Fukunaga might be just as impetuous when he saw Gorsinski sailing away from under his nose, from under his guns . . .

Bassinghorn halted in his stride and faced Halfhyde. "I see no other way now, Mr Halfhyde. We'll continue in accordance with Gorsinski's suggestions except in one respect: he will not be put aboard the *Ostrolenka* until we are about to enter territorial waters off Hong Kong. Bearing in mind Sir John Willard's wish to remain outside this business, I shall of course not enter Victoria harbour with Gorsinski aboard. But I shall put it to Sir John, in a way which he'll not be able to ignore, that the Admiralty will expect the China Squadron to back up what I have done—that is, to proceed to the island and assume control. That will not give Gorsinski much time to alter the status quo if he should feel so inclined. You follow, Mr Halfhyde?"

"I do, sir. In the meantime, have you precise orders?"

"Yes, Mr Halfhyde, I have. You will send my Engineer to me at once, and you will prepare the ship for sea so far as possible without it becoming obvious to the Japanese. At full dark you will shorten in without hosing down the cable, and be ready to weigh at a moment's notice thereafter, with the ship's company at General Quarters."

"And the civilian party, sir?"

Bassinghorn started. "Good God, I'd overlooked them entirely! I take it they'll be off by nightfall?"

"They asked for a boat to be inshore at two bells in the first watch, sir. They wished to put in a long day, and to reconnoitre the other side of the island, and—"

"Too late, Mr Halfhyde, much too late. You must send a cutter inshore now to have them found and brought back before dark—and remember, the boat's crew will be under the Japanese telescopes."

"Aye, aye, sir. I'll go myself, since I know something of the island—"

"No, Mr Halfhyde, I shall require you aboard. You'll send Mr Runcorn, if you please, who also knows something of the island."

The orders were passed without benefit of bugle or Boatswain's call. With the ship so recently in from sea, the preparations needed were little enough. Below in the stokehold, where the damaged boiler was still out of commission, the stokers banked the fires to bring the steam pressure up in readiness to proceed. Smoke billowed across the anchorage, thick, black, and heavy; there was no reaction from the Japanese battleships, which lay placidly at their anchors to seaward of the *Viceroy*. No further communication was received from Admiral Fukunaga, who appeared to be accepting the situation. Bassinghorn paced the quarterdeck with the First Lieutenant, wishing away the hours to dark, casting glances towards the Japanese ships, towards the *Ostrolenka,* towards the Union Flag and Runcorn's cutter waiting to collect Mr Mosscrop and his companions. Ashore on the island, Mr Midshipman Runcorn and six armed marines trudged the inhospitable lava deposits amid the lingering pervasive stench of burnt sulphur, trying, so far without success, to pick up the civilians' tracks. As the sun rose to its noon height the heat became almost unbearable: but there was no shelter anywhere, and in any case time might well be short with the civilians apparently having vanished. The party marched on, rifles slung from their shoulders, boots sliding on the hard surface, sweat streaming from every pore, looking, searching, and shouting for a response. By late afternoon Runcorn had brought his party round the island's northern coast towards the landing-place at which he and Halfhyde had originally come ashore from the *Viceroy:* here, at last, the shouts gained answer. Looking towards the source of that answer, Runcorn saw a man waving urgently from the foot of some high ground running towards the sheer perimeter of the land.

"Over here!"

Runcorn waved back. "All right, we're coming." He led the marines forward; scrambling over the jags of the lava, they reached the small party of civilians. One, Mr Mosscrop, was lying flat on the ground, his face as pale as ever and now filled with pain. Runcorn asked, "What happened?"

The botanist, a scraggy man named MacKillop, said, "He's broken a leg, lad."

"Can he be moved?"

"Better not. I'm no doctor, but in my opinion he can't be moved without a splint."

Runcorn bent down by the representative of the Director of Dockyards. "Is it bad, Mr Mosscrop?"

"God, it's agony. Don't move me, Mr Runcorn, if you've any pity . . ." The voice trailed away, and a spasm of pain passed across the face. Runcorn got to his feet, biting his lip. He pulled out his pocket-watch and looked at MacKillop.

"I have orders to return to the ship the soonest possible. I'm afraid Mr Mosscrop'll have to be moved. In any case, the sooner he has medical attention, the better."

"He could lose that leg either way," MacKillop said. "Can you go back to the ship and fetch the doctor?"

Runcorn shook his head. "It's a question of time, sir. Mr Mosscrop'll have to make the best of it."

"But look here, laddie, the man's in agony!"

"I know. But the Captain intends to sail as soon as it's dark, sir. He won't wait, I'm sure of that. There's enough of us to take spells at carrying Mr Mosscrop." An idea struck him, and he looked around at the waiting group of marines. "Rifles—we probably won't need them, there's been no sign of life here. We can lash two of them to Mr Mosscrop's leg, making shift of them as splints. Has anybody a length of codline?"

As the sun went down to the horizon, so the swift dark came. There was no moon: the island faded into blackness, the anchorage lay dappled with the lights of the warships—riding lights, gangway lights, lights from ports and hatchways. As soon as full dark came, a cutter left the *Viceroy's* quarter-boom with Prince Gorsinski's signed orders for the outward movement of the *Ostrolenka*. Aboard the British ship, the cable was very slowly shortened in, pulling the ship close above its anchor, with the minimum of men on the fo'c'sle, such as were indispensable being darkly dressed in home-service night clothing of blue serge without collars. These men moved like shadows, using canvas and cotton-waste and handfuls of oakum to muffle the sounds as the great links of cable came home from the sea-bottom. The steam capstan, its drum turning dead slow, could not be kept entirely silent: indeed, to Bassinghorn and Halfhyde waiting on the bridge, it seemed as though it must be shouting its message across the anchorage to Admiral Fukunaga; but there was no apparent reaction from the Japanese flagship. Bassinghorn paced the bridge back and forth, a prey to his anxieties: should he sail or should he not in the continuing absence of Runcorn and the civilians? A cutter still waited inshore for them, but there had been no contact from either party since they had been put ashore separately that morning.

"Mr Halfhyde, how is the cable now?"

"They'll report when shortened in, sir."

"The sea-boat's ready for lowering?"

"It is, sir."

"The Coxswain fully understands his orders?"

Halfhyde stifled a sigh. "He does, very fully. I promise you, no mistakes, sir."

"I trust that promise will be kept, Mr Halfhyde. Is there still no sign of the shore party?" Bassinghorn brought up his telescope and studied the land, finding nothing, unable now even to pick out the waiting cutter in the darkness. He closed the telescope with a snap and an oath. "Damnation take it, Mr Halfhyde, do we stay or do we sail? I'm damned if I like throwing everything away on Mr Mosscrop and his stomach upsets!"

"And Runcorn, sir, and the marines." Halfhyde moved away from the Captain, watched the progress of the cable party on the fo'c'sle. As he watched the report came: a ghost-like figure called up in muted tones, "Shortened in, sir, two shackles on deck."

"Thank you," Halfhyde said, his thoughts with Runcorn. "Stand by to weigh. When you get the order, heave in until the anchor's broken ground, but is held underfoot below the water-line, all right?"

"Aye, aye, sir."

Halfhyde approached the Captain. "Shortened in, sir." He waited for the next order, glanced sideways at the Chief Yeoman of Signals, standing ready to call the *Shimonoseki* by light and pass the message allegedly to indicate that Captain Bassinghorn was ready to send Prince Gorsinski across. Halfhyde found no response: Bassinghorn was staring towards the shore wrapped in its concealing darkness, straining his eyes for any slight gleam of green, the phosphorescence that would tell him that Runcorn was coming off with his landing party. Halfhyde felt strong apprehension: delay was dangerous. Now that dark had come Fukunaga would shortly lose his patience, might see darkness as a time for the British and Russians to take chances—and, on the opposite side of the coin, there would be a moon before long now. Nevertheless, some delay must be accepted. Men could not be left behind with inadequate arms and no provisions . . . not, that was, unless they were to be sacrificed for the greater aim. And that was the Captain's decision, not Halfhyde's.

Chapter 18

THERE WAS a faint loom out over the deep sea: on great waters there was seldom total darkness. With the sea all around, even though distant, Runcorn was helped on the high ground by this small luminosity. But it was little enough, and the march was an ordeal as, carrying the injured Mosscrop in shifts of two men each, they stumbled across the jagged landscape, skirting the high central peak. They suffered one delay after another: Mosscrop, in intense pain, moaned and wept; they were forced to put him down again and again and re-set the rifles around his leg, tightening the codline binding. At one point, climbing a steep incline covered with what felt like shifting clitter, they slid back, all of them in a floundering heap that upset Mosscrop in a screaming bundle at the foot of the slope, with the rifles sticking uselessly into the air and the broken leg twisted cruelly. As he was moved for the re-setting of his makeshift splints, Mosscrop, to the relief of them all, passed into unconsciousness, but only for a while. Coming back to a semiconscious state, he kept up a pitiful moan that set teeth on edge and made hands and would-be cautious footsteps clumsy.

"Will the Captain wait?" MacKillop asked for the hundredth time as they staggered on.

"I don't know, sir," was all Runcorn could say. He had said it so many times that he was almost at shouting pitch, though yet managing to hold onto his feelings. It was fifty-fifty:

Runcorn, given the facts by Lieutenant Halfhyde, knew the dangers of delay. Gorsinski could not be held beyond the un-forecastable but crucial point at which Admiral Fukunaga's patience gave way. When that point was reached, there would be bloodshed, and God alone could tell where that might lead. One midshipman, six privates of the Royal Marine Light Infantry, and a mixed bag of civilians might not weigh too heavily in the balance. Mr Midshipman Runcorn knew this, set his teeth hard, and made the best of it. A midshipman was a lowly thing in the Queen's Navy, but was yet a naval officer, and as such vastly superior to civilians, and Mr Runcorn had a long naval heritage to answer to, somewhere up aloft when his call came. He must not be reported wanting when the Almighty mustered by the Open List and each man's name was called . . .

Mr Midshipman Runcorn gave a savage grin into the night: he was letting his imagination run riot and that would never do. He struggled on, encouraging the small party, coming gradually around the heights in the island's heart. After a while, with the anchorage itself not yet in view, he became aware of a light in the distance, not a direct light but a light that seemed to reflect as off a cloud-base, up and down, on and off, visible for varying lengths of time, short and long. He swallowed, felt the lurch of his heart. "Fast as you can!" he called out. "We're not far off now and one of the ships is signalling—and that means we haven't much time left!"

Bassinghorn had made the decision, a painful one, after a delay that with every minute increased the chances against them. Turning heavily from his watch of the shore, the Captain had joined his First Lieutenant at the forward guardrail of the bridge and had given the order.

"Weigh anchor now, Mr Halfhyde."

"Aye, aye, sir." There was nothing else to say, no point now in speaking of Runcorn and the others. Halfhyde called the order down, quietly, and the acknowledgement came back. The Captain said, "Chief Yeoman, make the signal now to the Japanese flag."

"Aye, aye, sir." The Chief Yeoman flicked on his signal lamp, directed its mirrors at the *Shimonoseki*'s flag deck, and clacked the shutters in the Japanese ship's call sign. With little delay, the flagship's light flicked back in acknowledgement. The Chief Yeoman sent out Bassinghorn's signal, received the final acknowledgement, and reported, "Message passed, sir."

"Thank you, Chief Yeoman. Mr Halfhyde, do you confirm that everything's ready?"

"All correct, sir. Hands at General Quarters, ship secured for action, sea-boat's crew and lowerers standing by."

"Gorsinski?"

"Well guarded, sir, but he'll not be giving trouble just now!"

Bassinghorn nodded, seemed to pull his shoulders back, stood for a moment in silence, body turned towards the shore, eyes watching and hoping still but seeing nothing to delay him further; then his orders came: "Chief Yeoman, one executive flash to the *Ostrolenka*. Mr Halfhyde, lower the sea-boat on the falls. Mr Puckridge, main engines to stand by. All lights to be turned off and kept off until further orders. Mr Halfhyde, slip the sea-boat the moment the anchor breaks bottom."

He waited, standing stiffly by the rail with his hands clasped behind his back. There was extreme tension on the bridge as the cable rumbled home: the echoing drum-like clang as the links of the last shackle dropped back against the hull was like a knell. "Anchor's aweigh, sir!" Halfhyde reported. He turned aft, used his megaphone to call to the sea-boat's crew and lowerers. "Out pins . . . *slip!*"

There was a rattle and a splash as the sea-boat took the water, its fore-and-after knocked away from the slips. The phosphorescence showed the action of the oars as the crew gave way together and made out fast towards the Japanese battle squadron.

"Mr Puckridge, main engines slow ahead, wheel fifteen degrees to starboard."

The order was repeated; the *Viceroy* began to shudder throughout as the main shaft turned over, biting the screw into the water. Smoke came thick from the funnels, smothering the bridge personnel. Bassinghorn watched the *Shimonoseki* through his telescope. Despite the smoke, the Japanese did not appear to have noticed anything amiss yet, though the moment could not now be far off. More lights were showing on her quarter-deck and men were assembling at the accommodation-ladder, and that was all. Bassinghorn swung his telescope: there was more smoke, streaming from the funnels of the *Ostrolenka* as she got under way to follow the *Viceroy* out in execution of Gorsinski's personal order. Halfhyde felt a loosening of his bowels: at any moment now, if Admiral Fukunaga should decide to take the risk, the guns would roar into action, pounding, pulverizing, shattering. Bassinghorn, however, seemed no longer worried, as though the fact of being on the move, of doing something positive, had released his mind. Turning to Halfhyde he said, "All's well, I fancy. Do you see the sea-boat?"

Halfhyde turned his glass towards the *Shimonoseki*. "I see the splashes of her oars, sir. She's still making for the flagship. She'll turn away across our course once she's passed the ladder."

"Very good, Mr Halfhyde, you'll be ready, if you please, to hook on and hoist when she does so. The moment she's on the falls, I'll increase to full. I believe we shall cause Admiral Fukunaga much surprise, and be nicely clear before he comes to any decisions, or—"

The Captain broke off suddenly, giving an exclamation of dismay. A light, a big one, had come on at the flagship's super-structure, probably from her flagdeck or signal bridge: a searchlight, which swept momentarily upwards and then brought its beam down across the dark water of the anchorage. It swept across the *Viceroy*, lighting her decks like day, went on towards the *Ostrolenka,* outlining her smoking funnels starkly, then swept down again and in, glittering on the water and set-tling on the *Viceroy's* sea-boat which had started altering away from the *Shinonoseki* to cross the outward track of the *Viceroy.* Bassinghorn's voice roared out "Stand by main and secondary armament—wheel ten degrees to port, stop main engines!" Tak-ing up a megaphone he shouted across the water to the sea-boat. "Come alongside and hook onto the falls, fast as you can. Mr Halfhyde, stand by to hoist!"

Halfhyde went down the bridge ladder at the rush, shouting ahead to the lowerers grouped around the sea-boat's davits. Mak-ing his way along the deck at the double, he glanced towards the shore, and stopped: there was, he felt certain, a splash of oars and a bow wave: a moment later his belief was confirmed as the *Shimonoseki's* searchlight, sweeping the anchorage like an avenging finger, picked out the *Viceroy's* cutter making all speed from the shore towards the moving ship. Runcorn, bathed in light as he stood in the stern-sheets beside the Coxswain, could be seen clearly giving the stroke, his body bending, coming upright, and bending again. As Halfhyde watched helplessly, firing started from the upper-deck of the *Shimonoseki:* rifle fire—most probably, Halfhyde fancied, directed towards the sea-boat said to contain Prince Gorsinski and now obviously making away from the flagship with no intention of putting the Russian aboard. Whether or not this was the Japanese point of aim, it was in fact Runcorn's cutter that was the first to be hit: Halfhyde heard a howl of pain clear across the water, and saw the boat beginning to settle, obviously holed below the water-line. Turning away, he ran on towards the sea-boat's davits, shouting at the lowerers.

"I'm going down. Remain standing by, but don't hoist."

Halfhyde grabbed for the falls, ready lowered for the sea-boat to hook on. Bringing the ropes inboard, he swung his body onto them, holding the running parts fast so that they would not move round the sheaves, and slid down them towards the water as the sea-boat headed fast for the ship. As the boat came beneath his feet, he dropped down, landing heavily on the bottom boards. He scrambled up. "We're heading back towards the shore," he told the Coxswain. "To pick up survivors!"

"Mr Runcorn, sir?"

"The cutter—it's been hit."

"We'll get to them, sir." The Coxswain held the tiller against his body, pointing the bows away from the ship's side. "With a will, now, lads—give way together!" They moved ahead fast, dropping past the *Viceroy*'s stern as she continued on her out-ward course. They lifted, rolling violently as they came across the tumbling wake. As they headed out to starboard of the ship, Halfhyde looked back at the bridge, saw the Captain standing square at the rail, conning his ship out towards the end of the arm of land, the natural breakwater that shielded the anchor-age. The ship's outward movement left a naked feeling behind it, a feeling of desertion at the last; but Bassinghorn's action was correct enough and called for resolution. The die had been cast:

Gorsinski could not be sacrificed now, Fukunaga could not be given in to—and he might yet be bluffing, unwilling to bring his heavy guns into action notwithstanding his small-arms fire which, when explanations were demanded, would be more easily explainable than the use of his turrets. Halfhyde, speeding to the Midshipman's assistance, had no quarrel with Bassinghorn but had an unpleasant feeling in his bones that finality lay ahead for all those left behind, for if death did not come that night by rifle fire, then to be captured by Admiral Fukunaga would at best be a living death, for all the Admiral's talk about friendship with Great Britain and the Queen. Straining his eyes, peering ahead to catch what sight he could of heads in the search-lit water, Halfhyde felt the wind of bullets passing overhead. He shouted at the boat's crew to keep their heads down: they pulled strongly, and within minutes were in amongst the upset occupants of the cutter, some of them holding fast to the gunwhale as it floated just above the surface.

Halfhyde stood in the stern-sheets, risking the bullets. "Mr Runcorn!"

"Here, sir—"

Halfhyde looked over the starboard side, where the Midshipman, submerged to his chest, was now seen clinging. "Get your men aboard, Mr Runcorn, and quickly!"

"Yes, sir."

Runcorn rolled over and swam away, calling out to his boat's crew. With three men supporting Mosscrop, once again unconscious, the bedraggled party were hauled over the gunwhale of the sea-boat and laid along the thwarts and in the bottom. The rifle fire had for some reason slackened now, though the odd bullet sped harmlessly over their heads as to Halfhyde's order the rowers pulled fast for the shore. Giving that order, Halfhyde caught Runcorn's eye. "It's too late to make the ship, Mr Runcorn."

"Yes, sir. But what are we going to do ashore, sir?"

Halfhyde shrugged. "Make ourselves scarce, get lost—and wait for the Captain."

"Wait until he reaches Hong Kong, sir?"

"Have you any better suggestion, Mr Runcorn?"

"Well, sir . . . no, sir."

"Then, sir, I suggest you make the best of it! It's all we can do—I know it's not much, but—" he broke off, felt the blood drain from his face. A vast shape was looming ahead, between themselves and the shoreline where, in the continuing searchlight beam, the British flag could be seen flying from its pole. The shape—the *Ostrolenka*—was bearing down on them fast. "Give way for your lives!" Halfhyde roared at the sea-boat's crew, and sent the tiller hard over, almost laying the craft onto its port side. Shouts of alarm came from the men, those not at the oars crowding back as though to put extra distance between themselves and the moving mass of steel. Halfhyde was aware of a strange silence from the Russian flagship, an aura of lifelessness: her engines had died, the culmination, no doubt, of the blow struck at them by the storm whilst at sea. She was out of control. Faces could be seen upon her bridge and along her decks, faces white in the hard brilliance of the Japanese searchlight. Halfhyde's boat, strongly pulled, made safe water just in time: the huge bulk of the hull slid past in its curious silence, a silence broken only by the hiss of the sea along her sides. Her way was coming off now, the first impetus of her engine-thrust already fading, but she was still massively on the move—and her course was taking her straight towards the anchored *Shimonoseki*'s starboard side, her bows aimed amidships.

Halfhyde looked towards the Japanese flagship, knowing what was going to happen: the forward gun-turret was coming round, slow, ponderous, menacing, pointing for the *Ostrolenka.* Aboard the *Shimonoseki,* they would not realize the stark simplicity of the facts, would not know the *Ostrolenka* was without power, would take her to be attacking and perhaps about to open as well as ram. Looking aft along the Russian's decks, Halfhyde saw seamen clustered around the after steering position, some of them hauling out the steering tackles to the quadrant, others pulling at the canvas coverings over the standby wheel and binnacle: he might have known! Along with the main engines, the *Ostrolenka's* steering engine had died and now her company were hastening to give her the means to turn away before she hit. Slow though she was now moving, the impetus of her thousands of tons of steel would send her ram deep into the *Shimonoseki's* side. Warned by a sixth sense that the Japanese were about to react, Halfhyde gave the order to his boat's crew to stop pulling and lie flat. He was just in time: as the crew and passengers flattened to the bottom boards, the *Shimonoseki's* forward turret opened on the Russian flagship. There was a brilliant flash of red and white, a mighty roar like close thunder, and hard upon its heels a tremendous crashing sound from the *Ostrolenka* as her foremast and fighting-top smashed down in a tangle of twisted metal and parted wires, to drop on the navigating bridge and its stunned personnel. There was a high, whistling shriek from the shells as they continued on their way; and then, only seconds later, an enormous explosion on the island followed by a blast of heated air that swept back on the sea-boat's crew like a gale from the mouth of a furnace, singeing hair and clothing and bringing with it an overpowering stench of sulphur.

Halfhyde, thinking vivid thoughts about volcanoes, heard the Midshipman's voice through the din, a voice shouting into his ear: "Sir—they've hit the central peak, sir! D'you think it'll erupt, sir?"

"We'll not ponder on that!" Halfhyde shouted back. He sent the boat's crew back to the thwarts. "Hell is right behind you!" he said. "Pull to seaward as though the devil himself is after you and gaining ground!" As the sea-boat turned and headed out, Halfhyde looked back over his shoulder. There was, so far, no eruption; but the whole peak was aglow for what seemed to be several hundred feet down its sides—glowing and smouldering like live coals in a grate, and there was a growing mutter like distant thunder, becoming louder each second, while the sulphur-stench increased so that they seemed to be breathing airless fumes that made them cough and choke, tears streaming from their eyes. This was followed by the emergence of thick clouds of vapour from the mouth of the glowing peak, like steam, like a thick fog that rolled down upon the anchorage and blotted everything from sight in a clinging film of damp, sticky heat. The thunder-sounds continued, now loud, now low. At the low times they heard other sounds: a weird grind of metal and the screams of men cutting through the night's blankness, and then came movement beneath their boat, a curious heave of ocean and a sliding sensation as the water lifted and flung them forward. Suddenly an extra blast of searing heat seemed to dissipate the weird steam-fog, and, as the cloud vanished almost in a twinkling, the horror of the night could be seen clearly and terribly: Prince Gorsinski's flagship, evidently deflected from her collision course towards the *Shimonoseki*, lay with her bows embedded in a high sector of land that Halfhyde could have sworn was not there earlier, while her remaining funnel sent up a vast jet of steam. Men were jumping from her decks as a surge of water, oddly disturbed by the natural forces now at work, lifted her keel and sent her port side flinging hard against sheer rock. Not far from her a battleship lay turned turtle, her bottom washed by disturbed seas; but away to the west of the *Ostrolenka* was the weirdest sight of all: the flagship of the Japanese Second Battle Squadron was practically vertical, standing upon her stern with her great bow heaving to the sky and the guns lolling from the turrets, all clearly visible in the outlandish glow from the island's central point. Somehow, the *Shimonoseki* appeared actually to have climbed the land itself, was high and dry and in torment, her very metal crying out with the stress and strain of her unnatural position. Screams rang out from her decks as boats and booms crashed around her crew; like the *Ostrolenka* she was belching steam. Halfhyde gaped in horror, and in pity for any of her stokers caught below when the furnaces and steam-pipes and boilers fractured, sending the burning coal and the skin-peeling vapour ripping out to boil and kill and flay. As, so helplessly, he watched, and wondered what had happened to his own ship, there was a further sliding sensation and, with a violent jerk, the sea-boat hit something unknown. Halfhyde was thrown from his position in the stern-sheets: his body flew through the air to fetch up hard and head first on the unknown solidity, and he lost consciousness.

Somebody was wiping his face: it was Runcorn, looking relieved when he saw Halfhyde's eyes open. They remained open a short time only, for the sunlight hurt. It was a beautiful dawn had he been able to appreciate it, and the sky was full of colour around the horizons. There was quietness and peace also, and a slight movement and a sound of oars in crutches told Halfhyde that he was lying on the bottom boards of the sea-boat—or anyway, a boat of some sort. Briefly, he opened his eyes again, and saw only sky and sun.

"The island," he said. "Has it gone—after all that damn trouble?"

"Gone, sir?"

"They do," Halfhyde said weakly. "Volcanic islands sometimes vanish again . . . when they've caused enough bother to mankind!"

"Oh, no, sir, it hasn't gone, sir. It's—changed a little, that's all. As a matter of fact, sir, it's changed rather a lot." There was something in Runcorn's voice, some quality of sheer awe and wonder, that made Halfhyde fight down his nausea and the pain in his head and bring his body up to a sitting position. Shielding his eyes from the increasing sunlight, he stared around. The first thing he noticed was the central peak, or rather its absence: just there, the island had flattened out, forming a wide plateau with the heights dropping away to give it the appearance of Cape Town's Table Mountain. Halfhyde looked further, saw that the anchorage itself had changed: the jut of land that had formed the natural breakwater had grown to much greater proportions, higher, longer. In the anchorage itself lay the *Ostrolenka,* quietly now, her decks a shambles, alongside a natural rock wall similar to that on the far side of the island. The *Shimonoseki* still sat, or stood, up-and-down upon her prop of rock, looking as though she were about to slide back into the water at any moment, her masts broken and hanging from stumps, her guns askew. The wide hump of the overturned battleship's bottom lay breaking water like the carcass of a harpooned whale. Fukunaga's four remaining ships, in various degrees of disarray, two of them apparently fast alongside each other with smashed boats and davits as witness to a collision, appeared like drunks after a debauch. The *Shimonoseki* was abandoned now; her company were clustered a safe distance off, remnant of a thousand men, silent, apprehensive, bedraggled, homeless. Standing apart from them was their Admiral, in a group of his officers, all just staring at what the dawn had revealed.

"Where, by God Mr Runcorn, is the *Viceroy?*" Halfhyde asked.

"She cleared the anchorage just in time, sir. The others weren't at a high enough state of readiness, sir. The Captain took her through, sir, just before the gap closed."

"Closed?"

Runcorn pointed. "Yes, sir. It's not an anchorage any more, sir. It's a *pond,* sir—or a lake!"

Shaking his head in incredulous astonishment, Halfhyde looked. They were completely land-locked: short of the use of many tons of dynamite, which could prove disastrous, neither Gorsinski's flagship nor Fukunaga's would go to sea again. Formally Halfhyde addressed his Midshipman: "Mr Runcorn, we must report back aboard at once. No doubt the Captain will be standing off the island. We must climb the land—and wave!"

From the man-of-war anchorage off Kowloon, Captain Henry Bassinghorn and his First Lieutenant were landed in the naval dockyard on the Victoria side, whence they took a ricksha to the Commodore's residence—once again, bidden to dinner. As on the last occasion, Sir John Willard stood with a cold face before his fireplace; the portrait of Her Majesty hung still, the expression haughty and the eyes compelling beneath the white hair and lace cap, the blue riband of the Garter taut across the breast. As before the Commodore stood flanked by wife and daughter: this was no official reporting occasion, and a private dinner carried no official requirement or connotation such as would have been the case in the Commodore's office.

"Glad to see you safely back, Bassinghorn," Sir John said distantly.

"Thank you, sir." Bassinghorn bowed towards Lady Willard and Miss Mildred. Miss Mildred, catching Halfhyde's eye, gave him a coy smile. Sighing inwardly, Halfhyde did his best to be gallant and attentive. Fifteen minutes' chit-chat accompanied the sherry, and Halfhyde grew more and more bored as, inevitably, horses and hunting rode into Miss Mildred's dreadful conversation. Boredom, as dinner succeeded sherry, grew into irritation: it was no wonder that Miss Mildred Willard at twenty-nine remained unmarried . . . At last, however, the ladies withdrew, the port was passed, and the officers were alone.

Sir John offered cigars. Blowing smoke and with his eyes hooded, he said, "Well now, Bassinghorn."

"Yes, sir?"

"I've read your report. I gather the island's fairly useless?"

"I've not indicated that precisely, sir. Dangerous, possibly, but only a much longer and more penetrating survey will tell us that for certain."

"Well, it's not my business," the Commodore said, shrugging. "What's more important—to Their Lordships, not to me, you understand—is what you've done to the Russian and Japanese flagships, Bassinghorn."

"Not I, sir. It was Admiral Fukunaga's guns."

"A quibble." Sir John waved a gold-encrusted cuff. "Their Lordships will put their own interpretation upon it, of course, but it seems to me that your own actions had a precipitating effect." His eyes narrowed. "What about Prince Gorsinski—hey?"

"As I wrote in my report, sir, it was his wish to return to his flagship, for what use a land-locked flagship might be, but I feared the reactions of Admiral Fukunaga. You will appreciate the peculiar circumstances—"

"Peculiar circumstances or not, Bassinghorn, you will rid my command of him at the earliest possible moment, is that clear?"

"Quite clear, sir."

"What do you propose?"

"A cable to Okhotsk, sir, where the *Czarevitch* and *Gregoriev* should have arrived by now, suggesting a rendezvous at sea."

"And then?"

Bassinghorn said, "The local Chinese have seagoing junks, sir, and would prove susceptible to a guinea or two in gold."

"Undignified—for a prince!"

"Very, sir, I agree. And I dare say his welcome back to St Petersburg may lack warmth—but the alternative was worse in my view, much though he may have deserved it. I stress that he was the first aggressor, sir, and responsible for many casualties to my ship's company—"

"Which is one reason why I want him out of Hong Kong. Make arrangements for your junk, Bassinghorn, and I shall see to it that a cable is sent to Okhotsk in your name." Sir John stood up dismissingly: dinner, now the air had been cleared, was over. "There is for your consideration—not for mine—the further question of Halfhyde's action in killing two Russian seamen, is there not?"

"In attempting to escape, sir," Halfhyde said with his tongue in his cheek.

"Escape?" Willard gave a short laugh and his eyes went hard. "You may call it that if you wish—but I would not!"

"I had been improperly taken, sir."

"Yes, yes. You will be discussing this with Their Lordships in due course." The Commodore accompanied his guests to the hall for their boat-cloaks, intimating on the way that the *Viceroy* was under orders to leave for Spithead via Singapore and the Suez Canal as soon as Prince Gorsinski had sailed away in his fly-blown junk. The naval dockyard at Hong Kong was too busy to repair the damaged boiler: the base at Malta would see to that if necessary, and never mind how far away Malta was: the slow speed into the Mediterrenean and perhaps beyond was acceptable . . . Going back to the jetty in the ricksha, Halfhyde fell prey to intense depression. Once again, Mrs Mavitty and Camden Town loomed: the result of his and Bassinghorn's mission had not been unalloyed success on the diplomatic front! And clearly they were a monstrous embarrassment to Sir John Willard, who cared not a jot even for their casualties in action, casualties and action that by mutual consent of authority in Hong Kong and Whitehall would be glossed over, or, if they could not be entirely glossed over, then laid at the door of serving officers and their miscarriage of orders. There was no glory, and times had changed since Nelson had sailed the seas. Looking sideways, Halfhyde was aware from the set, baffled look on Bassinghorn's face that he was suffering similar thoughts. Their eyes met as they came into the dim glow from the kerosene lanterns in the Street of the Prostitutes.

"Mission, and dinner, not entirely successful, sir!"

Bassinghorn gave a half-smile. "We'll not fret, Halfhyde. And don't worry unduly about the two men, the Russian escort."

"Humanly speaking, sir, I must worry."

"Yes. It's greatly to be regretted, as I've said before and shall not say again. But I doubt if the Admiralty will take too serious a view in the circumstances." He sighed, heavily. "We did our duty. That's what counts."

"Rule, Britannia—I suppose?"

"Yes. It's still a case of that, isn't it?"

"The island, sir?"

"The flag was still there when we left, was it not? A miracle—but a fact! Almost the only thing that was!" The ricksha rolled on its way, passing throngs of bluejackets seeking wine, women, and song, bawdy men awash with drink, in from sea, back from danger and hardship and often despair. *They* were still there too: the Fleet was still in being. That had not changed, nor in the essence of its seagoing officers and men had the Navy.